DEEP IN THE SHADOW OF THE FALLEN

THE LEGACY OF ZYANTHIA BOOK THREE

CHANTELLE GRIFFIN

Published by Chantelle Griffin in 2017

Interior layout by Chantelle Griffin
www.chantellegriffin.com

Cover artwork by Matthew K. Hoddy
www.spacepyrates.com

Catalogue-in-Publication details available
from the National Library of Australia

paperback ISBN: 978-0-9943921-4-5

Also available in ebook
ebook ISBN: 978-0-9943921-5-2

The night sky whirred to life as blasts of wizardry pummelled through the air. Saranon dare not look as the dragon swerved and they made it past the first barrier. She glanced down as a blast roared up through the dark sky. Before she could attack Mitch struck out at the blast. The impact knocked the dragon off balance. She lost her grip and fell, rolling as the dragon skidded along the dusty plain. Mitch asked, 'Are you hurt?'

She glared at him as the wizards protecting the border circled in. Mark's voice rang out in the dark, 'Saranon!'

Enter an epic tale of sword and sorcery. More than two hundred years ago a powerful sorceress freed her people then vanished. As time passed truth turned into myth and myth became legend. The time has come again. Saranon must claim her rightful place before Zyanthia falls.

www.chantellegriffin.com

For my sister

For all that has been before, for all the pain and sorrow, may you rise above them all. For the path less travelled brings hardship, adventure and triumph.

THE ZYANTHIAN REGION, TORDOREN

CHAPTER ONE

Across the border

Saranon raised the fine glass to Lady Davene. The most powerful sorceress in Balquene entered the marble courtyard. The Lady's flowing burnt orange dress trailed over the polished mosaic floor. The tiles added to the vibrant colourful scene and a warm breeze ran over the shallow pool. It came through the open columns leading into the grounds that surrounded the grand mansion. It was a wonderful way to celebrate the end of training. Yet she continued to struggle with her sorcery. A fact she tried to hide in a country that once belonged to Dresha, an empire long gone. It disintegrated with disappearance of the last Angeon, the only link to her ancestry.

Maya broke through the crowd as the feast was brought to the table. The centre piece was positioned at the end of the courtyard. Music played they strode out into the afternoon sun. 'What do you think?' Maya asked.

'It's beautiful,' Saranon said as she gazed upon the low fields on the edge of the grounds.

'Does it make you want to stay?' Maya asked waiting for her to answer.

It was not the first time she had been asked, and her response remained the same. 'I have to return.'

'A pity,' Maya exclaimed.

An awkward silence fell and she made her way into the busy room. As people danced to the soft music and sat on the cushions by the walls. The table had been laden with fruit in front of the deep colours of the fresco. She gazed up in awe. The mansion had been untouched by the ancient war between Dresha and Zyanthia. She wondered what it would have been like if Zyanthia had not fallen. Yet there she stood, one of two Angeon when there had been none for more than two hundred years.

A glass fell shattering across the mosaic floor as the wizard moved away. Saranon caught a glimpse of his tall muscular frame. Then she came face to face with Lady Davene. 'You have outworn your welcome,' the Lady's voice cut through the crowded noise.

She stood between her wizard, Mitch, and the Lady as the blood began to run down his arm. If Saranon spoke she would regret every word. She held Lady Davene's infuriating glare and gave a swift nod in a partial bow of respect. It was more than the Lady deserved, but she was not about to risk it. She had gained a momentary truce when her wizard's life was at stake. She hesitated long enough to allow Mitch to make good distance. He headed toward the marble columns surrounding the sheltered courtyard.

Balquene was no place for a wizard. She glanced around the room reluctant to take her gaze from the Lady. The setting sun ran its golden fingers along the polished mosaic floor. It sprawled over the scenes of victory and spreading her shadow toward the heavily laden feast. The party was over and all eyes were on her. A large frame eclipsed the sun. Covering the courtyard in darkness as the great dragon came into view. Katholomu stepped forward and the crowd fell in a hushed tone. She waited as the lights of the sorcerer Keep flared glinting of the dragon's eyes. She bowed once more before the dragon raised her on his shoulders. He made for the sky in a mighty swoop his wings outstretched their full length.

Mitch stayed silent as she concentrated on leading the dragon Kat south. She glanced back and Mitch answered, 'They are not following.'

She was not convinced and signalled for the great beast to fly on. They increased the distance from the stronghold of the sorceress Lady Davene. After a time she asked, 'What did you do?'

There was no response and they flew on. Mitch spoke, 'It's what I didn't do.'

Saranon stifled a laugh and gagged. 'I...' She cleared her throat, 'I'm glad you have standards.'

She could not help but laugh at the wizard's predicament. He was seven years her senior and it was last the thing she had expected.

The low torrid ground with its stark remnants of grass vanished into darkness. The sun disappeared over the horizon. Katholomu lowered his descent toward the low rocky hills, that marked the outlying area of Balquene before the border. The wind swept around the sparse hillside breaking the evening warmth. The great dragon hid as best he could, lying low to the ground but there was little cover. She rested underneath his wing. As Mitch scanned the horizon in the fading light that remained. It was not the end to her journey that had expected. She pulled out her small sova bag that fitted inside her pocket. The bag grew larger and she reached inside for the map. The border to Normisia was close and they had been told to return via Magladen. They could still make it west to the wizard Keep Karaden.

Mitch peered down at the map lit by a small sacra seal over the pebbly ground. The ink stood out on the thick parchment as she ran her hand over the border with Normisia. 'We cannot go there,' Mitch said.

She did not intend to but spoke her thoughts aloud, 'We may have to.'

He crossed his arms in fierce stance. He would follow her if she went. They both knew the border between Balquene and Normisia was out of bounds. The closest the two countries had ever been to reaching an agreement. It remained an unspoken stalemate. If they flew across the border they would meet the Imperial Normisian Army head on.

The sky was clear as they settled in for the night.

Kat's muscles remained tense underneath his sprawling pose. Taking advantage of the sun's heat left behind in the large boulders. Mitch leaned in, he was about to speak and stopped. An awkward silence fell. 'You could have waited until after dinner,' she said.

As her stomach grumbled, reminding her that she had not eaten. He took out some bread from his pack and broke it in two. 'That is not what I meant,' she said.

'I know,' he replied.

She rested against his shoulder drifting into a shallow sleep. It was so difficult to read the wizards thoughts. It resembled a twisted haze and she gave up, sorcerers were not designed to read minds.

Mitch woke her up. The sky was pitch black. She could just make out the dragon's silhouette, as he crouched off to the side. She could sense the sorcerers approaching from the north. Mitch could not ask her to do what they both knew. She clambered onto the dragon sitting high between his shoulder blades. Mitch sat close behind her. Saranon could sense the sorcerers panning out. Soon the path to the west would be blocked. She had to make the choice. She took one last look out into the dark expanse as the sorcerers made ground. She signalled for Katholomu to turn. He leaped into the sky heading south, straight for the border. The great dragon flew hard and Mitch clung on. He whispered, 'Thanks.'

She concentrated on the horizon. There was no sign of Mitch's homeland, but it would not be long. She could feel the tension in every beat of the dragon's wings as Kat picked up speed. She held onto the thick folds around his neck. The great beast moved with a precision that belied his bulky frame. The low hills rose and fell. They revealed the final outposts guarding the edge of the border. For a moment there was nothing then the Balquene side sprang to life. Fires flared up lighting the night sky. Yet it was the only sign to great them as Katholomu headed toward them. Saranon lowered her head as the dragon flew toward the border at speed. Mitch remained silent soon they would be there.

Katholomu flew into darkness, Normisia stayed quiet underneath. It created an earie void. The only sound came from the wind sweeping past the great dragon's wings. She began to relax yet Mitch remained tense. She glanced down over Kat's shoulder unsure if her mind was playing tricks. There appeared to be a line of movement along the ground. She pointed and Mitch spoke, 'Hold on.'

A haze radiated along the ground sweeping through the open field. It crept through the air. The movement pulled at the Kat's wings and he struggled to gain height. A line of wizardry sparked through the night, the barrier expanded as they approached. It was too late to turn back. She steered Kat straight into it. The night sky whirred to life as blasts of wizardry pummelled through the air. She dare not look as the dragon swerved, and they made it past the first barrier. She glanced down as a blast roared up through the dark sky. It was heading straight for them. She raised her sorcery from within. Before she could attack, Mitch struck out at the blast. The impact imploded, knocking the dragon off balance and he dived toward the ground.

She lost her grip and fell, rolling as the dragon skidded along the dusty plain. She just managed to soften the fall before hitting the rough surface. A cloud of dirt filled her lungs and she coughed. She tried to stand and her legs collapsed hitting the hard earth. Her head spun and the dust settled. Katholomu stayed low to the ground leaving a trail of dust behind him. Mitch held on until the dragon came to rest then ran toward her. 'Are you hurt?' He asked.

Her mouth was dry and no sound came out. A line along the ground moved as the wizards emerged from the dark. She stood still waiting as they closed the distance. The cryzinelan wizards were Mitch's clan. Though it had been made clear they had to return via Magladen.

They greeted Mitch and the tension swept away before it changed in an instant. The soldier kicked Mitch to the ground and her temper rose. She hurled her sorcery to form a shield and the soldier flew backward. She had had enough. The line broke and wizardry sparked along the shield as she knelt to the ground. The urge to fight back grew and she gritted her teeth under the strain. The wizards stepped away and a silence fell. All she could hear was the thud of her heart in her ears. Mitch held her and it was enough to calm her thoughts, the sorcery slipped away. A dragon rider plunged to the ground landing behind the line of wizards. The wizard rider approached as the line fell back to let him through.

She glared at him as the wizards protecting the border circled in. Mark's voice rang out in the dark, 'Saranon!'

She flinched at the sound. Mitch stood up, 'It was my decision to head south.'

She shouted, 'No!'

'You were warned,' Mark said.

He marched Saranon over to where Katholomu watched. He stood close, 'Welcome back. Now get on the dragon before I change my mind.'

CHAPTER TWO

A wizard's welcome

Saranon peered over the dragon's wing. She watched the barren ground change into a sprawl of green fields below. The great beast Katholomu responded to Mark's commands. She fumed at having to relinquish control. The wizard Mark took delight in flying Kat toward the Keep Hedavin. They drew further away from the northern border. The aged dragon trainer directed Kat with ease. 'I know how to fly Kat,' she exclaimed.

He chuckled, 'I'm sure you do, but you were to return via Magladen.'

'I already told you we met with Lady Davene,' she retorted.

'That does not give you permission to cross the border with Balquene,' he said.

Saranon glanced over at Splodge. Mark's dragon was

terrifying in the air and on the ground. 'How come Mitch gets to ride your dragon?'

He chuckled again, 'Splodge does what I tell him to.'

'Like when he almost killed you,' she responded.

Mark became silent before he replied, 'You have a lot to learn about dragons.'

Splodge flew close to Katholomu, the two glided back and forth through the sky. The warm air gave the first hint of spring carrying with it the scent of blossoming trees. The hill hiding Hedavin in the woods came into view all too soon. Saranon slid down the marmoz dragon as they landed. 'Wait there sorceress,' Mark said.

She watched Splodge swooping in from the sky, 'He's a bit close.'

Mark pushed her flat to the ground as the dragon sped down over them. She asked, 'Did you tell him to do that?'

'Don't be smart,' Mark replied as he stood up.

It was all she could to not to laugh. The wizards could read her immediate thoughts. She caught a few glares as they landed. Normisia brought back mixed memories as she gazed at the woods closing them in. Mitch was seven years older and towered over her. The wizard made no attempt to hide his joy at returning. The Cryzinelan wizards gave him a warm welcome. In stark contrast to the way they greeted her.

Mark patted her on the shoulder, 'It's good to have you back. The border with Balquene is off limits.'

'Thanks,' she replied with a flat tone.

'Now, you get to wash your dragon,' he grinned.

Saranon began to remember how annoying wizards could be. She strode around the stone courtyard amidst the undergrowth of the woods. She had left so much behind and it haunted her still. Tasha left her a hard task and she had failed, leaving Normisia far behind. Mitch had accepted the bond of a Hilazen, as though it were intended. She rubbed her arms and longed for a warm bed.

She paced with a hint of caution as the wind stirred with a widening rustle. It wrapped around the length of the building and they approached. The leaves fluttered as they hung to the trees in the woodland. The giant Keep Hedavin appeared empty with no one in sight. The graceful Keep lay with its true magnificence hidden. It gave the appearance of a sleeping giant. The Keep lay covered by the scrubby, woodland forest that wrapped around. The roads were narrow with worn stone. It fed the illusion of a small building nestled in the hillside. She waited as a small creak emanated from the door. She glanced up at the massive dragon in a playful mood. The image masked his quick temper and restless mind. He ducked his head between Saranon and the open door.

The black marmoz dragon frightened the occupants on the other side. Saranon admitted that this was not a difficult feat. Even when Katholomu was being cheerful, she was not sure which mood was worse. Mark Staragen bought the massive beast as a gift. This was after she had saved the wizard from being squashed by Splodge. Kat raised his claws and the door slammed shut so hard, she thought the handle would fly off. 'Now you've done it,' she hissed.

Kat stared at her with his black sorrowful eyes. She nudged his head to the side and gave an exasperated sigh. A small gap broke, showing a crease along the edge of the door. A familiar voice filled the air, 'Oh for goodness sake Jerald, open the door.'

Saranon let out a giggle at hearing Captain Mirshendy's first name. Saranon's friend Rachel had a warm and tender voice. The memory of the wizardess melted away her fears. She raced to peer over Mitch's shoulder. Only to lock eyes with the stone faced Captain. Who, for reasons she did not understand, was blocking their path. Rachel's beaming face shone through. The wizardess raced over giving Mitch a warm embrace. For an awkward moment Saranon and the Captain stood next to each other. The thought of hugging him did not interest her.

Captain Mirshendy had never once warmed to her and he kept a respectable distance. Rachel broke their silent gaze as she greeted the sorceress. She led them further into the confines of the Keep. Saranon followed Rachel's lead. She could feel the Captain's eyes watching her all the way along the corridor. Rachel leaned close and whispered, 'He's been busy and it's not you this time.'

Saranon was caught halfway in a relieved sigh when her mind caught up to the response. 'What do you mean it's not me?' She asked.

Rachel laughed, 'You are not the only sorcerer who can cause trouble.'

It was a strange form of compliment. She thought no

more on the matter when a hearty smell wafted through from the kitchen door. For an instant the wizard Keep felt like the most appealing place. Even with all its strangeness. She relaxed her weary muscles and filled her empty stomach. Mitch had managed to disappear, she could not blame him. This was his home and now he was in the company of old friends. A gruff sound reached her ears through the warm air wafting through the windows. She peered out from the balcony to watch Kat standing over another dragon.

The beast did not take much to stir and his size was enough to scare even the largest opponent. The wizardess, Gabriel, waved and shouted for Saranon to join her in the courtyard. It was not the sight of her friend that worried her. It was more the thought that Gabriel's Uncle was Captain Graddon. The man had been irritating and she hoped that he was not around. Even though her muscles ached from the ride, she went out to meet her friend. While Katholomu rested, curled up the sunniest spot he could find. The courtyard's size was hidden by the lack of boundaries. The growing shrubs covered the edge wrapping around the paving.

Gabriel was only just younger than her. With as much enthusiasm as anyone could have. She had shown Saranon through the hills of Normisia further south with her dragon. Mitsy's medium size was far smaller than her personality. Gabriel smiled, 'Thanks for bringing back Mitch.'

She peered around eyeing Mitsy. The beautiful shazel dragon recognised her with a warm welcome. 'Did you come all this way to meet us?' Saranon asked, it would not have surprised her if they had.

The wizardess broke out laughing, 'Don't be silly, I'm learning how to train dragons.'

It was not the reaction she had expected, but it was good to see her friend all the same. Even with Gabriel's constant questioning about her travels, well into the late evening.

Her weary body longed for the lure of a nice warm bed as she left the warm fire in the great hall. Gabriel had not been the only one wanting to know what had happened. She had sensed quite a few of the wizards listening in. Saranon opened the door to her apartment. She froze at the sight of Captain Mirshendy talking with Mitch. The Captain ceased the conversation and left and she gave Mitch an annoyed stare.

As she glared the wizard appeared serene, for now she would let it rest. Her weariness caught up with her and the sight of a soft bed was too appealing. The starry night shone through the open curtains with a comforting glow. It echoed the pattern of her homeland to the south. Darkonia seemed so far away. The memory of Tasha made its way back into her restless thoughts. The words of her friend from the grave still clung in the air, Kill the boy but leave the girl. She had let the boy slip through her grasp in the battle. If she had not, then Bianca would have died. A silent tear fell down her cheek for she had done neither of what Tasha's spirit had wanted.

A small comfort remained in knowing her friend Pennie was alive and well. Residing in the homeland, where she could not return after what she had done. Pennie was always resourceful. She had little doubt that if anyone could find a way to help, her friend could. The image relieved her tension. Every time she woke with mixed dreams of Indarin Keep in Serenphel. The country seemed so far away. Yet it plagued her still, seeping through her thoughts. The sorceress tried to push them away. It was an uneasy battle that kept her mind from a peaceful rest into the early morning. When she tip-toed out of the room in a clumsy grace.

Saranon half tripped as she clambered through the doorway. The dim glow darkened the silhouette of the wizard as he sat peering into an empty glass. The sorceress stood up straight, 'I take it you couldn't sleep either.'

Mitch smiled before making an excuse to go to bed. Not that there was much left of the night. The thought of a day without the wizard was appealing. Before the first rays of dawn broke through she had made a large breakfast. The journey had been far more tiring than she had let on, but it was worth the speedy return. The thought of having to face Merrick Calthazard again frightened her. Fighting the sorcerer in any form had been a good reason to leave Indarin. The second Angeon still filled her dreams with unease. She had been the one to spare him. Yet she did not think he would be so grateful for such a deed.

A small creak sounded from the door. She stood up to poke her head around the corner. Only to see nothing, before it opened further in the dark. This time she crept forward, the silhouette of a figure stood near the door.

Bently peered around whispering in a low voice and gave her fright. The tall lanky wizard was one of Captain Mirshendy's officers. Before she had time to berate him he had already spoken, 'The Captain wants to see you.'

She was not impressed and the thought of meeting Captain Mirshendy did not appeal. She followed in an awkward silence through the wide corridors. They wound along the outer rim. The high windows revealed the stars from far above. It did not take long to find the hub of wizard activity. She was led to a room via an open corridor on the edge of a magnificent internal courtyard. It was simple yet elegant with an aged feel where the stone worn. The place was well kept with a hint of pride. They made their way down the open stairs joining the internal balcony to courtyard. The surroundings were lit by a stream of lights along the columns and wall. The glow beamed from the energy of the Keep.

An opening, hidden in the outer wall covered over by the hill, displayed the fading stars outside, as the early morning drew near. The place shone with the sun's first light awakening the Keep. As she walked into the room her surprise turned to annoyance. The Captain who stood there, was not Captain Mirshendy. To begin with he was taller. What Captain Mirshendy lacked in height he made up for in strength and ability. The absence of an explanation, came as a reminder of an old scar that stayed fresh in her memory. Captain Tredeer stood in a welcoming gesture that felt too smug. He was almost the same height as Mitch and behaved as though he were an old friend. The sorceress hung back in hesitation then sat down.

She listened to yet another wizard trying to tell her what to do and kept a pleasant face. Saranon had to remind herself to slow down when she closed the door. She tried not to show her eagerness to leave, as most of the morning had been wasted. Captain Tredeer was someone she did not want to meet again, he was far too vague for her liking. She went down to the Captain she had intended to see. She bordered on a dislike for Captain Mirshendy. He was straight forward and for all his attempts, did not hide how he felt. She let out a short laugh at the thought of finding the wizard's company welcoming.

The noise of activity brought Hedavin to life. A warm vibrant movement of people bustled past. Great care was taken looking after the Keep that showed its age. In simple classical forms that noted every foyer or small entrance. The place was void of lavish colour. Yet the dull light hues suited walls and reflected natural light deeper still. The long hollows holding the opening, let in an abundance of warmth as it neared midday. She made her way down to a voice she knew well. Captain Mirshendy stood in the midst of a room filled with activity. The place was called a room, yet it was space, between other rooms. It had been adapted and filled with connections back to the inner workings of the Keep.

Panels shone with the energy from the central core below. It provided valuable feedback to the habitable area. Saranon had assisted Captain Mirshendy with fixing Greddin Fort in southern Normisia. The central core was a fascinating thing for those who saw it. She was aware that the wizards could not visit. The amount of sorcery required was mind boggling. Then careful preparation to build the structure that sat above. First the central core, then the imbenik chambers and the indolin chambers. Then last of all the habitable area which could be used by many. The giant conduits ran the stallic energy away from the liquid sheal. This fed through to the smaller pipes running through the Keep.

Once complete, the whole structure could last for centuries. People sometimes forgot there was a central core deep beneath. It lay hidden under the many layers, until something went wrong. Work was well underway with looking after the Keep. Captain Mirshendy only acknowledged her with a glance. She stepped sideways out of the way, stumbling as she put her hand out near a control panel. The sequence showing on the screens caught her eye. Her curiosity was short lived as the sorceress was asked to move.

She was about to say something when the power cut out, before flickering back to life. The pulse felt strange underneath her hand and she pulled back. She leaned against the wall and a sound sent shivers up her spine. The wizards around her responded with haste. She sped past to look out at a vacant space seeing nothing at first. In the ambient void the small sound clicked past, echoing through the floor. As she peered toward the source, two sorcerers emerged from the air. One held their prize, a wizard who still struggled to break free. The sight caught her breath and for a moment everyone froze as the shock set in.

The wizards around her moved forward in a lunge, only to hit a shield. The sorcery maintaining the shield came to life with electrifying speed. Two wizards made contact as it threw them backwards. The captive wizard made a small whimpering sound. Saranon peered through the shield. She glanced straight into the eyes of the sorcerer standing free. He moved close to the other side of the shield. Smiling with a haunting laugh as his eyes lit with a cruel delight. While their eyes met she held out Tellembre. She brought it forward with a smooth motion as she held the sorcerer's gaze. The bond-breaker was cool to the touch as she brought it out, hiding the heart stone blade.

She stabbed its blade at full length through the shield. The sword, made of heart stone, hit home with a final certainty and the sorcerer sank. The mark of the Dihan showed faint on his neck. The wizards took no time to run through as the shield faded. The remaining sorcerer vanished from sight as he fled. The captive wizard gave a thankful nod as he was freed. She gazed his way holding the bond-breaker as her nerves steadied within. Tellembre had a pearl finish, made at Ollanthia Keep in Darkonia. She let it sink back into the form of a dagger before placing it back out of sight. The energy she exerted was minimal, but the nuances of sorcery still escaped her. She turned looking at Bently, 'You failed to mention you had a problem.'

The tall wizard made an attempt to hide his expression. 'I didn't know we had one,' he replied.

The response did little to please Saranon's temper,

which lay just below the surface. Bently's words were the most the wizards were prepared to let slip. The Keep steadied itself into a peaceful rhythm. As she left to find the sorcerer quarters.

She had not expected to meet the Dihan, the Keep had given away no sign as it hummed away. Yet she was troubled by the attack. The sorcerer she had struck with the bond-breaker was Dihan. A chill fled down her spine, her first encounter had been horrendous. It was the reason for the bond with Mitch. The wizard had saved her life from being taken by the Dihan. For that his energy had linked to hers. The Dihan who had taunted the wizards did not appear to be the same and it plagued her mind. The sorceress passed through the internal foyer with its slender columns and light hues. As she peered up at the hexagonal ceiling a familiar voice spoke beside her. 'Beautiful isn't it?' Caleb asked.

The sorcerer looked far more mature than the boy she had first met at Zaidek Keep in Normisia. He stood tall with an air of confidence, yet his eyes gave away his youth. For her brief schooling in Normisia, Caleb had been a fellow student. It was an awkward time as Saranon had struggled to fit in. She smiled in response as Caleb showed her around. At least this time she did not feel like an outsider.

The warm winds of spring blew through the open windows. Carrying the fresh sweet smell of the rambling open garden as Saranon stepped outside. Cradling in amidst of the shrubs covering the edge of the path, she found Katholomu. The great marmoz dragon appeared well camouflaged amidst the shade. His dark coat belied his true length. Hedavin Keep was flanked by a vast team of dragons. The dense woodland covered the true scale of the place and its operations. Saranon wondered how the Dihan sorcerers managed to make their way into the fold. The response she received from the Keep would have been perfect. That was, if it had not been for the attack.

Kat rustled in the undergrowth. Then he stretched out grabbing hold of the first floor balcony. He flexed his wings partway open shifting them to a more comfortable spot as he stood. She held her hand out, placing it over his powerful claws. His tense muscles moved in a smooth motion. The dragon appeared for more content than he had for days. His sharp eye gave away his true composure. She stepped out onto his shoulders. The dragon etched his mark toward the sky in one fluid motion. He circled around in a massive arc mapping out the grounds of the Keep.

Katholomu had no interest in stopping. He gathered speed. He steadied himself on a high perch on the hillside covering part of the Keep. The dragon stretched his body low and the sorceress did the same. Blending into the darkness of his scales and fur, she held her head close to his. The steady sounds ran down from the Keep. She listened unsure of what had raised the dragon's attention. Two raised voices carried just above their location. It marked the end of a short argument with no sense. Still she stayed close to the great beast. He lowered his shoulder and she slid off. The dragon had less subtle ways of getting his point across.

She was not about to argue as she climbed a little higher.

She clung on and lifted her head over the small rise. Peering just above the top of the stone wall embedded half hidden in the hill. The low scattering of shrubs spread across the rocky ground as it met the wall. Then it led down offering little view of the open platform. At first the sight did not yield anything. She began to dismiss Kat's enthusiasm. Then the sun caught an object glinting back toward her with its own spark.

The clump of stone lay on its side with a faded glow, yet the energy should not be there. Saranon eyed it with great suspicion as she stayed close to wall. The cool stone numbed her cheek as she stayed still. She was caught in disbelief. The Keep should have registered the syphoned energy source, yet it did not. As silence filled the air she moved over the wall. She made her way down on the narrow steps on the other side. She glanced around as stood close enough to reach out her hand. The energy gave off a heat that infuriated her. It was too hot for a contraption that was less than half her height. The device had well fused with the Keep, she could remove it on her own and it did not make sense.

A change in the breeze made the hair on the back of her neck prickle and she caught her breath. She dashed toward the dragon scurrying over the wall as she went. She tried not to lose her grip as she half fell onto the dragon. For once Katholomu did not make a sound, not even a tiny grumble as he usually did. She leaned back into the warm folds of his side, as she stood looking out over the vast terrain. The haphazard forest trailed into the open fields. It surrounded the dense city in the distance. A city placed in the heart of nowhere. The warm breeze whipped along as a steady sound filtered up from the hillside. She clambered along and peered over the edge. Captain Tredeer's hand leaned forward with a silent speed. As he ascended, climbing at a steady pace.

Saranon gave the wizard a stark look of disbelief. She was not impressed at having her momentary thoughts interrupted. While the rest of the small group made it to the open ledge. The sorceress had wandered far from her discovery. She felt no burning desire to share as she eyed the wizard with a steady stare. The Captain, who she had only just met, was becoming less tolerable. The sorceress did not recall Captain Mirshendy being so annoying. Yet it had been some time since she had been in the midst of wizards. The dragon behind her gave no hint as he bathed in the sun's warm light. The Captain urged the sorceress to go with them as they climbed higher still.

She felt as though she had just been coerced into an awkward arrangement. She began to miss her solitude. After the final climb she stood, drawing in a long deep breath. The top yielded a full view of the surroundings. The fresh greenery blossomed after a cold winter. The wind whipped at a fast pace through her hair, as she stood admiring the view. Further down, she spotted the familiar shape of Captain Mirshendy near the dragon pens. She could sense him more than anything. The wizard had a habit of standing out from the rest, now that she knew him well enough. Captain Tredeer brought her back to reality. As he asked her about the journey to Indarin Keep in Serenphel.

Saranon had expected this. Still the tone made her even more uneasy as she responded. The conversation had taken far too long, as the afternoon grew dark. Her polite restraint was beginning to wane with fading light. Captain Tredeer made it sound as though he had only just begun. They returned to the Keep for dinner. For once she had lost her appetite, she returned to the apartment to eat alone. Except for Caleb she had not laid eyes on a sorcerer since her arrival. Yet that did not bother her after Serenphel.

Raised voices made their way through the open door. She peered out half listening out of sight, as the words reached her ears. The bold claims of Captain Tredeer had trickled down through the Keep. It was then that the anger rose, as she realised she had been tricked. The Captain had been quick to claim he had a hold over the sorceress. Saranon made her way down a narrow staircase that led below the habitable area of the Keep. Hedavin hummed away in a regular tone. It grated on her nerves since the reading it gave was false. She waited for the right moment to slip undetected along the corridor. The Keep responded with no sign of trouble which unnerved her even more.

She found the nearest panel and held out her hand searching through the Keep. The thought of having to deal with an annoying wizard, made her more determined. Yet the information Hedavin gave up took her by surprise as she let out a small gasp. The shuffle of feet broke the silence close by and she hid, not wanting to be found. The wizard could sense the slight disturbance even though the Keep gave nothing away. He lingered a while before moving on. The sorceress let out a sigh and relaxed. Things were becoming far more complicated as the Hedavin gave up an unexpected name. Major Kellaway, the wizard who stood at the centre of her annoyance.

The Major was encouraging Captain Tredeer, although she did not know why. Saranon knew where to head. There was one person she was after, but she would have to ask the Keep first. Hedavin did not like sorcerers in the wizard stronghold. It would mean a bitter compromise, but one she was willing to make.

For the time the Keep remained silent. She waited holding the frustration back from her face. The sorceress knew she would have to wait as Hedavin decided, it was not an easy ask. Her mind rattled over what she would do. Yet if the Keep accepted, there would be limits to her options. Still, extreme measures were not on the path she was willing to take. So the compromise would serve her well. Etching out of the darkness, came a tone from the heart of the central core. She smiled in response as she made her way to the wizard stronghold.

The dark pool lay in an internal courtyard. Light shone from above with a graceful opening skyward. The wizards worked at their fighting technique around pool in the centre. The place filled with daily life. The Major practised near the water's edge, stepping toward the pool. A sharp short cry rang out, as she pulled the Major under the water. On the surface, the wizards looked down to see the Major caught in a struggle with her. The wizard, Bently, ran into the pool. As soon as he entered the water the image on the surface broke away around him. He dived under staring into nothing and stepped out. 'They're in the surface,' he spoke with haste to Captain Mirshendy, who stayed close.

The Captain leaned down. He plunged his hand in, stopping short of the surface. He took hold of the Major's leg, dragging him with help back out of the pool. The Major's deep gasps for air echoed in the silence. Saranon raised her head from the water's edge. 'Next time send someone other than Captain Tredeer,' her harsh words cut through.

Her statement carried the deep anger inside as she ducked under the surface.

The wizards huddled around in shock and amazement. Major Kellaway shouted at Captain Mirshendy, 'She's your problem.'

A sigh escaped the Captain's lips. She watched on as the Captain began to search the stronghold. The Captain called out, and the sorceress replied. She had perched herself high. Not far from his gaze, as the wizard peered above toward the balustrade. Bently moved without hesitation, he stood in position behind her without making a sound. Captain Mirshendy gave a grim smile, 'This is a wizard stronghold. Go back to your room. We will discuss this in the morning.'

Saranon was not about to argue. She made her way

with ease past a rather grumpy looking Major, who spoke only with his eyes. In the silence the only sound that escaped, emanated from the walls of the Keep.

She stopped herself just before colliding into Mitch who stood in the doorway. The wizard was in no mood to argue. He stayed with a steady restraint, the frustration gleaming from his eyes. 'Next time, tell me if you have an issue. The Major will not forget,' he spoke, with a firm tone that needed no reply.

She was not about to step headlong into an argument. So she tried to veer away from the conversation.

She had almost slipped through the door to her room. As he spoke, 'Were you standing up for Jerald?'

Saranon felt her face go red. As she heard Captain Mirshendy's name and the words stuck in her throat, 'Well…'

The wizard smiled in disbelief. He patted her on the back, 'Sleep well, no doubt we will have an early start.'

She hoped Mitch was wrong, but the chances of that were non-existent.

CHAPTER THREE

The disparity

The vibrant light from the first rays of the sun swept through the curtains of the window. It hit Saranon's eyes with a vengeance and she knew she had overslept. The slight disturbances of footsteps rocked across the floor from the lounge. It suggested that she was last to rise. She sat rubbing her forehead as an almighty headache loomed into place. The thumping sent a shake down her shoulders. Mitch rose as she entered the room, with a knowing expression. He said, 'You didn't think the Major would leave you without a parting gift?'

The wizard's odd sense of humour was half expected. After a moment's hesitation she picked up the toast. Mitch watched with a slow smile. She was about to leave. Then he spoke, 'Captain Mirshendy has asked you to patrol the perimeter with Gabriel.'

Before she uttered a word she thought better of it. She did not particularly want to meet the Major twice in two days. Katholomu had been getting restless. Without a second thought she responded, 'You're coming with me.'

The wizard looked speechless for once. Then she added, 'You know this place better than I.'

He agreed on one condition, that he rode his own dragon.

They went out into the clear morning light. It played through patchwork of trees shrouding the courtyard with a shadowy rim. A robust male shazel dragon sat steady near the opening of the dragon pens. His crisp elegant mane gleamed with a rugged pride. The dragon lifted his head in anticipation. Mitch reached out his hand as Holdvar beckoned him to ride. The wizard took his place on the dragon's muscular shoulders. The beast eyed Saranon as if tempting fate. He made his mark on the open sky with a sturdy, defiant grace. Leaving little doubt in her mind the two were well suited. She eyed Katholomu in the distance and wondered what the dragon said about her.

The mighty marmoz dragon was a fraction too big for even the largest of dragons. His size alone would have made him undesirable to train and he had a temper to match. All his elegant marks of fine breeding were smeared in a thick coat of dirt. Giving away the dragon's favourite past time. His dark coat shone black from a distance. Yet on close inspection the colour was deep dark brown. His wingspan terrified most, dragons and people alike. The size of his claws stretched along the ground. All together the great beast looked spectacular until he moved, giving away his clumsiness. There was also a sense of unreliability for the dragon could not always be found. This amazed her, for his size alone would be difficult to hide anywhere.

She climbed up his shoulder sitting comfortable, on top of his thick sturdy neck. The fresh winds swept across her face as the great beast launched into the sky. She leaned forward as her headache hit hard. She managed to steady the pain while the sun pelted down with a warm glow. Kat flew in a smooth formation following Holdvar's lead. A familiar pain etched its way across her stomach. She lurched forward closing her eyes. The sinking sensation grew as she tried to hold it back. Katholomu bent back his ears and twisted sideways as the sorceress vomited. The dragon made a quick dive low to the ground without missing a beat. He flew upside down and threw the sorceress to the ground.

Saranon tumbled down the rocky hill. She grazed both her arms before coming to halt while Kat flew off leaving her far behind. She managed to sit, holding her heading her hands. The dragon was in no hurry to return as he skimmed through the sky with an easy grace. He curved around in an arc giving her a cursory glance as he glided past. He taunted her for such indignation. She could not blame him as he circled again. He held out his claws as he skidded down the hill, digging in as he slowed to greet her. Katholomu gave her one final look before rubbing the back of his neck down her top. He wiped the last of the vomit on the sorceress. She glared at him while removing her jacket.

Katholomu let out a low grumble. Then side stepped the sorceress when she tried to get back on. He lowered his head near her, and took a sniff before allowing her to ride again. The sorceress could not blame him. As she reached for Kat's shoulder a sound scraped out from the Keep. It bolted through her senses more than she heard it. The dragon curled his tail around him, waiting in the soft winds. She ventured out toward the disturbance. In amongst the scrub she could see the signs of the outer areas of the Keep. It revealed just above the surface.

She reached out touching the panel that gave every appearance of an ordinary rock. A door opened with a distinct hissing sound. The air felt hot and humid as it rushed against her face. The place appeared almost deserted. She instinctively brushed her hand against the wall of the Keep. A muffled response came through piercing its way into her thoughts. It was small, but it was enough.

The fear hidden in Hedavin's response gave a sense of urgency. As the pressure rose deep beneath the surface. The anger swelled within her. The concentration of energy made sense filling her mind with a whole new picture. She left the outer region. The door closed with a tiny whisper of acknowledgement from the wind. There was no trace behind her of where she had been.

Katholomu strayed from his vigilant watch to let her clamber aboard. The great beast heaved his wings into the air and glided along with ease. She could spot Mitch waiting out in the open, with a wave of his hand the dragon dived down. He flew at a dangerous speed ploughing deep into the muddy ground. Kat rolled his chest in the dirt before Saranon managed to climb down. She swung sideways and leaped off. He asked, 'How are you feeling?'

As she stared at him he gave a knowing grin. 'I'm fine,' she snapped.

'You could apologise to the Major?' He suggested.

The headache dissipated, but that was not what darkened her mood. She stood beside him. 'The Keep is in trouble,' she spoke in a grave tone.

Mitch did not budge, he eyed her before he responded, 'You have a lot to learn.'

She was not about to argue with him. Yet the sensations from the Keep had said otherwise, and she knew where that led. A shadow appeared across the sky. Gabriel landed Mitsy close by with a graceful ease.

The wizardess smiled. She scouted the terrain with a thoughtful gaze, 'So what do you think?'

She was not sure how to answer, 'I think we need to take care.'

Gabriel laughed, 'You were the one that picked on the Major.'

Saranon grimaced at the remark. Their journey led them down toward the edge of the city. Mitch showed a reluctance to go any farther, so she did not press the matter.

Upon returning to Hedavin she slipped out of the way as he walked on. On the surface Hedavin felt smooth to the touch. With a methodical hum that should have denoted a functioning Keep. The day's events had ignited her suspicions after the death of the sorcerer.

As she returned, the apartment felt warm and welcoming. The small balcony held the gaze of the midday sun. She took a bite to eat and sat peering across the grounds with its mass of foliage. A sound from the kitchen made her jump as Mitch smiled. For someone so large the wizard could be rather quiet and put her own efforts to shame. She glared at him in annoyance, 'So how is Captain Mirshendy?'

A creak escaped from the room behind them, and the sorceress spun around. She breathed a sigh of relief and sat back down while Rachel joined them on the balcony. 'If you want I can take you to see Jerald?' Rachel asked with hint of sadness.

The expression was lost on Saranon. She bounded forward in eager anticipation, hoping that the Captain would be more forthcoming. Rachel had helped her at Greddin Fort. The Cryzinelan wizards had been intent on capturing her. She was still unsure if that idea had been put to rest. Either way the wizards found it awkward having to deal with her. Yet that did not bother Rachel as the wizardess smiled in return. She shared a warm moment as they passed through the large passageways. They walked further as the corridors became less grand.

The plain walls changed with the appearance of an odd layer of grime. That squished in her fingers as she picked at it. A stale smell wafted under her nose and she flung it to the ground. Without warning, the sounds of voices floated up from beneath. She found herself standing near the bottom of the stairs. She stared at a group of wizards in the midst of cleaning up. The gunk clinging from wall to wall had all the appearances of a murky cesspool. Yet it did not have the pungent odour. It took a while to make out who was who in the dim light. Bently raised a welcoming hand and invited her down into the muck.

The sorceress took the whole site in with an astonished awe. Rachel stood calm and perplexed, waiting for something that Saranon could not figure out. Then Rachel was gone, making her way back up the stairs. She faced the small band of wizards in silence, it was hard to tell what she had just entered into. 'Right, well then,' was all the conversation she could manage. She walked toward the mess in bewilderment.

She stood for a moment looking into the swirling mess. She moved toward the edge. The sorceress peered below while a bubble broke the surface of the murky sludge. She watched as it faded in slow motion and grimaced. It was not the outcome she had expected. As she breathed her lungs could feel the grime sifting up through the air. The stale smell sank into every part of her clothing. The wizards were clearly overwhelmed by the task. It was not the response Saranon was hoping for. She saw Captain Mirshendy avoiding her gaze in the distance.

Such an abundance of muck spilling through the innards of the Keep did not bode well. As she stood thinking she could feel several pairs of eyes watching her. While the wizards worked away at the task. She walked further into the confines of the Keep. The sorceress trudged with a heavy weight on her shoulders as she thought. The screens she had found were showing only a weak connection back to the central core. This explained the build-up. There was not enough energy for Hedavin to maintain the flow. Any attempt by Hedavin to clean up the mess would have to be setup manually.

She let out a groan as she realised that would mean wading through knee deep muck. She had to get to the other side of the open drain where the levers were. The bridge still held, though it was covered under the rising sludge. Saranon searched the pile of equipment for suitable gear to wear. The return journey did not take long. She cringed before stepping down into the sludge. It felt as bad as it sounded. She squelched her way across and heaved up to the other side. The levers were easy to find, but not marked. She concentrated, reaching out her senses to look for some direction from Hedavin. In the glimmer of an instance she found it and moved the levers in place. She poked her head around the corner, as though expecting something to occur, but nothing did.

A sorcerer called out, wanting her to get out of the lower area of the Keep. Saranon's work was done. Yet, she made it clear to Weylin she was not impressed as she made her way back up the stairs. The fresh air hit with a welcome relief, as she washed down her gear, peeling it off her clothes. The smell lingered, even after changing.

Her heart warmed at the sight of Rachel, who always seemed to have enough time to speak to her. She asked the wizardess about Weylin Druyard. The sorcerer had been put out by her presence below the habitable areas. Rachel smiled and responded without answering the question. It was a sign that Saranon was on her own. Still she did not push any further, as the wizardess would have told her if she could. She sat biding her time in thought. A commotion rang through the main doors of the medical area.

Her eyes transfixed on the pain held in the wizard's face, as he was wheeled past. The image locked with her thoughts. She sensed the bond of a sorcerer running deep inside with the pain. The sorceress had seen too much, she ran out before Rachel had time to stop her. She ran to find Mitch, almost instinctively. Just to reassure herself that he was all right. The frustration showed on her voice as she spoke, 'Have I ever treated you ill?'

'Well…' The wizard hesitated.

'I was being serious,' she exclaimed.

'No,' he replied.

The mood had gone stale as she entered the great hall for dinner. There was definitely a distinct tone left hanging in the air. It filled the gaps of silence funnelling its way through the conversation. Like a pause that had been left too long. Saranon managed to find Gabriel across the crowded room. The wizardess seemed unaware of the fuss.

Her friend spent most of her time with the dragons, so she may not have known yet. She waited until her friend had eaten before mentioning it. Gabriel's stunned look answered for her. Mark eyed them from the other side of the table. He hushed the conversation with a stern look. Saranon thought he would say something. Instead the he stood and room fell silent as he left the great hall. It was not the response she had expected. Her mind began processing the information. Gabriel leaned over and whispered, 'No good comes when that happens.'

She agreed with the resounding statement, as she too left. This time no one noticed as she scampered from the room. The Keep lay in silence as she tried to reach out. She had not expected much given its current state, but a little sign would have been nice. She searched around away from the medical area. She circled back through via a more discreet path. As she drew close Saranon expanded her senses. The glimpse shot through with resounding clarity. The pain pierced her mind in an instant.

She opened her eyes not realising she had closed them in the shock. She could sense the wizard breathing in a low ragged tone and she had her answer. The wizard was bonded and he fought with every breath to hold on. The sound of footsteps crept close by. She ran from the scene before anyone could follow. As she returned, the sanctuary of her apartment was not as appealing. She flicked the light on and almost jumped. As Captain Mirshendy appeared from the dark shadow washed along the moonlit wall.

The Captain glared down at her, 'Stay away from Rowan. You are here as a guest.' He spoke with such a stern voice that Saranon was taken aback. It was not what she had expected. 'The bond needs to be broken,' she responded.

'Do not interfere with the Cryzinelan,' his voice was final as he left. She was not ready to admit defeat, but she did not want to meet the Captain head on. She almost jumped at a rustling sound behind her and stared at Mitch as he froze. The wizard vanished into his room before she could talk. She opened the door and she peeped through the gap, the wizard sat not uttering a word.

She asked as she stared straight into his eyes. 'Would Captain Mirshendy let you suffer at the hands of a sorcerer?'

Mitch had not expected the question. He answered, 'No.' The wizard spoke after her, 'Don't go near Rowan.'

'I wasn't planning to,' her words drifted as she left for a restless sleep.

The bed did not feel anywhere near as comfortable. While the wind played through the branches of the trees. The shadows moved along the walls irritating her. She reached out searching for something unknown.

Sleep caved in and a sharp image broke through the surface, as a hand reached out and pulled her in. The rush was so sudden it left her breathless as she hit the ground in an ageless dream. She stood near the running water that made no sound. She looked up to the fallen ceiling marking the edge of the ruins. A figure stood in the centre facing away, as the sun shone through. Tasha's fawn coloured hair sparkled in the light breaking through the roofless structure. As Tasha approached Saranon turned to see a man lying on the altar. He hardly moved except for a ragged breathing. Tasha turned to face the man, he does not have time.

Saranon faced her old friend who showed no sign of the death that had taken her. Then Tasha's lips moved and the words prickled down her skin, kill the boy. She knew what it meant. She had left the task undone. Tasha had always been the leader and now more than ever she felt the burden she had run from. The sorceress knelt down on one knee as she had done when the task was hers to bear. Tasha reached over and tapped her shoulder. The shock ran through Saranon's body pulling her awake and into the dark morning.

She steadied herself, while wiping the sweat from the back of her neck. She crept out, to see the corridors void of life at such a dismal hour. The only sound haunting the darkness came from the rustling breeze. Saranon dashed out into the open. It swept away the last remnants of sleep as her mind cleared. In the distance a sound made its way through the air like a small mumble. As she ran through the darkened edges of the woods more voices travelled. The sound was ever so low among the swaying leaves.

Saranon crouched out of sight. The hidden door into the Keep lay wide open. Tellembre twitched by her side. The bond-breaker hummed with delight, sensing the events before she did. A dim light stretched up ahead. It roamed from the gathering of sorcerers in the cover of darkness.

As the sorcerers parted she caught a glimpse of Edan. The sorcerer stood near the centre. A movement caught her eye. The faint sorcerer's light shone upon the boy's face. Tasha's words were still strong in her mind as she held her breath. The glow flickered as the boy moved. The build of a sorcery stirred from the ground. As the vapour rose its tentacles skyward. The spiral grew taking form and Saranon stood. The last remnant of fear left her eyes as she stared out in the distance. Tellembre's pearl blade sang as she drew the blade and it formed into a sword. The bond-breaker made at Ollanthia was light and durable, fitting snug in her hand. She honed in on the boy's face. She had let Tasha down in the battle at Zaidek. The blade swung as she held it by her side.

The sorcerers began to close in a tight circle. Around the trail of sorcery as it lit its way into the sky. She raised the pearl blade and it shimmered in the light. Saranon swung in tight as the first two sorcerers turned to face her. Their eyes stayed with the bond-breaker. Her energy rose with one purpose as the blade swung. Then the blast followed through. It hit the sorcery swirling from the ground and deflected. The blast hit the sorcerer to the left of Edan. The sorcerer took the full force as he crumpled into a heap. She sensed the wizard Rowan and her face went pale. Captain Mirshendy had told her to stay away.

Edan disappeared as the group of sorcerers broke away from the huddle. She grimaced as she lost sight of him. The two sorcerers next to her regained their composure. They hurled their sorcery toward her. The blasts spiralled before she managed to block them. A cataclysm of sparks radiated through the air. The sorcery settled to show the place had been abandoned. Tellembre shone as she fumed. She had failed Tasha again, and she would have to face the Cryzinelan wizards.

She swung Tellembre high in the form of a sword, and staggered back. Tellembre came to life in the darkness of night before the dawn. Her heart pumped loud in her chest. Katholomu swooped down following the glow from the bond-breaker. His mighty claws dug in hard as he ground to a halt. His wings stretched their full length to lessen the impact. The dragon lowered his head and glared into her eyes. She transformed the blade back into a dagger and Kat lifted her up onto his shoulders. His coat was smothered in grit and blood, yet she did not question him. Her mind was filled with the silence of knowing she had failed again. The great beast grunted as he leaped into the sky. She patted him and the blood soaked her hand.

'We have both been busy tonight,' she spoke to the dragon and he snorted in acknowledgement. 'Perhaps I should have gone with you?'

Kathomolu gave a low chuckle that rumbled through his belly, and coughed. 'Great, even my dragon won't fight with me,' she grumbled.

The dark silhouette of Hedavin loomed overhead and her heart sank. She would have to face the wizards.

CHAPTER FOUR

End the night

The grey sky hid them and they made their way to the dragon pens before the morning sun broke. Saranon waited for the dragon to stop instead he squeezed under the gate. She clung on as she shouted. Kat ran toward the pool of water with a flying leap. He rolled and she managed to jump clear plummeting straight into the water. The great beast ducked his head under and scooped her up. He placed her near the edge. She wanted to shout at him, but he needed a bath or there would be questions. 'You owe me,' she said as she picked up a scrubbing brush.

'At least you don't have to face the Cryzinelan,' she said as a thought struck her. 'Please tell me you don't.'

Katholomu snorted in disgust.

The dragon showed enormous patience as she dried him off. Taking care to pick out the last signs of what he had been up to. He curled up in the courtyard welcoming her to rest with him. She was exhausted and accepted knowing she have to face the wizards later. The air filled with shouting as the great beast gave no sign of his hidden guest. The shallow hint of dawn splayed through the tiny openings. She remained silent, well after the commotion had passed. Mark's voice cut through the air urging the dragon to move. At first Katholomu gave no response. It only prompted the wizard to walk closer as he shouted. Kat stared the wizard down in a bemused fashion before uncurling his large body.

Saranon knew Mark Staragen well from Greddin Fort. The wizard was the best dragon trainer in Normisia. A reputation the wizard did not need to boast, he was also stubborn and irritating. The only reason she had warmed to him was because he had bought Katholomu for her. It was an act of kindness that left her baffled. The wizard had a grim presence and she was sure he could back up the unspoken threat. She climbed up onto the dragon's shoulders. She stared down at Mark, before the great beast launched into the grey sky. She was in no mood to answer questions as the night's events weighed on her thoughts.

Katholomu landed on a nearby hill before he lost his footing skidding to a stop. His sheer size made the landing difficult to judge. She patted the great beast. Then stared down into the valley where she had been the night before. The deep forest hid the area from the sky, as she stood with the wind sweeping through her hair.

A dark figure overshadowed the sky, she peered up

to see Splodge's underbelly. She could recognise Mark's dragon anywhere. He dived down beside Katholomu, giving a friendly nudge with his shoulder. Splodge stood his ground showing off his height, before letting Mark slide down. The wizard was one of the few Saranon had not argued with. His statue and appearance gave him a stronger presence than any other she had met. He was almost the same height Mitch. With a stocky robust built that gave the impression he could withstand anything. 'You need to return to the Keep, Mitch is in trouble,' the wizard spoke with a gruff rigid tone.

'Are you sure?' she asked completely stunned.

'He is blamed for Rowan's death,' Mark responded.

'Mitch wouldn't do that,' the sorceress spoke, still in shock.

'Then I suggest you return to the Keep,' the wizard's answer was final. He stood waiting for Saranon to move first.

Katholomu saw no need to rush. He waited before bolting into the sky, toward the open courtyard. Gabriel ran to meet her before she was stopped by a wave of Bently's hand. Captain Mirshendy's officer stood strong as the sorceress strode towards him. 'Come with me,' he spoke in curt voice.

The silence faded into a dull chant of shouts, emanating from the wizard stronghold. Saranon did not have much time to wonder, as a searing sea of eyes fell straight upon her. Then the shouting began as the realisation came too late. Bently strode behind her blocking her escape. She made her way to the front of the audience. The crowd parted with a great reluctance. None were brave enough to block her path.

She almost landed into Captain Tredeer, side stepping at the last second. She spied Mitch kneeling down on the platform. The chants grew around her before the Major's voice cut through the noise. Her mind was still catching up as she looked around. In amongst the crowd Captain Mirshendy stared back. Major Kellaway's words rang out. He boomed over the crowd as he stood on the platform near Mitch. He ordered the sorceress to stand on the platform before her. The crowd waited in eager anticipation.

She stepped forward turning back to face the Major. A hush fell through the crowd of waiting faces as Saranon waited. The buzzing silence lingered too long. As she braced herself for what may come. She remembered the agreement she had made with the Keep. She held back a smile, eyeing the Major as nothing occurred. Captain Tredeer broke the silence with his rage. The Keep would not harm the sorceress. He lunged toward her, as the Major ordered Captain Mirshendy to take Saranon and Mitch from the hall. Captain Mirshendy wrapped his strong arm around hers. They ducked away as the mood in the crowd changed too frustration. To her surprise the wizard took them back to his quarters in the wizard stronghold.

She could contain herself no longer and smiled. As she spoke, 'I always wondered what you did for entertainment.'

For once the Captain did not growl. Instead Mitch filled the gap, 'This is serious.'

'Did you kill Rowan?' She asked.

'No,' he replied.

'Then what is the problem?' the sorceress exclaimed as she faced the Captain.

Captain Mirshendy was about to answer when Rachel rushed through the door. She beckoned them to follow, as an array of harsh voices rose from the corridor.

Before Saranon had the chance to ask, the wizards ran ahead. They left her bewildered as she caught up. She peered around the wall, her mouth dropped at the sight of a sobbing wizardess. Cynthia, the Major's daughter, turned and looked her way. The Major's humiliated face told her more than she needed. Cynthia had ended Rowan's life.

She stood close to Mitch, and whispered, 'Will they do the same to her?'

'No,' he whispered in return, as the room fell silent.

The Major looked up at the Captain, 'We'll have to find another way.'

Captain Mirshendy nodded his agreement.

'Ah…' Saranon was about to speak up as Mitch read her thoughts.

'You didn't,' he exclaimed.

'I was only told to stay away from Rowan,' the sorceress glared at him.

Cynthia broke out into a painful sob as she realised the sorcerer was dead. Rowan would have survived. 'Take them from the room?' Major Kellaway addressed Captain Mirshendy. The Captain ushered Saranon and Mitch away. 'Tomorrow I expect you both to help with the clean-up,' the Captain spoke to the pair. Their mouths gaped in silent protest.

Saranon turned to Mitch, 'This is your fault.'

As the two exchanged short words, neither noticed Mark wandering up behind them. He said, 'I have two dragons that need cleaning, go and sort it out.'

Mark had not stopped moving as he moved them toward the pens. Mitch made his way down the stairs. She was not so convinced, 'Katholomu was clean this morning.'

'Why don't you take a look,' Mark spoke as he stood at the top of the stairs.

She was not about to argue any further as another person approached. Mark began shouting. She hurried down toward the dragon pens. Saranon almost ran into Gabriel who looked relieved to see her. The wizardess was a fraction younger even though she was an apprentice trainer. She had a natural gift for working with dragons.

The horrid smell of damp dragon stuck in her throat as she tried not gag. Gabriel smiled, 'You haven't seen Kat yet have you?'

It was a knowing comment more than a question. The sorceress did not need to wonder much longer. The great dragon was hunched back rubbing an itch on his shoulder. He kept dropping clumps of gunk. It had matted across his fine coat, and taken away all its shine. If she did not know better, Saranon would have sworn the dragon had done it on purpose. He had trudged through the mess the Captain asked her to clean up. Her mouth gaped, then she shut it, as a putrid smell caked her tongue. The dragon turned around and grinned.

Kat wiped a grubby cheek all the way along her side, making sure not to miss any part of her clothing. The wet substance sank through the fabric. She cringed as it stuck to her hands and she pushed the dragon away. Gabriel tried to stifle a laugh as she stepped back. The sorceress held out her grubby arms and her friend let out a short squeal then ran. Gabriel could not get away fast enough. As Saranon made her way to the change room covered from head to toe with muck. She winced at the thought. She hurled herself into the giant task of cleaning the dragon.

The sorceress looked up after dry reaching for the second time. To see Katholomu standing, soaking wet. The hose rinsed away the bulk of the smell, as she lathered his rough skin. It foamed with the sweet smelling liquid over his hard scales. The dragon did not mind being clean. For all his love of dirt, it was an excuse to find another way of getting grubby. He swished his tail along the ground in a curved arc. The sorceress groomed around his ears. Katholomu's ear twitched but she took no notice as she brushed up his markings. A gentle hand reached up and patted the dragon. Saranon almost fell off with surprise at the sight. Rachel had appeared without making a sound.

'Thank you for helping with Rowan,' the wizardess had been crying. Yet her eyes shone true.

'Will Cynthia be okay?' Saranon asked.

'Yes,' Rachel responded. The weight of a heavy day filtered through. As the wizardess asked the question she had come for. 'How is it that you were not affected by the

Keep?'

Saranon smiled as she glided down off the dragon's silky back. 'I made an agreement with Hedavin,' she said.

'You were lucky,' Rachel remarked and welcomed her to an evening meal.

The sorceress scoffed into the dish. Captain Mirshendy joined them with a thud as he sat down. The Captain glanced at her, 'You made the Major look like a fool,' the Captain spoke.

'Jerald,' Rachel responded.

'He has more empathy than I do,' at no stage had the Captain lost his harsh edge.

It was as close to friendship as she would see from the Captain. So she kept the response to herself. The night was growing dim as she left, with her weary muscles calling out for sleep. As she went into the apartment Mitch gave her a warm hug of appreciation, 'Thanks.'

'You could've cleaned my dragon?' Saranon suggested in astonishment.

'He's your responsibility,' the wizard smiled.

A tear escaped falling onto the pillow as lay awake in a warm bed. Rowan had lost his life for nothing. She hoped tomorrow would be more welcoming as she left.

A figure blocked the light. She blinked opening her eyes, letting in the morning light. She remembered where she was meant to be and groaned. Mitch smiled he did not have to say anything, as he waited. 'Why do wizards always have to be annoying,' she muttered under her breath. She followed Mitch downstairs.

'Well, you are in wizard Keep,' Bently's voice startled her, 'Did you sleep in?'

Mitch turned around and smiled with a soft chuckle. She was about to grab some equipment when Bently shook his head. They stepped into the underground chamber. While her mind took a while to catch up with what she was seeing.

Saranon peered over the hard edge into the darkness. She made out the trail of muck that had receded to the depths below. She was about to ask the wizard how, when she recalled her previous visit and smiled. The mess had been dissipating since she had manually engaged the Keep. It picked up a higher level of waste. Bently slid down and walked along the lower ledge. They followed as the sorceress tried not to touch anything grubby. It was impossible as she wiped her sleeve. Up ahead she heard a familiar voice. Captain Mirshendy gave a nod of recognition between orders.

The Captain appeared far more relaxed and at home in the slimy belly of the Keep. The wizards worked hard to open the doors. They washed out the grime from the chambers underneath. She peered around the corner, and stood stunned. The roaring sub-station whirred away underneath her feet. She knelt down, peeking over the edge. 'Impressive isn't it?' Bently spoke next to her before the Captain interrupted.

Impressive was not the first word that sprang to Saranon's mind. As she took note of the load the sub-station was picking up.

'I need you to go further down,' the Captain spoke in a flat tone.

'I can see why,' the sorceress answered without taking her eyes off the engine.

'If this is not fixed there will be another Rowan,' the Captain spoke. The other wizards fell silent.

The sorceress felt the weight of his words on her shoulders, she stood up and nodded. Mitch peered over the edge next to the Captain. He stared out into the gloom just as Saranon fell into knee deep muck and shouted.

She could hear the wizard laugh with nervous relief from above. As she waded out to the other side and cleaned herself off. She trudged along, trying not slip as remnants of the grime squelched beneath her. It covered the base of the lower floor and pooled in the lower areas. A sound crept up from the pipes leading deep underground. She caught her breath, then letting out a sigh into the silence. She steadied herself climbing downward along a stale dry passage. A musty smell wafted from the opening and prickled up the back of her neck.

Saranon froze, before stepping into an alcove. The large sealed doors were lying in her path. The sorceress stood in the alcove of the great archway. The doors blocked her entrance down to the central core. She held out her hand and it felt hot to the touch. As she examined the seal around the doors the stress lines showed. The weakness embedded in the tiny grooves. She stood back in awe as the Keep held the pressure at bay. It remained locked within the central core. A small tapping sound echoed from above.

She moved away and started back to the surface.

Captain Mirshendy was waiting in the silence, 'We have to leave.'

Before she could speak, Mitch whisked her out of sight. A familiar sound crept through the space and the colour drained from her face. They darted away in the midst of the confusion. A warning prickled at the edge of Saranon's senses. She ran in front of the wizard as the sorcery hit in a fit of rage. It melted, trickling down as the sparks hit the barrier. It faded, as she shielded Mitch from the blow. The heated shouts from the other wizards reached their ears. The group reunited in the ambush. The Captain's cold harsh stare glimmered in the light, as a scream cut through the air.

Saranon recognised who it was, as she peered beyond the group. She could just make out Cynthia, made visible in a moment hesitation. In the verge up ahead she could make out Captain Tredeer. She cringed knowing that the sorcerers who attacked had the advantage. Just as an attacker spotted Captain Tredeer's hiding place. Saranon ran with all her might. Time slowed as the pain seared through. The familiar agony that coursed through her and an old memory came to life. As her energy resonated with Hedavin she sucked the energy of the Keep in. She churned it out with immense force.

The Keep let out a violent thunderous roar. The wind whipped through the air and shards of Hedavin with it. The sparks broke across the walls in an array of light. For in the space between time and nothing the Angeon held out her hands. She grasped the energy. The pain melded with the air and the smell of fear pulsing through the pressure. The blades formed from the whirring haze. The brilliant razer-sharp blue of Normisia, called forth in two strong bond-breakers. As Saranon raised them Captain Mirshendy leaped forward. He took the one to the right, wielding the blade as he sheared through his opponent. Captain Tredeer took the one in her left hand. The sorceress could not raise her voice amidst the dim haze. The two Captains had finished their work.

She was in no frame of mind to argue over losing her new bond-breakers. She walked over to Cynthia and held out her hand. The wizardess stood in amazement at the scene. As the other wizards cleared the area, with almost no sign left of the disturbance. In the silence that followed Cynthia asked, 'Does there have to be another Hilazen?'

Captain Mirshendy did not answer, his hard stare spoke for him. Mitch stayed by the sorceress. As Captain Tredeer led Cynthia away, 'I thought you didn't like him?'

Saranon was not about to argue with the wizard. Yet he could be infuriating, 'Of course I don't.'

Then she realised she had spoken the words too loud.

CHAPTER FIVE

Company

Mitch was still laughing to himself after Saranon's outburst, much to her disgust. The sun shone bright at the start of a new day. The glimmering rays belied the subtle tone, that had swept through the Keep from the day before. It was not what she had wanted in many ways. Captain Kane Tredeer had begun boasting of his acquired prize. At least Captain Mirshendy kept his hidden from sight. Although there was a distinct jovialness to his step that appeared out of place. She smiled shaking her head in disbelief. A thought had crossed her mind to take the bond-breakers back. Yet Mitch's glare suggested otherwise. The wizard had become good at answering her sudden nondescript thoughts.

The fresh air flowing around the grounds outside swept beneath her feet. She strode toward the dragon pens and a familiar sound rang out. Only this time it was Mitsy the shazel dragon, who had a rough elegance about her. The dragon greeted the Saranon before expecting her to follow.

Mitsy skittered around the corner disappearing with a short flick of her tail. She was full grown but the size of a teenager compared to Kat. She woke Katholomu who lifted his sleepy head with one eye open. The dragon had been sunbaking on his side and he stretched out his body with a vibrant shake. Saranon stepped back and Kat had already stooped down. He picked her up, tilting her onto his large shoulders. The sorceress smiled as Gabriel's voice echoed nearby. She asked, 'I thought you would like to go for a ride?'

'That sounds great,' Saranon smiled in return. The clear blue sky beckoned from above.

It was good to feel the air move. Even if the dragon's launch made her stomach squirm as he bounded for the sky. The wizardess, Gabriel, glided along with ease as Mitsy flew in perfect formation. Kat grunted beneath her. They flew to the edge of the bustling city, where the two dragons did not appear out of place. It had been ages since she had the chance to roam through Normisia. She let Gabriel lead the way. The street was clean with a rough edge. She reflected the hardiness of the people living in the north.

Saranon rushed ahead in the maze of shops and activities. It took her a while to notice that Gabriel was not following. She looked around then went back reaching out with her senses. She narrowed down her search walking up to the corner of a building. In the alleyway stood a sorceress she gasped at the sight. Bianca shushed her as they stood in silence. Saranon could not see the point of staying in the dreary alley. Bianca disappeared into the wall, leaving the sorceress alone with Gabriel. Before she had time to ask, a sound came from along the ground in a slow hiss.

She reached out and dragged Gabriel into a rear entrance of the building. They listened to the sound of soft gravel footsteps approaching. Then it stopped. The sorceress did not need to tell her friend to be silent, as they stayed hidden. The sound resonated from their breath, as every minute felt like an hour. When the footsteps had headed away she breathed a sigh relief. Bianca stood beside them as Gabriel let out a small gasp in recognition. 'What are you doing here?' The wizardess asked.

'It's all right they're gone,' Bianca said.

She tried to sound convincing, with the doubt showing in her eyes. The thin smile did little to reassure Saranon, who saw the signs of a hidden fear. 'I think now would be a good time to head back,' she spoke her thoughts aloud.

'No,' Bianca said with a strained voice, 'How about we stay a little longer?'

'Okay?' Gabriel responded hoping for more of an explanation.

Bianca smiled as they crept outside with the fading light. They stepped into a warm welcoming air. A complete contrast to the last few hours. Saranon stayed several paces behind in an agitated state as she surveyed the area.

She remained unconvinced that the trouble had vanished, but her senses revealed nothing. Gabriel was intent on having fun as she joined a group of friends. From the edge of her energy Saranon felt something. She grabbed Bianca's arm, 'You need to go.'

Her tone was so final that her friend did not argue, as the three of them made it back to the dragons. Bianca sat atop Katholomu. The scent of sorcery that had been picked up earlier grew stronger. She motioned for Kat to go and the great dragon wasted no time. Mitsy followed in unison. Saranon stayed, watching them as they grew distant in the sky.

The air buzzed around her as she glanced back not seeing anything. The Angeon crept to the surface with delight knowing what it had been called for. The energy of old ran through her. A sound sparked her attention in the dim shadows of the late afternoon. It spread across the ground from the buildings. The sound grew as the wind rushed around her, sweeping a steady path. Growing in the hollow drone as a figure appeared in the distance. The sorcerer came closer with every step. Saranon was waiting. As she did the figure blended into the background leaving behind no trace.

She stepped forward toward the last trace. The air prickled against her skin as the cold set in. Damon stood in the shadows as she waited, she could sense him. Damon raised his sorcery from the ground as it twisted around. He strode forward facing her. Saranon let out a gasp as he stood too close for comfort. 'Stay out of my way,' he waited for her to back down, then shook his head. 'I gave you a choice.'

'Another time,' Saranon replied.

She raised her sorcery to remove the barrier he had placed around her. It took more effort than she expected, yet she shrugged it off in Damon's presence.

'Very well,' he spoke.

He raised his arms and the ground trembled, Saranon was thrown back. She managed to buffer the fall before slamming into the dirt. She stood catching her breath and braced herself. She created a barrier to give her time. Damon could sense the shield and he flinched. He gave one blast that shook the shield just enough to frighten her. She took the warning and fled. 'Run, run while you can girl,' Damon's voiced echoed after her.

It was not what she had wanted, but then there was no point chasing Damon as her senses reached out. She ran to the nearest lay-line, and rushed to the Keep Hedavin hoping her friend was safe. She did not have to wait long to find out. She made it to the apartment, where Bianca was talking to Mitch. He appeared at home with the Palascene sorceress in his presence. He was far more comfortable than he was around her. Bianca stood to thank Saranon. While avoiding any direct questions about who had been following her.

Saranon felt a great reluctance to push the point. All the while Bianca's calmness made her feel more on edge. At Zaidek the Palascene sorceress had been scathing at times with her remarks. The sight of the same person with sadness haunting her eyes ran shivers done her spine. Her friend changed the subject, 'You are lucky to have Mitch.'

Lucky was not how she would describe the wizard. The word irritating was more appropriate. Bianca laughed at her expression as the thought showed on her face, 'I need your help.'

'I guessed that,' Saranon looked up from making the bed. Her friend watched in amusement.

'I need a Hilazen,' Bianca said.

As the words left the friend's mouth she almost fainted. She asked, 'Why in Tordoren would you want that?'

'My kin want me to bond a wizard,' she replied.

Saranon froze, as all her thoughts escaped in the stillness that followed. She was not sure what to say in the awkward pause.

She said the first word that entered her head while her mouth gaped, 'Oh.'

'Do not tell anyone.' Bianca added, 'Not even Mitch.'

'Well that makes it difficult. Is there anything else?' She asked with a hint of sarcasm.

'I would like some toast,' Bianca's request reminded her not to ask silly questions.

Mitch was keeping busy in the kitchen. She almost ran straight into him and the wizard side-stepped. Saranon changed her tune as she waited for the toast. The wizard could appear uninterested as he lingered. She darted back to the room where Bianca sat. Her friend showed no hint of their conversation. She settled down into her warm cosy bed and turned over. The rain crept through the quiet night, lapping at the window.

The restful sleep turned into a rampant dream. All

she could see in the image was a figure running. As she chased the figure ran farther away. She was left alone as she caught her breath and turned back. She was under attack. She flung her arms to hold off the surge of energy as it catapulted toward her. Something moved in the real world above her head. She opened her eyes with a start. Her energy raged just beneath the surface as she reached out her senses. She walked over to the large window and peered out into the darkness. No sign came so she eased her way back into bed. Whatever had alerted her would have to wait as she drifted off into sleep.

The sound of rushing water woke Saranon, as she remembered she had a guest. Bianca looked far more like her former perfect self as she left the room. By the time Saranon managed to run out to the lounge room Bianca was gone. Her heart skipped a beat with panic before Mitch reassured her. He led the sorceress to the main control room, like the one she had seen at Zaidek. At the threshold of the door she stopped glancing in. Bianca and Captain Mirshendy were deep in conversation.

For a brief moment Saranon saw a small spark of energy between them. Then it was replaced by a sense annoyance that swept through her. The Captain was calm and polite around her friend. Just as she was about to speak Mitch asked, 'You two have become good friends?'

He knew the pair had clashed at Zaidek. As she tried changing the subject, 'So what are we doing here?'

'We need to gain access to the lower areas,' he answered.

She was not convinced with Bianca not having to brave the grimy chambers below. He spoke as though reading her thoughts, 'The controls are our best chance.'

The scowl remained on her face as she let it go. She peered down at the screen running the length of the bench. She ran her hand over it to search through the information. A shadow passed over and she glanced up to see Cynthia.

The wizardess tapped on the control panel, 'Mind if I help?'

She felt a sadness knowing Cynthia's loss and nodded. If anyone would be able to help the Major's daughter could. Cynthia saw her cringe as Bianca's laugh cut through the air. The wizardess asked, 'What did you do to annoy the Captain?'

'I don't know,' Saranon answered while Mitch coughed interrupting them.

Cynthia smiled at him. As the sorceress retorted, 'You became my Hilazen afterward so that doesn't count.'

Mitch coughed again, and she glared at him. Cynthia laughed, shaking her head. As she went back to work and remarked, 'It's like all the accesses are jammed.'

Saranon felt like hitting her head against the screen. She refrained from acting on the thought. The wizardess was trying to help. She glanced sideways to find Bianca had discovered a way into the maze. Captain Mirshendy greeted it with jubilation.

The Captain's reaction annoyed her even more. As Cynthia broke the silence, 'You don't like him do you?'

She turned to answer, 'I'm not sure.'

Her response was not what Mitch had expected. Before he spoke Bianca began showing them how to gain access to the system. With a way in, Saranon did not need much encouragement. Cynthia watched with excitement.

The paths that lay hidden underground came to life. It showed in sequences cascading along the screen. Still it held a few glaring disadvantages, as she began plotting the way in her mind. No doubt she would be expected to make the journey down. Bianca's voice chatted away in the background. She sighed as her friend gave the appearance not being in trouble. There had been no sign of Damon since to her relief. The morning progressed with a graceful ease. Cynthia's conversation came to a mute halt as she peered up.

Captain Mirshendy had lost none of his hard edge. Even with the new bond-breaker sitting by his side. The Captain gave no sign of appreciation. He suggested proceeding with another attempt down in the Keep. All the while staring at Cynthia as the fear shot up through her eyes. Saranon pursed her lips together as the Captain spoke. He appeared as though the fate of another wizard had been decided. The silence gave away far more than his words. As she eyed Mitch with a knowing glare, 'I don't look so bad now?'

'Well…' He began.

Saranon thumped him on the arm before he could answer. His laughter only annoyed her more. The midday sun in the garden offered a refreshing change, as she moved away from the group. Spending the afternoon in the control room did not appeal. She strode toward the dragon pens. Gabriel was grappling with one of the dragons. She intervened and held on to the dragon's hind leg as the beast admitted defeat. 'Thanks,' Gabriel called from the other side.

A loud snort ran warm air straight down her back as she turned to see Splodge. Mark's dragon, Splodge, was hard to miss. He had the same no nonsense attitude as his rider. The beast had a soft spot for her after their first meeting at Greddin Fort. The dragon had almost killed Mark. Being trapped between two dragons gave Saranon an uneasy feeling. She heard voices from across the courtyard. Gabriel poked her head over the dragon Dredger, 'Are you hiding from something?'

'Hard work,' she answered.

'You've come to the wrong place,' before Gabriel laughed.

Mark motioned for his dragon Splodge to leave and he spied the sorceress.

'Why aren't you with Mitch?' He did not wait for a response. Before making the firm suggestion that the dragon pens needed cleaning.

Saranon was still trying to think of a response when Mark had left. 'I wouldn't bother he's been out of sorts,' Gabriel added.

Dredger was more of a hindrance than a help. She used a small amount of her energy to push the dragon out of the way.

The beast did not make any attempt to snap at them.

Gabriel laughed at the sight before diving in to give a hand. The place wafted of a musty smell, although it looked far tidier than it had before. She had to find a solution for both the wizard clan and Bianca. She mused over it as she rinsed the floor. While trying to avoid soaking Splodge as he lay to the side watching the spray of water. She placed the bucket back on its stand and peered around in search of Gabriel.

A sound drew her attention from the corridor. As she stepped into the Mark's office finding no one. A paper caught her eye on the desk and she could not resist the opportunity to peek. She let out a gasp, as the muffled thud of footsteps approached and she ran outside. Mark's booming voice echoed in the distance. She was too shocked to take any notice. Saranon ran straight for an end node of the Keep. As she reached it she fell in a weary heap and collapsed out of breath. The sorcerer's stone had a dull finish resembling paving. It was smaller than the end nodes she had seen at Indarin. She rested her legs trying to think as the image stuck in her head.

She drew a heavy breath, as a light breeze blew around her. The afternoon shadow grew into a murky glimmer of evening. Thoughts whirled around her head. She had to help Bianca. The air trickled with an unseen stillness by the natural sky. Her senses began to prickle at the edges. There was no time to waste as she made her way down in the confines of the Keep. She touched the wall of the Keep, and sent a faint signal hoping that it would reach Bianca in time.

If her idea did not work it would be too late. The sorceress could sense the wizards in the background, keeping their distance. A figure emerged up ahead and she smiled with as Bianca met her in the outer region of Hedavin. Bianca spoke, 'It's good to see you.'

Saranon whispered, 'I think you should bond Jerald.'

Her friend let out a small gasp. The wizards revealed themselves from the background. Just as she had expected the Captain approached first.

Captain Mirshendy's eyes pierced the darkness as he went for Saranon. She was ready for him, and in no mood to yield to the wizard as she gripped him in a tight hold. The other wizards closed in. As Bianca cried out, 'I can't do it, I can't do it,' and sobbed slipping to the floor.

The hesitation of the whole group was instant. As Saranon turned to the Captain and retorted, 'Well you're no good.'

She loosened her grip, and tossed him to the side. The Captain did not go far as she stared him down in an attempt to negate a second round.

'What's going on?' Captain Mirshendy's mind did not miss anything. It bought a temporary truce.

'Bianca needs to bond a wizard and I thought you would do,' she exclaimed.

The Captain's jaw dropped. To Saranon's amazement he approached Bianca and held out his hand. Before she had time to think Bianca and the Captain bonded. She was speechless at the sight.

Bently stood beside her. As she noticed the wizards

had blocked the most obvious path of escape. She eyed the wizard as he led them off to the wizard stronghold. They peered down over the balcony. Listening as Bianca and Captain Mirshendy explained what had happened. She was so focused on the pair that she only sensed Mark when he stood right next her. Saranon did not know what to say as he listened. Bianca was accepted into the midst of the Cryzinelan.

Mark leaned over and whispered in her ear, 'I was meant to be bonded to you.'

The words cascaded through her brain like a torrent as her face went pale. All she could manage was a whisper, 'Why?'

'Because you can access the central core,' his words were so definite. That it made her wonder if she could enter the core under pressure.

She turned, the wizard walked away without saying anything more. Yet what he had said was enough.

Saranon was so bewildered that she lost track of time as she entered the apartment. Mitch took on a scary appearance when he was angry, he slammed a mug down so hard it almost broke. 'I'm sorry,' she spoke assuming he was angry with her.

'It isn't you,' Mitch explained.

'Are you sure?' She asked.

The wizard managed a smile in return.

She stood watching him for a while before sitting at the table. 'I couldn't stand to have more than one wizard.'

Mitch nodded staring before looking up with eyes

that showed a heavy burden. It was not what she wanted as she her thoughts turned to the central core. 'I may be gone for a while,' she said.

'Are you going to spend time with your friend?' He asked.

'I meant Hedavin,' she responded as she eyed his knowing look.

The pair sat in silence as she thought of Captain Mirshendy and Bianca. She wondered who her friend was afraid of. As the night crept in, Saranon began feeling the harshness of the day. It rested heavy on her shoulders. The Captain had given her a thumping bruise that would still be there in the morning. She wondered what the Cryzinelan had been thinking and what lay below in Hedavin.

CHAPTER SIX

A virtuous ground

The branches clipped the window in the night breeze. As the moon still shine outside. Saranon had not bothered to close the curtains. Her dreams had been filled with darkness from her days in the detention camps. She felt the marks in palms that were no longer there. Mark's words still clung in her head and echoed through her ears. She reached for her bond-breaker, the dagger stayed in its dormant form. She opened the door jumping with fright. In the darkness stood a figure, Captain Mirshendy, his silhouette form stood like stone.

It was not the first time the Captain had snuck up on her, as she caught her breath while he spoke. 'Mark should not have warned you,' the wizard said with a firm stance.

Saranon's mouth gaped before she closed it. 'You don't get to make that decision,' she retorted and headed past the

Captain.

Bently materialised out of the shadows and blocked her path. She eyed him while her anger rose to the surface.

Her energy surged escaping from her hands. It stunned Bently as he clambered to the ground. Silence followed before the Captain pinned her to the wall in one swift motion. The Angeon waited just beneath the surface calling to be let out. Saranon held it back as the two stood face to face. Letting go of her energy could kill the Captain, and that was not what she wanted. The Captain was not gaining any ground and she laughed right in his ear. 'I'm not the little girl you first met,' she remarked.

The Captain knew that he had met an impasse. He was reluctant to acknowledge the fact, as he kept hold of the sorceress. A door opened and she sighed as Mitch made an appearance. 'Can you tell him to let go?' she asked Mitch as he stared with a curious smirk.

Before he had time to ask Captain Mirshendy eased off a little. Her head was still thumping and she could sense the headache was unnatural.

The wizards were caught in a power play without words. She felt as though she had been left out of the conversation. Saranon felt like running for the door, but Bently stood in the way with a bemused look. The Captain began to speak then his legs crumpled. He collapsed with bewilderment as Saranon's headache went away. She knelt down, 'You forgot about the bonding.' she said as the wizard still showed signs of weakness.

Mitch helped lie his friend down on the couch as

the sorceress lifted his feet off the ground. 'So what have you decided?' She asked the wizards as they appeared inexplicably dumbfounded. 'Well my plan is to get into the central core,' she spoke as she stood up. '...And that does not involve Mark.'

She stated the last words as she leaned over Captain Mirshendy.

She waited for a moment expecting some kind of response. Yet the Captain gave none as she eyed Mitch, 'Can you make sure he stays out of trouble?'

'What makes you think it's going to work?' The Captain asked unconvinced.

'Because you are not going to be in the way,' she retorted.

She wanted to add a whole lot more but stopped herself. She closed the door and a face appeared from around the corner, she let out a blunt cry. Bianca smiled, 'You didn't think I was going to let you go alone?'

'How do you...?' Then she remembered the Captain, 'Never mind.'

Bianca smiled with an air of confidence. They went in search of equipment to ready themselves. Her gaze flittered up the wall. They approached the small foyer created by the merging corridors. The graceful columns lined the perimeter making the space warm and welcoming. It held a simple elegance with a plain finish as the lights of the Keep shone around the edges. Her heart raced inside her head but she dared not show it as she followed. The last trace of anger slipped away as she focused on the ladder leading down. She tried not to lose her step.

She ran her fingers along the wall, and a soft sound resonated from beyond. It was so faint she almost missed it. The thrill of meeting the central core crossed her mind. Before the enormity of what it meant sank in. She began to ask a question. Bianca motioned for quiet while listening in the darkness. They were not far below the habitable area. The muffled sounds of life echoed from above. A sharp sound rose above the rest and Bianca let out a gasp. Her friend stepped back and almost knocked her flying as she hung on.

Saranon peered around the corner, the open room appeared empty. If only she could hear the Keep. A shadow stretched along the corridor and a glimpse ran along the periphery. Her senses found nothing. They continued downward until all signs of life above had vanished. The shimmering warm glow from the array of small lights led downward. It formed patterns in the dark and they followed.

The remnants of the grime caked itself to the edges of the floor. In a murky trail building as they went. The soft dry air began to creep up from the outer rim of the core and Bianca began to relax. Her shoulders slumped in recognition as they sat in the depths of Hedavin. A tiny clink sparked Saranon's attention as her friend laughed aloud. She smiled in response, still wondering how she would enter into the central core. As though reading her thoughts Bianca answered the question. The easiest way would be through there. Bianca pointed to a small opening that ran parallel with the arterial cable.

The access point was one of the least used by sorcerers. It was located near the Cryzinelan. The walls were still smeared with grime. She cringed as her hand slipped in the substance and wiped it off. It revealed the broken body of a small skada. A mechanical spider that repaired the Keep lay covered in the muck. Hedavin had been awfully scarce of the little critters that worked in groups. She turned the metallic body over. Running her hand along the charred edges left from sorcery.

The hollow remains crumbled away in her hands as the fragile shell lost its shape. She placed it back as her hand touched something solid and hidden in the grime. She wiped it clean as a small emblem protruded on the fragment. As she held it up to the light it moved and almost fell as she caught it. A tiny spark of sorcery flowed within the fragment as she recognised the mark.

Bianca did not notice as they went on their way following the pipes. For such a large Keep little energy flowed through. Saranon tapped the edge of the gauge hoping it would move. Instead it stayed below halfway. She was being left behind and rushed to keep up. She slipped, diving over to the side. Both hands squelched along in the grime. Her shoulder caught the side of the wall and she winced. A flash of golden raging light boomed overhead. In a fiery instant, the surge of sorcery drove a wedge between them.

The crackle roared past with a deafening tone. Saranon managed to shield herself from the blast. The heat radiated through the room as she gulped. The hot air hit her lungs and she wanted to cry out. Her heart pounded hard as she stretched out her energy. She reached out to the Keep but it did not answer. Her breathing slowed as she waited, searching in the dim light for a sign of the assailant.

She could sense him in the darkness. She closed her eyes and winced. She had run away in the chaos at Zaidek Keep. As she understood with a rising dread what Tasha had meant. She tried again to reach out to the central core and no response came. Saranon breathed in the warm air. The last remnants from the sorcery faded in the distance. She took in a deep breath and the Angeon rose to the surface. The energy swirled as it coursed through her body.

The sorcerer Edan stood at the opposite end of the darkness. He held up his hand as a fireball flared lighting up the room in a smothered embrace. The sorcery sparked outward as it wrapped around the Angeon. It dragged her in to the centre of the room. He stepped out from the darkness taking aim as she floundered. His sorcery stormed through as a ceaseless source. The blast struck her, catching Saranon off-guard as she staggered to her feet. The shield around Edan held its strength as he ran forward. The air crystallised and shattered in the intense heat. She held out her arms to block the full blow. The wave of energy slammed her back to wall and the air rushed out of her lungs. The pain edged its way through her muscles as she clenched her jaw.

Edan sealed off the way ahead and her only chance to enter the central core. She stumbled and Edan struck.

The blast fractured through her shield and hit hard sending her to the ground. The pain seared along the surface as the Angeon took hold. She ran as the pain faded and blasted her way through. Her energy smouldered around the edges of the seal. Edan retreated further into the Keep. The Angeon raised her hands as the energy flowed. Spiralling as it lit up the underneath of Hedavin. It scorched the edges of the walls as it honed in, hitting Edan with enough force to knock him down. He staggered as she caught up.

Edan's eyes held a stubborn stance. In the darkness Tasha's words rose, kill the boy but not the girl. Something inside the Angeon snapped as she closed the gap and plunged both her hands around the hilt of Corsavere. Her bond-breaker shone a deep sea green in the darkness, as the blade in the form of a sword rose. He saw it in her eyes. The Angeon held the embrace with a cold strength. Shouting rang out from behind her as her focus fell to one task. The blade struck home.

There in the last essence as Edan's strength flowed the dark sorcery. The Angeon saw him as he truly was. The fear rose from within, yet she did not let it show. Edan gave a small gasp, but she did not loosen her grip. Tasha's words played in her head. She understood the message that had been sent from the grave. In the distant haze Bianca's scream cut through. As the exhaustion showed on her face, she did not want to admit it had taken a toll. It was not the ending Saranon had planned. The effect was instant as the marks of the Dihan marred the dead sorcerer's hands. The dark sorcery left its trail plain to see. She covered the body with her cloak. She showed all the care in the world as she whispered a final goodbye.

As the web that held the Keep unravelled, the shriek from the core below rang out. It pierced through the air. Bianca stood motioning for her to go on. Saranon wasted no time as she turned. The Keep cried in pain and that was all that mattered. As she trudged through the darkness the Keep gave off a dim light guiding her way. The pain screeched at her ears as she tried to remain calm. Yet the Keep was having none of it as it called, demanding her attention. It pinpointed her every move bellowing with an urgency that made the hair stand on end. She wasted no time as Hedavin urged her on ever closer to the pain.

Her heart thudded as she could only guess what lay beneath. Yet she had to go on in the eerie darkness. The sounds of the Keep filled the silence with a dread that filled her mind. She stood at the edge as the sounds bellowed up from below. She peered down into the resulting chaos. The sparks of stallic energy flew up arcing out from the deep. The heat rose through her hair at a constant rate. The stallic energy blew hot and sharp with razer precision. The energy swirled in the void before falling back into the Keep. Saranon, the Angeon, closed her eyes. She took a deep breath with the memory of Odana Temple pulling at her mind. With cold precision she leaped off the rim, diving straight into the darkness.

As the first wave hit her it jolted her back with the sudden impact. She dived further down a sheer drop. Then hit another arc of the Keep's energy. The pain seared through with an agonising slowness. Saranon reeled from the shock as she sank further into the darkness. She peered ahead and a massive ripple formed like a bubble with an eerie surface. The stallic energy held in a moving formation beneath. The Angeon rose with all her strength. Guiding her sorcery deep and she fell through. The sparks shot up around her and it was all she could do to hold on. She forgot to breath and gasped in the hot substance around her. It burned through her lungs as she writhed in a silent scream.

Before she could blink she found herself floating in a dense fog, with no up or down. The sparks lit up the murky clouds with sudden flares. The light glinted through the distance in an eerie motion. A heavy clunking sound resonated from the side. Saranon gasped at the sight of the central core. The dense storm held in a gigantic shell with no meaning of gravity. The stallic energy light up the air. It called with a shattered voice searching through the hidden nightmare. Help me, it called out in muted disbelief at the tiny visitor. The voice echoed inside her mind as it faded in a muffled tone. Before calling again and again like a steady tide. The Angeon managed to move with the strains on the Keep magnified in the core. A dark shadow moved closer as the cold touch of the Keep wrapped around her leg and dragged her in.

It was all she could do to keep from gagging in the filthy air. The tendrils of the inner core sucked her inside. The Angeon dropped with a short thud as gravity found itself again. The Keep had miscalculated the location of the floor. The control room lay hidden in the rod that struck down into Tordoren. Saranon stood as the Angeon left and made her way over to the controls. The small circular compartment wrapped around the solid core. Shaped like a massive impenetrable rod. It led into the hidden ground far below the surface. The core captured the arcs of energy from deep inside Tordoren. The energy was concentrated before sending it up through the Keep.

The sorceress reached for the nearest control. It moved as if not wanting to be held and she almost stumbled into the seat beside it. The room was cramped as she sat upright catching her breath, filled with apprehension. Her fingers felt numb from the decent. They still ached while she tried to figure out the controls. The sweat beaded down her back as the air grew warm from the charging of the central core. The power surged at an uneven rate sparking through the core. It crackled around her as she watched through the windows. Even in the confined space it was beginning to be unbearable.

Saranon tried again with the controls as they moved in an unfathomable rhythm. Yet somehow she had to figure them out. She rested her hand on a bar and leaned over for a closer inspection of the levers near the floor. She tried to move them, but it would not work, a deep crackling sound rose from below. The sparks blew a wave of light flashing pulsing through the windows. It shone through the slits in her fingers. The roar began with a low rumble resonating in a deep tone, as she opened her eyes and remembered to breathe.

The heat in the air hit her lungs as she lurched forward in a violent cough. Without warning three of the controls moved all at once. She froze waiting and listening, as the harsh wind tunnelled around the core. It bellowed with a menacing call as it whirred in the background. The flashes of stallic energy broke through leaving trails criss-crossing the harsh grey fog. The charge compounded in on itself. The air whistled again from below in the depths of Tordoren. The sound of the crackling clung in the distance.

Saranon's heart beat faster as she recognised the chaos below. She stood peering close to the window and tripped. The controls moved for the second time. The ball of light grew beneath her and she caught her breath. She gulped letting out a small whimper. The charge curled itself up the surface of the rod. It circled closer with every breath. The thunderous roar of pure stallic energy gained speed. The sound became louder as it swept toward her. The crackling buzz reached her ears, turning into pounding bellow with no pause. The solid rumble carried the heat far above, glowing with an electrifying intensity as it neared the control room.

She tried to concentrate. Yet the swirling inferno held her attention with a fatal beckoning. She knew she had to break free and time was slipping away. The crackling roar thundered through the floor. She felt herself lift as the sound around her became deafening. Hedavin spoke inside her head, I've got you. The white wall of energy hit, with an enveloping blast that shook every part of her body. For a moment the world stopped as she held out her hands and felt nothing. The panic hit with a jolt as the air rushed out of her lungs. The Angeon woke with a power so great she absorbed the energy.

In the insufferable moment the Angeon linked with the central core. As the massive clouds of energy poured down, condensing between her hands. The last traces of energy stemmed into the inescapable stronghold. A small sphere formed. The Angeon floated in a trance. She had lost the ability to move her limbs as the energy coursed its way through. The beautiful shiny Orb formed as the energy condensed, glowing from the continuing flow. The last particles wrapped within sealing the surface of the Orb as it cooled to the touch. The air in the central core brought with it a sudden chill.

Saranon stood waiting for her legs to catch up as the Angeon slipped away. It left behind darkness amidst the low humming of the central core. She peered over the edge of the controls in the small room. The whirling clouds of stallic energy had tipped upside down. They lay at a safe distance around the base of the rod. The Keep was at peace as it lulled to itself in a reassuring tone. The pressure had eased as she stepped back. She melded into the main rod of the central core, falling out the other side. Hedavin wasted no time as he spurned the little visitor out with all his might. The central core was content to be left alone once more. The force pelted her upward. The Keep sighed with the last signs of disgruntlement washing away.

She could sense from his mood that Hedavin would not be so easy to fool a second time. The journey finished as she came to a stop. She lay on the floor of the imbenik chamber above the central core. Saranon sat alone as she clasped the Orb in both her hands. It was smaller than the ones she had seen and wondered what to do with it. A gruff voice called from above. She tried to call back, but her voice was too hoarse. A figure reached down. She recognised Mark and stepped back almost slamming sideways into the wall. He shouted something, but the words were fuzzy in her head.

Saranon looked up at him with tired eyes and he shook his head as if reading her thoughts. She caught her breath, and clambered to the surface. The throbbing in her head made it difficult to grasp the flow of conversations. The words muddled in and out. The group of wizards crowded around as she recognised Captain Mirshendy. Without saying anything she placed the Orb in his hand. A stunned silence collapsed over the space. Major Kellaway strode up to inspect the Orb. He mulled it over in his hands. The Major studied Saranon's face before returning the Orb. 'The fun is over, now let's get Hedavin back on track,' he said.

She looked at Captain Mirshendy, who whispered, 'You did well.'

She smiled as the exhaustion shone through her eyes. Mitch guided her away from the hive of conversations blurring into one another. As much as she was itching to stay and listen, all she wanted now was a warm soft cosy bed. Before she could lie down a thought entered her head, 'Bianca.'

'She's all right,' the wizard whispered as he tucked her in.

Sleep crept in like a flood taking over. The sweet hum of the Keep was the last sound she remembered. A dream swept through her tired mind as a hand reached out. She looked up to see Tasha waiting on a windy path near the river. Her old friend held the Orb in her hands it glowed with a warm radiant light. She held out her hand, but she could not touch it. Tasha was too far away as she spoke, not yet. Saranon tried to reach for the Orb again, but Tasha moved farther away. In her dreams she ran and ran.

Then with one final leap she hurled herself forward catching the Orb. As she did she fell down a massive hole carved deep into the ground. Then she saw the large ockren. The essence of Hedavin stood, wrapped into an unnatural large panther like creature. It had sharp yellow eyes piercing through her soul. The creature bent its head forward until the tip of its nose almost touched the Orb. Its breath blew over her cold fingers. Saranon stood in silence not wanting to move as the ockren circled her in a slow stance. She backed away out of the cave and onto a sandy beach near the black ocean.

The waves crashed on the shore around them as the wind echoed along the dunes. A distance hung between them, then the ockren leaped in a fluid motion toward the sky. Saranon held the Orb up above her head shielding herself from the ockren. A jolt ran through her body and she woke with a gasp. The energy of the Angeon flared to the surface. As her eyes opened they made contact with the sorcerer in the room, Damon lunged in. She grabbed his arm in a powerful lock as he began to wince. Before she could concentrate he was knocked to the ground. It took her a while to realise Mitch had entered the room and a wave of relief swept over her.

CHAPTER SEVEN

The unexpected

Mitch held onto Damon with ease as Saranon's room became crowded with wizards. She darted out into the lounge room. She almost stumbled straight into Captain Mirshendy. He glared at her then stepped aside taking charge. Damon began rambling protests while the Captain clung onto him with a firm grip. She stayed out of the way not wanting to be the focus of attention. She kept close to Mitch waiting for the voices to fade in the hallway, before relaxing.

The dawn was breaking as she dressed. She followed Mitch down to the stronghold of the Cryzinelan wizards. The internal courtyard warmed with the morning light. While the Keep returned to its old self. The wizard clan appeared stronger than ever. To Saranon's amazement Damon spoke to the Major as a friend. Then he left the stronghold. Major Kellaway smiled as he spotted her gaping mouth. There were many things she did not understand, and letting Damon go was one of them.

She stood in astonishment as the anger dissipated. If it were not for the group of wizards she would be tempted to run after him. As though reading her thoughts Mitch stayed by her side. He could be annoying at times. She cringed while Mitch pretended not to notice. Her arms still ached from holding the sorcerer. When a wizard walked over and blocked the light streaming down from above. The Major was a tall man with a stubborn look as he gazed down at her. He leaned over and asked, 'Did you mean to kill Edan?'

The question stopped Saranon's thoughts from roaming as she stared back in defiance, 'Yes.'

It was a small reply that meant so much as the Major mulled it over. She swallowed and bit her lip. She was not about to tremble among so many wizards. The dragon pens did not seem so welcoming anymore. She went out into the warm courtyard, breathing a sigh of relief. As she stared toward the sky an array of small dots grew just above the horizon. Katholomu lying at the edge of the clearing, lifted his head. The dragon clambered as he uncurled himself. He arched his back in a long stretch that filtered through the whole of his body.

Up ahead the skies broke to make way for three riders flying in fast with their dragons. She watched in quiet anticipation as she turned an inquisitive eye toward Mitch. The wizard stared up into the crystal blue sky. He spoke in deep thought, 'I think it's for you.'

'What do you mean?' She snapped in annoyance.

'It's Pennie,' the wizard replied as smile touched his lips.

'You're making that up,' Saranon spoke.

She tried hard to glimpse the image in the distance. The wizard chuckled which only made it worse as she checked, trying to gauge a sign of any sort. He patted her on the shoulder, 'Why don't you go to the roof and take a look?'

She agreed as her dull walk turned into a quick run. She covered the last distance with ease up to a vibrant roof top. She came face to face with Captain Mirshendy. Bianca stood near the edge of the low wall. They watched peering out in the direction of the dragons.

She strode toward Bianca as she gazed out over the clear sky. Her friend looked on as Saranon asked, 'Do you think it's Pennie?'

'Of course it is,' Bianca quibbled.

She stared at her friend in annoyance, 'You didn't tell me.'

'I did not think I needed to,' Bianca replied.

The pair stood in an awkward silence as the gracious beasts swung overhead. The dragons flew down gliding into the courtyard. Pennie's blonde hair caught in the sunlight. She peered upward and straight at the sorceress.

Saranon made her way down to the dragon pens. Hoping she would not see Mark, which was almost impossible. Pennie stood tall and proud not far from

Captain Assinden. The Darkonian wizard held himself with a great ease so far from home. In a way he reminded her of Mitch. No words were needed as the two friends embraced. A familiar voice spoke behind her. 'I hope you're not going to stand there all day. The dragons need to rest,' Mark's voice was gentle, but it still made her cringe.

Pennie laughed as they sat down, 'So you made it back from Serenphel? I half expected you to stay, but then I heard about Merrick.'

Saranon grimaced at the sorcerer's name. It was not an easy memory to stomach. She had completely recovered from the ordeal. 'I would prefer not to think about it,' she replied.

'That's okay, I've got something else for you,' Pennie lowered her voice. 'We've got a problem.'

She leaned closer as her friend explained without giving too much away. Pennie was good with that. Yet as Saranon's mouth gaped she figured her friend need not have bothered. She mulled over the words in deep thought. Pennie waited with an endless patience. 'Well, it looks like I'll be going home,' she said.

'You'll need to stay close to the border, on the other side. If you get into trouble you're on your own.' Pennie replied.

The last part was said with such seriousness by Pennie that they both laughed. Captain Jacob Assinden gave a stern stare as he watched on. Pennie waved it off with a flick of her hand. Before she turned to her friend, 'I'm sure you'll be fine.'

Saranon breathed a huge sigh as she looked at the wizard, another reminder of home. Before she could think on it anymore, her friend changed the subject. The gesture was made to gloss over the raging problem. It did not go unnoticed. Captain Assinden gave away a small sign of annoyance that creased along his brow. Saranon had not forgotten his strength as she stayed at a distance. The talk turned to Pennie's birthday just gone. With her friend describing a party of such grandeur that she found it hard to imagine.

She smiled wondering if her friend's effort had turned into a tall tale. She tried not to interrupt. It was wonderful seeing Pennie so content. The small scrape of footsteps behind her brought her back to reality. She turned at the thought of Mark being there. She jumped off her chair so fast she almost lost her balance. Captain Mirshendy spoke, 'I need to have a word with you.'

Pennie did not flinch at all as she stared at the wizard in a serene fashion. She gave nothing away under her gaze.

The Captain strode with a sturdy step then came to a halt. He gazed out of the large window in a meeting room that opened onto views of the garden below. 'You cannot travel to Darkonia with Pennie,' He said.

The edge of his voice filled with a finality. Before she had time to ask him how he knew. He continued, 'We have received word of the Keep your friend is here to discuss. If you go there you need to stay out of Darkonia.'

Saranon's heart sank as she admitted to herself. That it was too early to return to the land in which she grew up in.

The deed was done she had taken down the Arthrose Council for hunting the Issola. Even in exile the threat still lingered. If she went into Darkonia the Arthrose would find her. Then she filled with annoyance at the wizard for being so knowledgeable. Yet he appeared ready for that response. A smile crept at the corners of his mouth. She placed her hands on her hips, in a silent defiance. 'I've arranged for you to travel with someone else,' the Captain said.

His words shocked her out of her stagnant mood. 'What do you mean?' She asked.

'Wait and see,' the Captain smiled then left her alone to wonder.

Her life appeared to be decided for her yet again. The temptation of crossing the border into Darkonia filled her with excitement. She went to find Mitch who to her dismay was engaged in a conversation with Mark. He stood beside Katholomu. The dragon had a rather suspicious looking full belly. She wondered where he had plundered the amount of food required to leave him in such a state. Mark explained that the beast had helped himself to three breakfasts. Scoffing all the food down before he had time to shoo the dragon away. She could believe Kat had done it, as he showed off his belly in the sunlight with a sleepy smile.

'Well he won't be flying anywhere with that on board,' Saranon spoke. She grimaced as Mark stood beside her.

'Do you want to know how close you came?' He asked in a low voice.

She knew what he meant and shook her head as

her cheeks began to feel hot under his gaze. He walked away without needing to say anymore. Her heart was still pounding. When Mitch broke into her thoughts, 'Have you been to Taria?'

'I beg your pardon,' she hissed, the wizard knew full well about her past.

'I meant we're going there,' he replied.

Saranon rolled her eyes in disgust at yet another wizard telling her what to do. She fobbed it off by reaching over to the great dragon and rubbing him under the chin. Kat obliged her by kicking in the air as Mitch side stepped to avoid contact. The great beast nuzzled his head around her. He did so in a comforting grasp while pretending to be asleep. The sun warmed his coat with a glistening touch. She reached over and hugged the dragon. He seemed not to care enough about his gruff image to show concern.

Mitch let them be, he had far too much to do to worry about. He shook his head in dismay. A voice cut through the open courtyard as Saranon glanced around. Not wanting to be disturbed. Damon stood on the edge of the stone paving, his face pale even in full light. She remained calm on the outside. Every essence of her being told her to run. She stood transfixed as though turning away would be worse.

The Palascene sorcerer, Damon, gave an eminent glare. He moved closer wrapped in a cold silence. Katholomu retracted behind her, experience told the dragon not to intervene. Saranon's first instinct was to step back then she stopped in midstride. Reminding herself there was no need to give the sorcerer ground. Yet his eyes pierced with a raging intensity. His anger quelled only by an air of superiority, as he approached. Damon raised his arms without a halt in his stride as he closed in. She could feel the energy rip through the air in front of her and held her ground.

The energy of the Angeon rushed through her as she met Damon's sorcery head on. She watched him hold under the strain. The build-up of energy spurred against him. He cringed then relented expecting the energy of the Angeon to consume him. Yet as he stood unharmed his smiled waned. This time it was Saranon's turn to smile knowing she could hold back the tide of the Angeon. Without any warning a large dark matted scaly tail swept the sorcerer off his feet. The dragon sent him flying high into the air.

Kathomolu stood up heaving his giant chest in victory. His strong tail curled up beside him. He bent down in a casual stance as Saranon gaped in amazement. She was too shocked to tell off the dragon who gave her a quizzical look. 'Well I guess that's one way of dealing with him,' she responded in awe.

Pennie ran to the courtyard peering out to where the sorcerer had landed. Trying not to laugh she said, 'I was about to give you a hand, but I can't beat that.'

A small laughed escaped Saranon's lips as Bianca rushed out. Damon walked off with a slight limp toward his quarters. Bianca smiled, 'If he bothers you again let me know.'

After a small cough she agreed, even though she

thought it would not be needed. The sky began to grow dark as they went inside for a heartfelt feast. Pennie enjoyed sitting with her as they laughed again. Captain Mirshendy had asked about the day's events.

They giggled with delight. As the Captain realised Damon deserved the consequences of his actions. It made a great tale as they ate. Just as Saranon took a breath and regained her composure. A hush fell on the crowd at their table as a wizardess entered the room. The Captain wasted no time introducing himself to the new arrival. Zara had travelled a far distance with a buoyant smile. Zara had an adventurous air around her full of enthusiasm. She headed straight for the sorceress placing a gentle hand on her shoulder.

Saranon looked at her in surprise, wondering who she was. As the Captain spoke, 'Zara will be taking you to Taria.'

It was more a statement than a request. As Pennie filled in the gap, 'Zara is Lord Glyrondagar's sister. Her clan can get you close to the border with ease.'

Her friend spoke as though she had known all along. Then she was used to Pennie making arrangements. As she looked around the table she noticed Mitch gazing up at the wizardess. She felt like the odd one out.

Mitch spent the rest of the night chatting away to Zara. Saranon found an excuse to leave. She tried not to sound annoyed at the situation. She was about to step out of the path of a sorcerer, he appeared out of place. He looked straight at her with a calm grace as he introduced himself.

The Denowan sorcerer known as Garth Arbidan explained that he was bonded to Zara. He would be accompanying her to Taria. For a sorcerer Garth seemed rather meek and quite. He was content to wander in Zara's shadow.

To her surprise the sorcerer explained that there were few of his clan in Taria. Saranon could not imagine a land full of wizards. Then Normisia felt like it at times as she peered around the room. She left feeling perplexed and tried to block her thoughts out. Her head hit the pillow with a welcome sleep. The dreams of the night before clung in a faded bubble. She glimpsed them from afar, drifting further into a restful slumber. Later in the night two sets of footsteps made their way around the apartment. The moon shone bright through the open curtains with a soft welcoming glow.

She sat up with the morning light. She stared around an empty room, checking under the bed to make sure it was safe. Not that she thought someone would hide there. Yet finding Damon lurking around before had unnerved her. Clanging noises sounded from underneath the door with the making of breakfast. Zara helped lay the table with a comforting smile. She was too shocked to say anything and Mitch was not offering any answers.

Before any words came to mind a hearty breakfast was laid out in front of her as the three began to eat. The toast was warm and the butter melted as she took a bite while eyeing him with suspicion. 'Are you ready to head south?' Zara asked waiting for a response.

She swallowed a mouthful and coughed, 'Where are

we going?'

'To my home,' the wizardess replied.

Saranon stared at Mitch, 'Are we going to be staying at a wizard Keep?'

'Isn't it wonderful,' Zara smiled.

She did not look impressed. She thought about having to get to know yet another group of wizards. Garth would be there for company. He seemed far more interested in talking than being a sorcerer. Mitch leaned over. 'You are welcome to leave the table,' he smiled.

Then he indulged in a conversation with Zara. She rushed out the door and realised she had forgotten to ask when they were leaving. She was in no hurry to go back and glanced out over the balcony into the open courtyard below. A familiar voice made her smile. As Rachel approached, 'Sorry I haven't had a chance to catch up with you.'

The Captain's voice interrupted her thoughts as she stared beyond her friend. He appeared to be caught off guard by her. He stood beside Rachel holding her with his arm. The sorceress peered down at the bond-breaker, she had made for the Captain, as it glistened on his belt, 'Have you given it a name?'

He smiled as Rachel answered for him, 'Stayer.'

Saranon spoke to the Captain, 'Do you think the Keep will be attacked again?'

His mood darkened with an eminent sadness. For once he was at a loss to hide his thoughts as she looked on. 'Hedavin has a long memory,' as he spoke the words he leaned over. He gave Rachel a soft kiss before leaving the two in peace. Rachel watched him go, 'Thank you for looking after him. We haven't much time since you leave tonight.'

Saranon's mouth dropped open in astonished disbelief. Yet she could not stay annoyed for long. Rachel had taken the day off to spend with her. The wizardess was a welcome relief in a storm of chaos. They made their way down the stairs. It took a moment to realise she was heading toward the dragon pens. She had been trying to avoid Mark, which was much harder to do than she thought. He seemed to appear almost everywhere.

It was as though he knew she had been trying to stay away. She was not angry with him, but at the whole notion of not being asked which annoyed her still. Rachel stepped aside and before Saranon knew it she was staring straight at Mark. Who appeared undeterred by the whole passing of events. In fact he looked quite comfortable. He was at home as he patted her on the head while she ducked to the side. He gave a knowing smile, 'You have nothing to worry about.'

She was not convinced, as she spotted Gabriel in the background. She found an excuse to runoff, darting past as he let her leave. Saranon surveyed the pens. To find the dragons glistening in the morning light through the open doors. 'They're ready for when you leave,' Gabriel explained.

'Wow,' she was impressed at the sight of several clean, sweet smelling dragons.

She knew the hard work would not last long.

She stared up at Katholomu whose eyes darted across to the open air. 'Mark did most of it, I think he felt sorry for you,' Gabriel spoke.

Mark patted her on the shoulder. Making Saranon jump with start, 'What do you think?'

She smiled and agreed. Hoping he would not do that again as he continued, 'Ready for your big debut?'

'Pardon,' she asked.

'You are going to Taria. The wizards don't have many sorcerers to contend with,' he spoke.

'I thought I was already,' Saranon exclaimed.

'Perhaps,' Mark replied in deep thought.

As they spoke Rachel patted Katholomu. The dragon appeared eager to comply as he rolled his head. The great beast was good company and Saranon was looking forward to the ride.

'That dragon cost me a good amount, but I knew someday the favour would be returned. You earned him when you took care of Hedavin,' Mark Staragen spoke.

The wizard showed a genuine respect. She peered up at the great beast as he lapped up the attention. He looked almost comical, knowing full well his short temper. She could not imagine life without the dirt loving, cranky and opportunistic dragon.

CHAPTER EIGHT

A careless grandeur

A warm wind blew with the sun's rays in the late afternoon as Saranon looked at Pennie. They both smiled with the thrill of excitement. The thought of being close to Darkonia pulled at the heart of her emotions. She still did not know who her parents were even though she was a Vandragamond. With any luck she would find out more. Her friend had tried so hard to search for them while she was gone. She was grateful, but now seemed like the right time to go. The sun lost its' strength with the last of the afternoon fading away.

The dragons preferred the cooler weather of night and she could not blame them. Saranon clambered aboard as Katholomu leaned down. This time she would ride alone, with Mitch and Zara riding together. Captain Assinden went with Pennie which left Garth to fly on his own.

The sorcerer was quite at home with this. As he urged his dragon forward with a mighty jolt upward into the fading sky. Saranon and Pennie followed. The two wizards made up the rear of the diamond formation. They flew southwest to the edge of the border near Taria.

Her heart pounded with a happy tune as Kat covered ground with ease. Way underneath his massive outstretched wings. She let the wind fly free whipping at the wisps of her hair. The beast appeared to absorb the excitement as he flew hard without a break. They glided down onto the Pendelon Plains, in south-east Normisia. The dragon's smell had soaked through her clothes by the time they landed. She clambered down as the wind sent a chill along her skin. They had stopped near a small township. She ran into the tavern where the owners were expecting them. Saranon was so relieved to have a warm bath and clean clothes as she sank into a soft bed. Taking no notice of the morning light as it broke outside.

The smell of baked bread wafted under her nose. Captain Assinden brought them a hearty lunch. He woke them from a restful sleep. It had been a while since the sorceress had been spent time with other Darkonians. Yet she still held a small grudge at the Captain, for tricking her before she had left for Alveron. The warm bread melted the butter that dripped down her hand before she caught it. He started to whisper in a low voice, but stopped as the door creaked open.

'Ah, you're awake,' Garth said. He sat down near the Captain, ' There's something I need to tell you about the

Glyrondagar. They are good at dealing with sorcerers so take care.'

Saranon choked on her mouthful of bread, as she coughed to clear her throat. 'I thought you would understand,' Garth replied. As he patted her on the back, '...And don't say I didn't warn you.'

His voice sang out as he left them in peace. She could not see how the wizard clan could be more annoying, than the ones she had already encountered, but Garth meant well.

She calmed her thoughts as she stood up and scrambled her things together. Captain Assinden had already packed and watched in an awkward silence. 'We have tried hard to find out who your parents are. Whoever knows is not giving anything away. It may be more than wizards that you need to worry about.' He spoke.

His voice carried a firm certainty as Saranon tried to brush it off. 'I can guess that I am about to walk into trouble. So if you don't mind I'd like to finish packing,' the sorceress eyed him as he bowed and left.

She could not bring herself to trust the wizard. She rushed down the stairs and almost knocked Pennie over in the process. 'Are you ready? We're all waiting for you,' Pennie beamed.

Her friend gave a large smile full of excitement to have her friend back. Saranon knew how it felt as her nerves gave way to a sense of excitement. She rubbed her hands together in anticipation. Katholomu gleamed in the dry afternoon sun glowing orange along the horizon. It tilted toward the call of the evening sky. She clambered up onto the dragons shoulder. Riding high on his back as the giant took one big leap showing off in full swing. He opened his massive wings with a rush of the wind beneath.

Her breath filled with enthusiasm as the darkened sky hid the border into Taria. A welcome chill crept along her arms as she held on tight not wanting to let go. Kat roared with excitement as he tasted the wind. He moved on at an impressive speed waiting for the other dragons to catch up. The hills rushed by beneath them in a blur, as she looked on, hoping for a glimpse of the Keep Ardaguar. Even though she knew it was far too early, it still did not stop her from hoping. The breeze swept through Saranon's hair as the other dragon's kept up. Katholomu paced himself for the last leg of the flight.

Pennie's dragon Veradae swooped close to the side enticing Kat to race. He called on with a renewed strength to fly ahead. Ardaguar Keep came in sight, a beautiful towering fortress over the grand landscape. The terrain was filled with the low lying hills that ran all the way through the border. The great dragon circled the open sky. She peered over the top of an open arena, that hung silent in the early hours of the morning. Katholomu glided in sliding along at ease. Then he ploughed his legs forward to a sudden stop. With a small tilt he dropped the sorceress down before she had the chance to protest.

The dragon shook himself spraying musty sweat in all directions. Saranon used her energy to shield herself just in time. She had not been so lucky before and was not about to be left with the stench that took hours to fade away. Zara ran up behind her, 'Come on you'll be late.'

Saranon asked, 'For what?'

The sorceress could not imagine being late for anything, but sleep, as she tried to catch up with the others, following behind. As she reached the entrance all the lights were on sparkling along the walls. The foyer opened up onto a great hall filled with trophies along the walls.

She was so overcome with the sight that she failed to hear the footsteps right beside her. Lord Dackren beamed down, his bulk towering over the young sorceress. The Lord did not look much older than Mitch. Yet his face was weathered and it displayed hints of more than one good fight. Lord Dackren smiled as he used his size to intimidate her. Saranon took a step back, he followed as Zara tapped him on the shoulder and he stopped. 'You are welcome here Vandragamond. There is one thing I want to know, where do you fit in?'

She stood in silence while trying to fight the urge to step back a good few paces. In fact the other room was starting to look appealing. Pennie spoke up as she let out a sigh of relief. 'We do not know, but if you are offering to help that would be appreciated,' said her friend.

Lord Dackren glanced her way with piercing deep brown eyes. He responded, 'If I help you, you will let me know.'

The last words sounded like a warning, and she was not about to argue as the Lord left them in peace.

Zara seemed oblivious to the whole drama. She showed

them to their rooms and wished them a good rest. Saranon did not want to sleep, but her tired eyes said otherwise and the bed was so cosy. Before she knew it her dreams were filled with the wild whisperings of the Keep. Ardaguar spoke to her with a tight grip. It tried to pull her down below the habitable area in her sleep. The Keep spoke the words in her head with a background whisper wrapping around her. It tried to drag her along on an unknown path. No matter how fast she moved it was far too slow for the Keep's liking. It called ever louder through the dream.

Saranon sat up gasping for air, as Ardaguar's voice faded in the distance. The knocking that had broken her sleep stopped, as she shouted out. A wizard's voice extended through the closed door. 'It's Killian, my sister asked me to tell you it's lunch time. If you want anything you'd better hurry up,' he spoke.

She wondered who the wizard was, then shrugged it off. She ran downstairs as the thought from her mind. The large row of tables held a gathering, that filled the air with the rumble of many conversations. She wound her way through the jubilant crowd.

A few wizards glanced her way, but she tried not to notice as she made her way through. Then she darted off with a small arm full. She juggled the food while finding her way to the open courtyard. The sun beamed down with its full might. As she glanced around to spy Mitch entangled in Zara's arms. It was almost enough to make her choke as she turned the other way. Across the courtyard a sorceress a few years older than she, stared back. Triona hesitated before walking away without saying a word. Saranon was tempted to follow. Yet just as she did a large welcoming arm gripped her far too close for comfort. Lord Dackren grinned down at her.

She managed to nudge her way free as she stared at him in a constrained silence. The Lord was a little too close for comfort. 'You'll want to check out the disc this afternoon,' she could smell his breath as he spoke.

'No,' she answered.

She was not sure what it was. She wanted to steer clear of anything Lord Dackren was involved with. 'That's a shame, perhaps I can entice you later,' he grinned as he left.

Saranon did not feel like eating the rest of her lunch as she ditched it in the bin. Killian stood beside her and asked, 'Do you want to check out the disc?'

'No, I'm fine,' she replied.

Killian smiled as she turned to look at him. 'I meant just to have a look, I don't fight on it, like my brother,' he added.

'Well that's reassuring,' she spoke, wondering what it was.

'No, I really mean it,' he continued.

Killian tried to reassure her, as he walked while keeping a respectful distance between them. She sighed as she relented. Wondering what she had gotten herself into. They left the bright courtyard for the more subdued light of the Keep. Killian brought her to a large room and the ceiling lifted high above. It allowed for tiers of seating wrapping around the walls. In the centre a circular stone pattern swirled along the floor. The anti-climax was astounding as she realised the carved stone floor was it. She attempted to sound interested as he waffled on about the history of the disc.

The dim lights above in the high ceiling gave the great room a dark atmosphere. Saranon walked over to the rough walls that had stood for so long. She ran her fingers along the edge as the Keep spoke. I see you, she flinched, recoiling straight back in Killion's arms. He smiled, but said nothing as the sorceress composed herself. Zara followed through the open doorway. The wizardess had an air of pride as she relaxed in the small row of seats near the disc.

'So would you ever part with Mitch?' Zara asked.

'Pardon?' Saranon exclaimed. She felt like she had just been dragged into an unspoken conversation.

'Have you ever had a lover?' The wizardess asked in a low whisper.

'No,' Saranon replied hoping she would not have to answer any more questions.

She began wondering if she could find another seat. A flurry of activity filled the room with a crowd gathering in around them.

Mitch leaned over from the opposite side of Zara. He whispered, 'Lord Dackren is up against Crevan, the ambassador for the Vandragamond.'

Saranon sighed with a lack of enthusiasm. Then she tried her best to look interested as the crowd went quiet with a hushed tone. She glanced through the faces, but could not see Pennie anywhere. Garth whispered a small greeting from the row behind. He waited in eager anticipation. She watched on as the crowd of wizards gave a deafening roar. Lord Dackren entered dressed for the occasion. He beamed with a jubilant pride and waved.

A second deafening cheer rang out and reverberated around the room. It was then that she noticed a small gathering of sorcerers. They made their way out to the opposite side of the disc. Crevan stood forward, a tall solid man almost the same size as Lord Dackren. With no hesitation he strode onto the disc. Crevan scouted the audience. He locked eyes on her before returning his gaze on his opponent. The Lord was more than eager to oblige as they stood for a brief moment. Eyeing each other across the centre of the disc carved into the floor. Then with a flash of wizardry the sorcerer was pelted back. The two were locked in an intense struggle to gain power over the other. They were intent on defeating their opponent.

Saranon's jaw dropped in a mix of surprise and horror. While wondering why anyone would do that for sport. Garth leaned over, 'You can breathe now,' he said in a gentle tone.

She gave him a smile, and then watched on in astonishment. She tried not to flinch when a streak of energy flashed along the edge of the disc. Both Lord Dackren and Crevan appeared to be enjoying every moment. It gave them the opportunity to show off their strength to a crowd that cried out for more. She looked around at the nearest exits and contemplated the idea of creeping out. With Zara by her side she doubted it would be well received.

The pair on the disc locked close together for a final struggle. Then it was over as Lord Dackren stood, he flung his arms up in victory. To her amazement Crevan stood up unscathed. Yet he looked jittery on his feet as he shook hands with the wizard and left to his side of the disc. Jack, a sorcerer not much older than Saranon eyed the wizard with contempt. Lord Dackren shouted out to the crowd daring anyone else to come forward and fight. He eyed Saranon and gestured, but she stayed right where she was. Jack Heath stepped forward onto the disc, 'I will take you on.'

He stood proud beyond his years, with a certainty that left no doubt he was ready. The Lord eyed him with a cool smile, 'So you think you're ready to take on the Lord Dackren?'

He shouted his last words raising his fist high in the air as the crowd roared in delight. Jack Heath stood silent waiting for the noise to subdue. Then he stepped up to the centre of the disc. The sorcerer did not hesitate as he struck first. The Lord had expected as much. Before Saranon could blink the two were engaged in a heated exchange.

The crowd watched on in wide-eyed awe as Jack lost ground. It was slow to watch as she winced at the sight. The Lord looked as though he was using every last bit of strength. The strain showed across his face. Yet Lord Dackren stood his ground and the crowd grew tense around her. The spectators began to stand as a low chant hummed through the air. A great creaking sound caught Saranon's attention. As she turned back to see the circular disc had tilted, dipping at Jack's end. She gasped as the end of the fight became clear. She stood up in a wide-eyed horror as the two locked in a power struggle. Jack moved closer to the lower edge of the disc.

Her whole body froze with shock as the disc creaked again and dropped. It tilted even further into the dark abyss. Jack stepped back as the Lord pushed him ever closer to the edge. Then the great disc tilted, and for a moment she lost sight of the sorcerer. Saranon rushed past Mitch's fleeting hand as he tried to hold her back. She ran and shouted, 'For the love of Odana stop!'

It was too late, the disc tilted at a sharp angle dropping the sorcerer clean off the edge. Jack grasped out with his energy and managed to grip a small ledge down in the darkness.

Saranon stood at the edge glaring at the wizard as he heaved himself up to the middle with ease. Then with a great groan that echoed off the walls the disc began to close. She felt her heart sink to the bottom of her toes as she tried to think. She reached out with her energy and Jack wasted no time as he formed the second half of the link. She hauled him up as she held her breath. With the disc closing behind him he darted away from the edge. He stood grinning beside her and held out his hand. He took no notice of the astonished gasps escaping from the crowd, 'I'm Jack Heath.'

Saranon was astounded. That he had just waved off the fact that he only just made it out of the dark tunnel. She shook his hand without speaking. The spectators began to fill the floor with a wave of excitement. He darted away and disappeared from sight. As she glanced around for a brief moment she locked eyes with Lord Dackren. She too left, not wanting to be caught up in the action. Mitch grabbed her arm and led her away as he spoke, 'What did you do that for?'

'You could've warned me,' she said as she yanked free of his hold.

He peered down at her, 'You're going to see more of that around here.'

Saranon was not sure what he meant and she did not want to find out. She ran off in search of Pennie. As she turned around the corner, a familiar face peered back at her. Jack smiled, 'I thought I might find you here.'

He was starting to get on her nerves. She refrained from making a comment as he led her toward the sorcerer quarters.

Triona opened the door to greet them as they entered the place. It was pleasant enough, yet it was smaller than the quarters set aside for the sorcerers at Hedavin Keep. Triona was around same age Jack. Crevan was twice that with a short crop of greying hair to match. It was a strange sensation wandering through rooms meant for the Vandragamond, the sorcerer clan she had been separated from for so long. Saranon was not sure if she was meant to behave like a visitor or one of their own. The turmoil was visible on her face as she found an excuse to leave.

She made her way back to the room she shared with Pennie. It was empty, but she did not mind as she slumped onto the bed. A silent tear dropped down. The urge to throw an object against the wall felt right. She lacked the energy to carry it through. She peered out the window and leaned on the sill. Ardaguar held an air of confidence, one that sided with the wizard clan. Yet the Keep itself, felt odd as she listened. She reached out her senses in the gaps of noise stemming from the courtyard below.

She searched the Keep with her energy, but the further she went the stronger it felt. It did not make sense. The thought tapered from her mind as the smell of tea wafted up from the kitchen. It mixed with the warm night air. Pennie welcomed her as they made their way to the table at the centre of the room. It was wonderful to hear her old friend laugh again. Mitch approached her and whispered, 'Lord Dackren wants you to sit at his table.'

He left assuming her compliance was a given.

She made her way over to the table, the Lord filled the large chair with his size. He leaned forward with an air of arrogance. From what Pennie had said the façade belied an intelligent man underneath. Lord Dackren tapped for an ale as he kept a careful eye on her between conversations. Killian sat beside her quite content to blend into the background. As she listened to his brother's bragging. Saranon did not believe half it, but preferred not to say so. The Lord continued with an eager audience.

As she finished her meal, Lord Dackren turned his attention to her. He asked, 'What of you sorceress, how many have you killed?'

Saranon hesitated not knowing how to answer. As

the Lord leaned forward and continued, 'The border is no place for a soft heart. Interfere with my fight again and I expect you to answer for it.'

She could feel her cheeks grow hot as all eyes turned to her. The Lord was not someone she wanted to face as she found an excuse to leave. Her words sounded meek even to her own ears, but it was better than having to stay and listen.

A flurry of footsteps followed her down the hall she could sense who it was before she saw him. Killian smiled as he stopped, 'Did you think my brother would let that go?'

Saranon glared at him in silence. 'Sorry I'll start again, let me show you around,' he showed no signs of relenting.

Ardaguar Keep was massive in size and stature. As much as she wanted to wander by herself, she would not know where to start. Below ground the Keep's voice would be stronger to guide her.

Killian spoke and it took a moment to break out of her train of thought. As he repeated himself, 'Lord Dackren wants to know who you are. There are many who went missing.'

She was speechless at the thought of what that meant. Pennie knew that not everyone had returned from the camps. Yet she had been hesitant to discuss it. Saranon slumped on the floor as the tears ran down her face. She asked herself, 'What have I come back to?'

CHAPTER NINE

Aspirations

The large entrance leading out into the hall loomed overhead. The place was filled with a grandness Saranon did not understand. She made her way up the stairs. The Keep beckoned, but she was not ready. Exhaustion set in. She could feel it all the way down to her fingertips as she moved through the doorway. Pennie sat in cold silence while she turned to greet her, 'It's getting worse.'

'Garduend Keep?' She asked.

'Yes, what did you think I meant?' Pennie spat the last words out with a hiss.

She hesitated not wanting to annoy her friend. Pennie replied in a soothing tone, 'I need you to look into it.'

Saranon did not like taking orders from anyone. Her friend was the only exception. As she rested on the bed, the silence of her dreams swept her away. In the darkness the whispers of the Keep Ardaguar spread out around her. In the early hour of the morning she woke with a start. The moon still covered the sky in shadows creeping across from the corners of the room. She made her way down stairs.

She crept along the creaking floor, while her leaving did not go unnoticed. A soft rustle escaped from around the corner just as she was confronted. Lord Dackren stood over her in a menacing tone, 'Where are you off to girl?'

He leaned too close for her liking as she replied and he remarked, 'You are not going alone.'

Before Saranon could muster an argument he began giving instructions to his right-hand man. Ben Waterworth wasted no time gathering the clan's best fighters.

She was reluctant to ask the wizards to stay behind. Even though all she wanted to do was travel alone. Somehow Lord Dackren managed to look even scarier in the darkness before dawn. As he hiked himself up on his dragon Ember. She was a sleek dragon with a large build. While Saranon clung on as Katholomu leaped into the sky before she was ready. She managed to sit upright as Kat flew at full strength. He made haste catching up with the wizards who showed no signs of slowing down.

The warm night air ran through her hair as they dived in close to the border. Lord Dackren had landed near the side of a hill, as she rushed to keep up. She looked straight ahead through the night sky. To a row of shimmering lights in the distance, the Lord turned to greet her, 'This is as far as we go.'

Saranon waved a short thank you, before darting off.

She fled into the darkness to the end node of the Keep Garduend. Her feet touched the stony edge. She hesitated with the realisation of being in Darkonia.

The thought evaporated as she remembered why she was here. She searched out with her senses and no sound came back. The only thing she could hear was her own breath. When she leaned down to touch the stone it felt wrong. The sensation felt like a heavy burden, sitting underneath the surface, held back by an invisible barrier crouched just below. In the distance a sound caught her attention, but it was just a misquew. Its sharp eyes stared with a warm glow as the large riding cat curled up to rest near the edge of the stone.

She found an entrance leading back into the Keep. As she placed her hand up the shield around it held strong. The misquew stretched out in response as it rose to greet her, before wandering off. She hesitated before following. The creature had an agile stride glancing back before sitting down near the bushes. Saranon peeked through as the bush prickled along the palm of her hand. The misquew laid down closing its eyes to rest once more. She moved the branches away from the stone and read the marker. It did not make sense, but then not much here did.

She walked further and a jarring pain ran through her leg as she stubbed her toe. She held her breath and nothing stirred. Saranon leaned down to find a large metal ring. It fitted around both her hands and she pulled. A cloud of air sprayed dust away from the side and she coughed trying to mask the sound. It was a vain attempt, yet by the look of the entrance it would not have mattered. The air was musty and dry with no sign of any sorcery guarding it. She ran her fingers along the wall. A bulging sensation reached out as she pulled her hand back.

The Keep felt unfamiliar as she glanced around. All the sounds of the normal running of the Keep were mixed up. The Keep lay empty while she moved about expecting someone to notice at any moment. The hair at the back of her neck stood on end and her heart pounded. She continued her descent into the depths of the Keep. Garduend rumbled around her in an eerie tone.

The place filled with a sadness that penetrated her mind and darkened her thoughts. There was not a soul in sight except for the empty mutterings of the Keep. She clambered downward and the oddness dawned on her. There was no flurry of skada, no sound of sleeping zennigh, not a peep. The Keep was void of the creatures that protected it. In the silence it was just her and Garduend. Saranon stepped further down aware of the time outside. This was not the place to contemplate what had happened, she had to move fast.

The strange clanking sound from below became louder. She jumped out into the dark cavern where the main conduit should have been. Her energy held her as she made a slow descent to the bottom. Peering down a gigantic tube filled with nothing but a shambled mess. The last remains of the conduit tying the Keep to the central core had wilted. To all but a thin tube charred at the edges. It glowed hot with the inability to shield the energy pulsing inside. She was able to protect herself from the heat as she walked along with a purposeful stride.

The conduit dipped down a long shaft, she stood at the edge holding on in thought. All the conduits would not last long. An idea crept into her mind one that would have scared her had she not helped Hedavin before. The Angeon enveloped her then she reached out with a tight grasp. She seared all the main conduits from the central core. The blast pounded out reverberating up through the walls. If no one knew she was here that would need to change, as she used the blast to catapult the energy upward. The deafening roar split through the conduits as the stallic energy poured out. It drenched the walls so hard the damage rang out behind her.

Saranon ran out the door closing it behind her. Not wanting to hear any more with the last traces still ringing in her ears. She turned to go and hesitated. A large figure stood in the first glimpse of light spraying out from the unwelcome dawn. Edred the administrator stood strong. The Vandragamond sorcerer was more than twice her age. Her eyes grew wide and she ran. The last traces of the Angeon shielded her from the sorcerer's blow. The energy faded, but she took no notice as she ran back to Katholomu. The dragon picked her up in a sideways scoop and flung himself hard into the air.

The great black dragon looked magnificent in the light of day. Yet that was not what she wanted, as her hearted thudded. A small glimmer up ahead revealed the wizards who had been reluctant to stay. She grumbled in annoyance. Kat gave a deep low growl in return. The dragon did not think much of acts of cowardice and had let her know more than once. The warm sun creased across the sky with its full rays just as they hit the ground. Katholomu held out his wings in a seething manner. He whipped his steel like talons hard against the Keep Ardaguar.

The effect was spontaneous as one wall cracked, with dust flying over the courtyard. The dragon moved his head in an ominous glare daring any of the wizards to challenge him. Saranon landed with a heavy thud as she swung down from the tense beast. Shew ran inside, in a lame attempt to hide. She slowed to a walk as she realised it would be useless. Mitch reached across grabbing her arm and pulling her out of sight. Before she had a chance to say anything he held a finger to his lips.

They both listened. She wanted to shout at the wizard. As the exhaustion wrapped around she reconsidered. Crevan's voice spoke over his talik. As only half the conversation was grasped while the sorcerer walked by. The small circular communication device fit in the palm of his hand. Saranon frowned, 'I think it's about Garduend.'

Mitch gave her a look that said otherwise, 'So how did you go?'

She muttered under her breath. He smiled before responding, 'You'll do better next time.'

She was hoping there would not be a next time. She had the distinct feeling that would be unavoidable. As she walked away the sorcerer at Garduend had looked familiar. She had seen that face somewhere before. She was deep in thought when an arm circled around her shoulders and she flinched. Lord Dackren began talking as she removed his arm from around her. 'Now,' spoke the Lord into her ear, 'When am I going to see you on the disc?'

She cringed before answering, 'No Lord Dackren.'

He gave a ruthful smile and winked as he left her in a state of mortified bewilderment.

The Lord was starting to get on her nerves. She was not sure how much more she was could put up with, as she shook her head. Saranon went outside in the golden sunlight. It streamed down just before midday, as Jack caught her attention. Now that was where she had seen the face before. Jack Heath looked like a younger version of the same sorcerer. He waved again with a warm smile, 'Lord Dackren won't rest until you fight him on the disc.'

'I know.' The reminder annoyed her as she added, 'This is your fault.'

Jack shrugged his shoulders at the accusation. As the smell of lunch wafted passed and consumed Saranon's thoughts. She had not eaten breakfast amid the rush to return to Ardaguar. Afterward she returned to her room. Resting on the small couch as her exhaustion took hold. The warm breeze glided through the window and she fell asleep. Her dreams were filled with a large gaping hole, as she let go, falling deep into the ground.

She landed at the end of a long journey down. Embedded in the soft dirt of Tordoren, a small shining spark glimmered. In the dream she reached out pushing the dirt away so she could hold the spark in her hands.

She held a solid form of life, warm to the touch. Then something grabbed her and she woke up. Pennie stood over her smiling, 'You almost fell off the couch.'

Saranon glanced around the room making sure nothing else was going to jump out at her. 'What's happening at Garduend?' She asked.

'I'm afraid we haven't been able to get close to find out,' Pennie explained.

An unknown problem in a Keep with a detached core spelt even more trouble. Her friend look at her while she was searching for an answer, it was not forthcoming. Pennie could read her face and the sadness welled up in her eyes. Saranon hated seeing her friend this way the internal torment made her heart sink.

The moment was broken as Mitch entered in a rush. Catching his breath while leaning against the wall, 'You're needed.'

He looked straight into Saranon's eyes and nodded. She gave him a quizzical stare oblivious to his reference. As Pennie rose taking her queue without hesitation, 'It is time.'

'What do you mean?' She asked.

'You entered the disc, now you will fight,' her friend explained.

She gave an exasperated sigh. Her mind ran through several arguments. Pennie's expression displayed an answer for them all. 'I'm not sure which one of you to blame for this,' she spoke in anguish.

Mitch stepped aside without saying a word. Saranon

strode down the corridor in a sullen frame of mind. A flurry of sound stemmed from the grand two-storey foyer. A familiar grunt from a dragon filled the air. Katholomu turned his head sideways staring straight at her.

The shouts grew louder as a group of wizards tried to move the great beast out of the main doors. The dragon paid no attention as he lowered his neck and she leaped on. For once she welcomed Kat's disregard. He twisted his body easing through the open doors. He jumped up high into the evening sky as the darkness of night wrapped around them. The voices of the wizards shouted through the wind. No one followed after them. The dragon flew too hard she could sense he had a purpose. She clung on tight as Katholomu swung a hard left, into Darkonia.

She peered down as the ground changed below. The low hills parted into a clearing then Kat swooped fast and smooth in the silence. Up ahead a dragon stirred on the outer edge of the hill, greeting them. She moved through the group of dragons with ease. She realised they served the Vandragamond. She moved closer listening to the sorcerers as she hid. They spoke in low voices and she recognised Edred Heath, the administrator. He stared right past her and she hoped he did not notice, it was all she could do to stay still.

A booming voice echoed in the darkness above. The harsh tones came from the sorcerer that towered over the rest. He said, 'Take the path down below, she's had enough fun. Next time you want a divorce, warn me.'

'Yes, sire,' Edred, the administrator answered with a

dry tone.

Lord Shakar stared off into the distance straight through her. Then his eyes locked on and he shouted, 'Gallagher!'

Allard Gallagher moved off from the side. Saranon wasted no time running toward Katholomu through the low scrub.

She clung to his shoulder as a sound crept up behind her. The dragon lunged. Gallagher stepped back as the great beast took off with a mighty roar. She was too shaken to understand the dragon's sense of delight. He swooped onto the nearest hill across the northern border. The dragon landed with a sudden pelt. The jolt threw her forward as she used her energy to slow her descent. The hard ground stung her hands as she left it too late. Katholomu stood arching his shoulders up to full height. He spoke the same word he had said before with a deep growl, 'Coward.'

It was one word and as much as Saranon tried to argue, it amounted to nothing, as her voice fell flat. In a last effort she shouted, 'I'm not a coward.'

The dragon laughed with the sound rumbling. It ran through his entire body from head to toe. Then he lied down in a casual stance staring at her with bemusement. She tried to stay angry, but the great beast pouted and her heart melted. She clambered up over his shoulders. 'Let's go, I have a wizard to fight,' she grumbled.

The dark night swept in around them as a light rain took the last of the heat from the day. The disc did not enthral her in any way. Lord Dackren had not left her alone since she arrived. Continuing to hide from the problem was not going to work. She smiled as she patted the dragon. Ardaguar came into view and she cringed at the thought. Sometimes it would be nice to be someone else. Katholomu glided down in silence sweeping through the night air.

The dragon flew low along the ground. As he headed straight for the place Saranon wanted to avoid. The beast ran along slowing as he went. He ducked straight into the great hall with the disc and he slid her down near the edge. She did not want to leave the comfort of the dragon. He stayed with the same expression reminding her of what he had said. She jumped as she realised she was not alone. A solitary figure stood in the shadows. Lord Dackren was hard to forget. As he stepped close to the outer rim of the disc, 'I didn't pick you for one to run away.'

She grimaced at the cold remark then walked onto the disc, 'I don't run.'

He grinned, 'We'll see.'

The Lord was no stranger to taking on a sorcerer as he moved with a graceful ease. Saranon watched in fascination, but she had little time to think. The first bolt hurled across the disc. The Lord's energy shattered as she shielded the blow. From that moment she locked her attention on the Lord. She moved forward hurtling her sorcery with certainty. Yet the Lord cut through it in lightning speed. He smiled in delight at her shocked expression.

The shards of energy ricocheted off the edges of the shield around the disc. They lit up the hall with a magnificent array of light. She struck hard, but it did no good. Lord Dackren shielded himself. 'Are you going to call on the Angeon?' He taunted.

She grimaced at his words as she tried to concentrate. She kept pace as they moved around the disc exchanging blows. A movement caught her attention at the corner of her eye. The noise and light had brought other occupants from Ardaguar to watch.

The Lord struck again more specific as if honing in on her. Saranon held her ground as she dodged the full impact of the blow and moved closer. The Lord smiled, consumed by the challenge. He circled in anticipating the end and this time she let him. In the heat of the excitement part of her wanted to see what the Lord could do. He lunged hurtling his energy hard and fast. Saranon gasped and in the gap between her thoughts Katholomu coughed. She turned to face the dragon only just escaping the blast. It lashed through, lighting up the shield in an almighty spray of light.

She rushed forward in the skirmish. She tried to grab hold of the wizard, but he was too agile and darted out of her grasp. He grinned as they moved around the disc. It had not been long, yet her body felt heavy from exhaustion. She refused to give in and she recognised something just for a moment. The Lord lunged in close with his energy and Saranon took hold, dragging him to the floor. She stared straight into his eyes and whispered amid the cheering crowd, 'Let go.'

'No,' he groaned through gritted teeth.

The latches holding the disc in place came free with a metallic ringing sound. Piercing through the crowd as the people roared with delight. 'Relent, and I will spare you the indignity,' she whispered to the Lord.

His attempts remained futile as they remained locked in a silent battle. He sighed, 'All right Vandragamond, I'll give you this one.'

The Lord ceased his fight, and the disc stopped its slow swaying. It returned to its permanent holding.

A roar stemmed up through the crowd so loud it hurt her ears. As they both stood Lord Dackren spoke, 'You have won this one.'

The words were not endearing, but for Saranon it meant an end to being hassled. For that she was relieved as she managed to catch her breath. Mitch found his way through the crowd and held out his hand, 'Come on.'

She followed as they darted away. The thrill of the excitement still buzzed around her head making her feel giddy.

Zara greeted them in the large entrance. With a warm smile, 'My brother rarely loses.'

Saranon was too exhausted to speak as she left for her room. A rose hung from the handle, she picked it up as she went inside. Pennie was studying and stole it from her, reading the note attached. Her friend burst out with laughter, 'I think you have an admirer.'

'What?' Saranon's face went red with embarrassment.

'See for yourself,' Pennie handed her the note.

She fell back on the bed, 'If it isn't one, it's the other.'

'What are you going to tell him?' Pennie asked.

'I'll think about it in the morning,' Saranon sighed.

Pennie burst out laughing, 'At least it's not Lord Dackren.'

She threw a pillow at her friend who would not stop laughing.

CHAPTER TEN

Rising to the challenge

A harsh round a shouting pierced through the open window. Saranon resisted opening her eyes to the morning light. Her body felt like a sack of potatoes as she lifted her arm and winced with the pain. She tried to figure out how the wizard had caused the bruising. Pennie glanced out to the courtyard below, 'Wow, you have to see this.'

She was not amused as she moved her aching shoulders and slid out of bed. The ranting had ceased, but the figures stood in plain view.

Saranon's head throbbed as the harsh light stung her eyes. Jack Heath seemed attracted to trouble. As Crevan walked away her friend made a sly comment, 'I don't think all is well.'

She was not convinced and paid no more attention to the idea as she ran downstairs. Jack was still standing in the courtyard. As he spoke, 'I understand you've been to Garduend.'

'Who told you that?' Saranon asked.

Jack gave a sad smile, 'It's everybody's business to know about the Keep. I was wondering if I could go with you?'

She wondered why anybody would want to go straight into a troubled Keep. She agreed to the request. There was something about the sorcerer's determination that changed her mind. She was not sure what she was getting into herself. If Jack was familiar with the Keep it could be of some use.

She sensed someone approaching and blushed. Saranon had forgotten about the rose as she turned to meet Killian. He greeted her with an open bow and she could feel her cheeks grow red as he asked to walk with her. Her mind went blank and she could think of no reason not to, so she accepted his company. He was not much older than her.

The mystery of Garduend Keep still racked her mind. She almost lost track of Killian's words. He had a quiet manner though he was not shy, Lord Dackren would have made sure of that. He was intent on showing her the beautiful gardens that surrounded the Keep. They were hidden away throughout the many courtyards. The blissful rays of the sun warmed her face as they meandered along the path. Saranon took the opportunity to quiz him about her homeland. A tear trickled down her cheek as she wiped it, hoping Killian would not see.

'I could not imagine what it would be like without my kin,' he spoke with a hint of sadness.

She sensed something, 'You do know?'

He hung his head in shame before answering. 'I was held by Lord Shakar when my father angered him,' he spoke.

Saranon was not sure how to answer.

She held out her hand and he held onto it not wanting to let go. Neither of them knew what to say. Part of her did not want it to end, but then she had no idea what she was doing. At best she managed a small goodbye before leaving him behind. When she was out of sight she smiled as her cheeks grew warm.

A still air hung over the warm afternoon as she looked for a distraction and found none. Pennie was meticulous in her method of packing as they prepared for the inevitable. Her friend had been too absorbed in the details to ask her whereabouts. It was just as well, because she was not sure how to approach the subject. Instead she found some of her belongings and pretended to be busy. Pennie's voice made her cringe, 'Will you stop doing that! I need those boxes packed over there.'

She gave a meek smile while helping.

Saranon followed her friend all the way down underneath the Keep. They passed through the grand foyer. A large simple staircase led them to the armoury below. The lower Keep was more spacious. Only the great columns broke the immediate view. Pennie strode with a purpose. They stopped while two wizards opened the massive doors to a large room.

'Wow,' Saranon exclaimed in awe.

She stared at a room full from ceiling to floor of weapons. 'See anything you fancy?' Her friend asked.

While examining a tool she had just picked up. She had travelled to Indarin with what she had and saw no reason to change. Yet the offer was enticing. She hesitated in thought then left the room and all its glory behind.

Jack stood ready though a little nervous around the edges. It was the first time she had seen him show fear. The late afternoon was still light. This meant swinging around the long way into Darkonia, then back toward the south of the Keep. Pennie had been plotting the path, not wanting to lose time once they were in the air. Katholomu glanced at her as she entered the courtyard, this time he was calm. She held on tight as the great dragon flew hard into the sky.

The ground swirled past below, but she paid no attention as the wind picked up. Kat flew with a majestic grace. They surged over the border straight into Darkonia. It was a fair way in before they needed to turn. The air filled with the flight of dragons missing one another as they went. She was relieved to see that many did not have riders. The last thing she wanted was to be spotted. Pennie showed no hesitation as she bolted through the sky with a purpose. Jack blended in with ease.

Still the anxiety made her queasy and she wished she could be like her friends. The untouched hillside beneath them broke down with the signs of settlement. They stayed on the outskirts flying at a swift pace. Before she knew it, the dragon dropped into a glide, hitting the ground running. Then he arched his great body to a mighty halt. The muscles tensed and she clung on closing her eyes until Katholomu came to a rest. Pennie landed closer still to the Keep's edge. Saranon followed as the strange noises emanating from Garduend resounded through the air.

A snapping sound came from close by but her companions paid it no attention. She quickened her pace not wanting to be left behind. The Keep had an odd stillness that crept over them, with the looming darkness of night. Her senses prickled at the edges. She felt the crisscrossing energy of the Keep leaking through. The path they took along the edge of the forest felt dense. The energy wafted up through the ground. Jack reached over taking his time to read the inscription. He used his energy to shuffle the words around. Something creaked from behind the door and she jumped.

Pennie gave her a stern look before making her way inside. The air was musty with a slight acrid smell, that tasted metallic on her tongue when she breathed it in. She held out her hand. A strange sinking feeling stemmed back through her senses. The odd sensation made her tingle and her eyes locked with Pennie. The taint was something they had seen before. Saranon did not want to admit it, but she was scared. The only thing that had stopped her fear at Antavagon was a deep wild rage. That she had released after Tasha's death.

Tasha's face still haunted her from the grave even though she did not want to admit it. Jack found a hatch leading down to a substation. He knew the layout, the Keep was so faint and it would be easy to become lost. A spark grew from up ahead as she caught her breath and braced herself in the glow. She could just make out her companions as they managed to dodge the blast. It rippled past as the blow hit hard. She staggered back as the last remnants swept through. In the distance she could hear Pennie and Jack running away. She hesitated then darted after them.

Part of her wanted to stay behind. As they escaped out of the Keep, another blast pelted down the passageway. It seared the sides of the building. Kat eyed her with suspicion before whisking her up onto his shoulder. The dragon had no intention of taking her back to Ardaguar. He circled out of sight landing close to the Keep Garduend. Saranon watched in anguish as her friends flew through the sky disappearing from view. Katholomu stood his ground. The dragon lived to fight and he would not back down, much to her astonishment.

She patted the dragon's sturdy shoulder then clambered onto the grass below. The still night air closed in around her as she plucked up the courage to move forward. In the dim light the distant voices travelled to her ears. She crouched in the darkness. It was beyond her how the large dragon could blend into the background. Yet Katholomu did it with ease much to her annoyance. Dragons were so common, that even if he had been seen she doubted it would draw attention. She tried not to make a sound and waited in the shadows on the edge of the Keep.

The voices became people. She watched on as two travellers arrived holding a strange glowing bundle. A sorcerer came out to meet them, then all three darted inside. Saranon hid for what seemed like hours. Then she gathered the strength to climb onto Kat. Her mind filled with unanswered questions as the dragon flew into the air. Just as they picked up speed her thoughts were broken by a stirring of noise on the ground. Katholomu wasted no time leaving Darkonia behind as she clung on tight. The wind whipped around her with a vibrant energy of its own. She could feel the strength of the dragon. He moved with a powerful grace, with the excitement still buzzing in her head.

Saranon wondered what she would have done if Katholomu had been shy. Then she could not imagine him any other way. The great dragon glided into the warm open courtyard of Ardaguar. Jack waited, he was a tall lanky figure and stood back as the dragon came to rest, 'I let you down.'

'What do you mean?' She asked in surprise.

'I know someone at the Keep, and I didn't want to see anyone get hurt,' he explained.

It was not what she had expected, but then she could not blame him.

'I saw something. I was wondering if you could help?' She asked changing the subject.

He smiled, 'I'll see what I can do.'

Jack led her down below the habitable area of the Keep. It was warm and dry with a soft flow of fresh air.

Then he sat dangling his legs over the edge of floor. The warm dark mass of sheal shimmered, swirling below. If she reached too far she could touch it, but it did not scare her. Saranon sat near the edge leaning up against the column waiting to see what he would do. He projected the sheal and transformed it into an image. Asking her if it looked like what she had seen. She shook her head and he created another. This went on as she tried not to laugh. Then her voice stuck in her throat as she waved out her arm and almost lost her balance.

Jack whispered something under his breath. She was too busy staring at the image. She was caught in a trance as it sparkled with an eerie glow. He gave her a knowing look, one she did not expect. He explained, not wanting to stare at the image as it melted back into the sheal. Somehow Jack knew that next time she could not take him with her. He looked heartbroken in the midst of so much unsaid.

A clicking sound cut the Keep's hum short. It startled both of them as they glanced at each other. She had heard the sound before. Her mind raced through the possibilities. The low hum filled the background once more. It did not quell her suspicions. Jack spoke, 'Let me show you something?'

He reached out his sorcery weaving it into the sheal as it glowed fusing into a sphere of light. Jack brought the sphere around holding it out toward her. She was mesmerised by the light.

Saranon had not seen anything like it and the sphere of sorcery intrigued her. She held out her hand and it responded, 'How did you do that?' She asked.

Jack smiled, 'You need to find that out on your own.'

They made their way to the door as a small trail of bubbles popped along the surface of the sheal. She glanced out of the corner of her eye. She stopped as it held her curiosity then left for a well-earned sleep.

The beautiful stars twinkling in the night sky had vanished. They faded into the brilliant mid-morning sun. It played through the open window, reaching the dull carpet. Saranon felt half asleep as her eyes played tricks on her with the light. She blinked and the message was still clear there, marked by a pattern in the shadow. As she stepped towards it, the lines vanished. She lowered her head to the floor trying to trace the source. Pennie opened the door and burst out laughing, 'What are you doing?'

When she explained Pennie smiled, 'It may be one of the wizards.'

Saranon was not so sure, but she did not see any harm in following the instruction. She made her downstairs. It seemed an odd way of communicating. Her annoyance showed on her face as she went below the habitable areas of the Keep. The great doors had been left open with voices echoing above the hum of the Keep. The substation whirred with a strong steady sound. She was not sure if she was meant to say something, but the wizards appeared to be expecting her. Killian strode through the door, 'Beautiful isn't it?'

She was about to complain about the message on the floor, but before she could he walked away. Killian smiled,

'I wanted you to check something for us.'

'Who is us?' Saranon asked.

'The Glyrondagar. We think something is wrong with the Keep and we thought you could help,' he responded.

It did not matter which country she was in, wizards had a habit of finding ways to be irritating. The small group stared at her in anticipation. Until she relented, 'All right I'll take a look.'

She had nothing better to do while waiting to gain access into Garduend Keep. She sat down near the control panels. It was a short way down, positioned near a main connector between the conduits. It was below the spider's web of small connections above. Saranon started flicking the buttons. She froze as Killian slid in the seat beside her. She could feel Killian's eyes boring into the side of her head. He waited with a hint of excitement.

She was tempted to clout him for leading her astray and thought better of it. She immersed herself in the task at hand and listened to the Keep. It hummed along as Killian waited. She moved the levers, switching connections before Ardaguar was ready. Saranon listened to the gaps between, the missing notes in the hum of the Keep. She tried to concentrate as Killian's hand moved across the controls, breaking her concentration. 'Will you stop doing that,' she exclaimed.

Just then an audible clunk broke the silence. The hum of the Keep whirred into action. 'Did you hear that?' he asked.

'Shush…' She held her finger to her lips.

She waited then moved the levers in a different sequence. This time the clunking rattled deep within the Keep, echoing up through the floor. The Keep tried to engage, but it could not. The hum broke into several false starts and the colour drained from her face. She worked the control panel creating a surge from the depths of the Keep. The great roar echoed up. She held her breath as the stallic energy whirred the Keep into life.

Saranon gasped and she stepped out catching her breath. Before she could blink Killian had leaped into action. He wasted no time directing the wizards around them to locate the source. Then turned to her, 'Are you coming?'

'Are you mad?' She asked in exasperation.

He gave a faint smile, 'Maybe.'

She trailed after the wizards. Ben gave her a sideways glance in acknowledgement as he darted ahead.

She had the distinct sinking feeling of rushing into something unprepared. The sensation sank to the pit of her stomach. The uneasiness made her lag behind, no matter how much she tried to keep up. A small clinking sound skittered along the floor. As she turned around to see her talik bouncing down the corridor. She leaned down to scoop it up. A high shrill escaped through the air. Saranon shielded herself from the blow of raging light. The energy sparked along the top of her shield as she dared to open her eyes. The air was thick and metallic. It left a sharp taste in her mouth as she searched through the spray of light.

Her talik buzzed in her hand, but she ignored it. The

air crackled around her as the energy dissipated. She showed no fear as she strode forward toward the shadowy light. The only sound came from her rapid heartbeat pulsing up through her ears. The haze dimmed the way ahead as she searched with her senses. There were figures nearby, but she had no way of telling who was who. Wizardry arched through the air giving the sorceress a small glimpse. It was all she needed as she honed in on her target.

The roar from her energy was electrifying as it cleared the air in an instant. It absorbed the other sorcery. Crevan's eyes became all too clear as they filled with an intense frustration. His blast erupted shaking the ground. Saranon met the sorcerer's blow in kind as Crevan struggled while losing ground. The wizards kept a respectful distance away and she eased off as he stood in defiance. Her mind was still racing, trying to catch up. The wizards reacted before she did, using their energy to block the blow.

Saranon had had enough. She held out her arms absorbing the blow and combining it with her own. The result was pure hot vengeance as Crevan fell limp on the floor. Ben Waterworth ran up to check and gave acknowledgement that he was alive. Her voice sounded hoarse and remote as Ben smiled in response. He remarked, 'Crevan has been syphoning the Keep's energy for himself. We had it narrowed down, but we needed to know which one.'

It still did not make sense. She was willing to accept his judgement after having been attacked. 'Perhaps you need to join the night watch and get some practice?' Ben suggested.

'I'd like to see you take on the Keep's energy,' she coughed.

'That's not possible,' Killian spoke.

'Next time warn me,' she spoke with a tired voice.

Ben smiled, 'I will add that at the top of my list.'

CHAPTER ELEVEN

The old world still burns

It was not long before the whole of Ardaguar was abuzz with the news. Jack's hands trembled as he tried to hide them he was still shaken by the events. Saranon could not blame him, but at the same time she was not about to give the wizards any ground. Lord Dackren's voice boomed across the room. It felt like she was the only one strong enough to answer. She found herself shouting at the Lord. He stared at her, 'I suppose you want me to shower you with praise?'

'Some respect would be a start,' she spoke aloud with a hint of annoyance.

Her body still felt the effects of the fight as she stood her ground, staring the Lord in the eye. Lord Dackren was not about to budge which infuriated her even more. She had been refused access to the lower levels of the Keep.

She could always ignore the Lord's word, but she did not have time to get caught up in a dispute. She was about to say more, then stopped. She did not want to get bogged down in the Lord's antics. 'I expected you to be more forthcoming,' Saranon grated her teeth in frustration.

Lord Dackren took genuine pleasure in his position. He enjoyed telling sorcerers what to do in his Keep. He leaned forward, 'For a guest you make many of demands.'

Pennie broke through the crowd. She stood in front of Saranon, 'We are indeed grateful for your hospitality. As you can appreciate we will leave as soon the matter at Garduend has been resolved.'

To her amazement Pennie bowed and grabbed Saranon's arm. Pennie yanked her down in a clumsy bow, guiding her away from the Lord's gaze.

'What are you doing?' Pennie hissed.

'You can't blame me for that,' she retorted.

Not wanting to start an argument with her friend. Pennie glared at her in astonishment. Then let out a heavy sigh, 'We'd better go before one of you starts round two.'

She did not think the statement was fair. Her head still buzzed from the confrontation. If she had known helping the wizard clan would land her in trouble. She would not have bothered helping.

The room offered little escape from the sentiments of Lord Dackren, that echoed the mood of the clan. The sensations running through the Keep did nothing to calm her mind. Pennie left as though making noise would provoke her frustration. She leaned back on the bed and closed her eyes. A knock broke her rest as Mitch entered, 'I think you'd better come downstairs.'

He left before she could ask. A noise erupted through the open foyer and it only meant one thing.

She ran along the upper level which joined up to the balcony around the stadium for the disc. She could sense who it was, before glancing down. Jack Heath stood on the side of the disc closest to her. She felt awkward as she looked around and found no other sorcerers in her midst. She sat down preferring not to be the centre of attention this time. All eyes focused on the fight below. Sparks flew bouncing off the shield around the disc. The roar from the audience erupted with excitement.

The noise and the sensations running from Ardaguar changed. She could tell the Lord was starting to close in. This time she would have to leave Jack to his own fate. The thought did not sit well with her. Then a tiny spark of wizardry flickered from the corner of her eye. All her irritation narrowed in on the culprit. Her sorcery reached out extinguishing the wizard's work. He tried again without success and looked around. By this time she was well hidden. The wizard was growing frustrated as Saranon remained calm. A loud gasp of astonishment rang up through the crowd as Lord Dackren lost to his opponent.

She darted away in the commotion with a smile of satisfaction. She should have guessed the fights were rigged. She made her way downstairs where Mitch caught her still smiling. 'That was not what I had in mind,' he exclaimed.

He guided her out to the courtyard toward the disc.

Saranon could not understand what the problem was. She glanced at a rather shaken Lord Dackren. The Lord focused on her and their eyes locked. He glared at her. As he moved away from the disc, 'You've just made a sorcerer even more arrogant.'

She leaned close and could smell his breath on her shoulder. As he fumed, 'You were not going to win that fight, at least this way Jack thinks it's fair.'

Lord Dackren looked as though he was about to say something as the sweat soaked his top. Then the conversation was over as he strode through the crowd. She stayed out of his way with no intention of fighting the Lord again. Jack clasped her shoulder from behind and she jumped. 'I didn't scare you did I?' He grinned, 'I've wanted to beat him for a long time.'

Mitch stared at the younger man and responded, 'I hadn't noticed.'

Jack smiled, 'Perhaps next time I'll take you on?'

Mitch gazed from Jack to Saranon then walked off. As she spoke for him, 'I don't think you should, he took down a Dihan.'

'I'm impressed. I need to talk to you about Garduend,' this time he spoke with a sobering tone.

He changed the subject when evening had fallen on Ardaguar. The drunken spectators spilled into the warm night air. They had no inclination to rest. The pair made their way over to a quieter courtyard where the stars lit their way. Together with the small glowing lights along the ground. He looked as though he was about to say something, but stopped. Then tried again as she wondered how long it would take. Jack fumbled around with his hands and let out a sigh. The first hint he had ever given of an inner turmoil. Saranon stared on in bewilderment as Jack Heath began to make sense. Her fragile smile turned into a deep frown.

Footsteps rushed towards them and Jack stopped. He behaved as though nothing had happened as he greeted Pennie. Her friend grabbed hold of her hand. She did not have time to react. 'We need to go now, if we're going to make it to the Keep,' Pennie said.

She tried not to stumble as she ran along the shadowy path. Katholomu snorted in the dark and pushed his way into greet her. The dragon shifted his shoulder sideways scooping her up. She clung on while he took off with a jolt, leaping up into the beautiful still night sky.

She clambered around on the dragon's back and saw Pennie catching up. Her friend wasted no time taking the lead. With Kat following so close the wing tips almost touched. Veradae snorted in disgust. She was almost as large as Katholomu with a sleek black coat. Pennie headed across the border as Saranon's mind raced, full of jumbled thoughts. She left out of the discussion yet again. Blind trust was one thing, but she was beginning to feel as though she had been left well behind. The warm empty night gave her too much time to think. The still air uttered few sounds as the sleepy darkness shadowed her mind. It was not the Darkonia she had entered before.

Without warning Katholomu veered away from the

small group at a sharp angle. She did not try to stop the massive beast, if she could feel the sensation then so could he. She surrendered to the dragon's flight. If not a little bemused by his instinctive decision as she held onto his shoulder. A faint series of lights broke along the hillside. She could feel the great beast beginning to descend. He lunged out his hind legs absorbing the blow. Kat reduced his short sprint to a walk as she stayed low near his shoulder blades. This time she let the dragon lead and the warmth of his skin gave her comfort.

A damp sensation gripped her skin as it dawned on her she was hugging a sweaty dragon. She cringed in disgust. The dragon was searching for something. She was beginning to feel silly clinging to his back. A movement caught her eye in the distance as Katholomu leaned forward. A moment of sheer jealousy ran through her body. As she felt more than heard the dragon rumbling a happy purr deep within his throat. She reached out her senses, and recognised who it was, 'Galven.'

She jumped in surprise not expecting company as he answered, 'Saranon.'

His voice was filled with relief, 'We thought we'd missed you.'

It was an odd statement. 'What do you mean?' She asked.

'Come down,' Galven spoke in a soft tone as he plucked her down off the dragon.

She would always remember him as one of the unfortunate. Branded an Issola like her, and taken to the detention camps. Since then he had changed so much. There was no sign of the scared little boy as she stared into his eyes searching for an answer. He moved forward crouching low, and she did the same. The Keep was still some way off, but there were signs of activity below in the shallow valley.

She watched comprehending what Galven wanted to show her. There in the valley, gathering in their numbers. They were some of the most powerful sorcerers she had ever sensed. They were trying to shield their whereabouts. It was clear that someone else did not approve of the goings on at Garduend. A branch snapped underfoot nearby and her heart leaped into her throat. As she stared into the eyes of the administrator, only a few strides away. Galven grabbed her arm, and they ran. They melded straight through a stone wall before Saranon had time to blink.

While they waited Galven explained as Saranon spoke aloud, 'He looks like Jack Heath.'

He gave a soft laugh, 'Jack is the administrator's son.'

'Are you telling me we just ran for our lives and we didn't need to?' She asked.

'No,' he remarked as he walked down a small path leading deeper into the hillside.

It was wonderful to see Galven again. Maybe someday they would be able meet under ordinary circumstances.

They went down into the small Keep hidden underneath the hill. As she followed along, hoping to avoid getting lost. She glanced at a few familiar faces in the narrow passages. Galven announced an end to their journey. He presented her with a small unassuming doorway. Saranon stepped out into the warm night air, bidding him a short goodbye. Garduend was becoming far too busy. She wondered if she would still be needed when a tall dark figure stood in her way. The administrator loomed over her, and she froze in an odd silence.

'You seem to have misplaced your dragon?' Edred, the administrator spoke.

Saranon looked around her, but there was no sign of Katholomu anywhere. He stood so close this time there was nowhere to run. The soft noise of footsteps behind her only confirmed her situation. Gallagher went to hold her arm. He stopped short as her energy blocked him. 'Don't be stupid girl,' he remarked.

Instead she walked ahead of him, 'Suit yourself,' he commented from over her shoulder.

As they approached the small camp she could make out Pennie and the Captain. Still there was no sign of her dragon.

A large figure approached them in the dark. The sorcerer strode with a fierce pace, showing all the signs of his stature. Lord Shakar's glare cut through the faint light webbing its way around the camp. Without warning the night moved. The Lord sent a blast of his energy toward her, cutting into the air. The Angeon rose inside her shielding the blow. To her astonishment the Lord stammered backwards. As he held his ground the Lord wiped a streak of blood from his chin. 'Don't ever do that again,' Lord Shakar spoke.

'I should say that for you?' Saranon almost shouted the words as she spat them out.

Gallagher tried to tackle her and she gripped his hand. She crushed it with her sorcery until he relented in a shriek of pain. She turned her full attention to Lord Shakar, as they exchanged a verbal argument. Both were prepared to back the exchange with their sorcery. The Lord unsheathed his bond-breaker holding Evermoor in the form of a sword. The blade shone in the reflection of light. It was then that Saranon remembered. The words told to her by Theron, the Prophet in waiting. The blade was like hers. In an abrupt shock she burst out laughing. It was not the reaction the Lord had been expecting.

She smiled realising that Lord Shakar was none the wiser. Captain Assinden's calm voice intruded, 'I think you'd better tell them.'

Mitch was not the only wizard who could read her immediate thoughts. She said, 'I don't think that's necessary.'

She was annoyed, but at that moment the Lord stepped so close. She could feel his irate breath as he glared at her. She held out Corsavere in all its brilliance, gleaming in the form of a sword. She held it up with the ambient light radiating along the blade.

It glowed in a brilliant sea green. The same colour as Lord Shakar's bond-breaker. In the soft glow Saranon saw his expression change. The Lord nodded in acknowledgement as she was left alone. She placed Corsavere away by her side. Gallagher leaned over her shoulder, 'Welcome to the clan.'

'Thanks,' she whispered back, although she was not sure how she felt.

Her would be father had wandered off without uttering another word. So she followed Gallagher to meet her friends. Pennie gave her a giant hug that almost bowled her over in midstride. 'That was great,' her friend said so that no one else could hear.

She looked up in the background to see a large shadowy figure sprawling into view. Katholomu barged his way through claiming a warm spot near the open fire. 'I take it that's your dragon,' Gallagher asked.

He gave the massive beast a gentle pat of affection. 'I think it's a mutual agreement,' she was not convinced the dragon was her pet.

Kat treated it as a convenient arrangement. Gallagher laughed, 'It always is.'

Everything in his body language gave her the impression. That he would not take her on again. 'How do you know Lord Shakar?' It seemed a silly question as soon as she asked.

'That answer is not for a young sorceress,' he explained.

Before she could ask again Pennie interrupted. Her friend said, 'How do you plan to deal with Garduend?'

Gallagher walked over to her friend. 'You'll see,' he spoke.

As though it was a given and strode off leaving the pair bewildered. She wondered why there were no guards around them. Pennie laughed, 'Do the Vandragamond need them?'

In a more serious tone she whispered, 'I should have known there was something odd. That the clan didn't know you.'

She was inclined to agree as Captain Assinden stayed close by. He did not appear fazed by the whole ordeal. Katholomu looked far more content. He would have blended in with the other dragons if it were not for his size. His attitude showed with a small curve at the edge of long jaw.

The still night air caught an odd conversation as she remained quiet. 'How could it happen?' Lord Shakar's voice carried in the dark.

'With your lifestyle anything would be possible sire,' the administrator replied.

Saranon gave a small chuckle as she listened in. Then another voice broke into the conversation. Pennie whispered, 'That's Garridan, Lord Shaker's son.'

She peered up at the great dragon resting. She strode over to the tent before Pennie could say anything. Saranon felt the energy shielding the place. She warped it as she went through, out of annoyance. Wondering how she could have heard the conversation. As she entered the occupants looked none the wiser. She made no attempt to greet them as she searched the room for an answer. The administrator coughed, 'People do not snoop in the Lord's tent.'

She spoke aloud, 'Why could we hear you?'

Lord Shakar glared at Edred, the administrator. He moved quicker than she had seen before. Once Edred knew what to hone in on he made her attempts appear feeble, as he produced a small device. Placing it in a dense black box, 'That was a delight for the evening. I wonder what else they heard.'

Saranon found herself standing near Garridan who gave her a sympathetic smile. The resemblance was there as she gaped in astonishment.

'You mean Hollie, your ex-wife has a name,' the Lord shouted.

There was an awkward silence. Before Lord Shakar spoke again, 'Garridan look after Saranon and our other guests.'

He stared straight at her, but that was as much acknowledgement as he was prepared to give. All she wanted to do was find a warm place to sleep, like Katholomu who had since rolled onto his side. Garridan showed them to a tent then left. She was not about to argue and Pennie relaxed after he had gone.

The events of the night crept through into her dreams as her mind fought them. It was no use too much had happened and the images flashed through. She was left hanging in limbo with a sea of unfinished realities sneaking in. She imagined what it would have been like growing up in the north. Then every time she managed to cling onto an image it vanished. The torment kept her from falling into a deep sleep as her eyes slipped open. A figure moved by her bed.

She jumped upright as Captain Assinden knelt down. He whispered, 'I didn't want to alarm you, Lord Shakar has gone.'

She raced to get dressed then ran out into the night air and ran toward her dragon. Faeryn stood up and was almost about to stop her. Katholomu arched his body up to its full height. He broke into a run with a massive leap into the sky. The dragon's mood mirrored hers as she fumed.

The air swooped over Kat's wing. She clung in tight to his shoulders in the silence that followed. Garduend had given up nothing. The frustration ate away at her as the dragon tilted preparing for the descent. A faint row of lights made their way across the fortress of the Keep. It was an eerie glow that held her full attention and her stomach churned. All her senses honed in on the Keep. Kat spread out his wings and floated the remaining distance to the ground. The grassy hillside hid them with a scattering of trees. The dragon hid well, yet she was sure she could be seen.

There was no hint of the dragons marking Lord Shakar's arrival. She wondered if they were here. She crept forward and a small hum emanated from the Keep. It was more than she had heard before, yet still she could not sense any words from Garduend. Saranon entered the Keep as the clanging began in a faint chaotic rhythm. A shiver ran down her back and she ran further in. The door was blocked and she pounded at the seal. A chip flung to the side thudding against the wall yet still it held. She pounded her energy again and the seal shattered around her. The opening appeared and charged through.

Faint voices travelled along the Keep haunting her from

a distance. The clanging came again reverberating upward from the deep. The walls shuddered and she ran. A voice screamed up ahead, but it was too late. Saranon ducked as Gallagher's blade swung full circle. She ran as the room filled with the Razen sorcerers from the Keep. Gallagher was too far away and the sorcerers were too many. They were blocking her path to the Keep. She caught her breath and turned as the Razen sorcerers honed in. Isen Quinn's voice rang out above the noise as he attacked Gallagher.

Saranon dare not look as she ran. The group of dark Razen sorcerers moved in as the room fell silent. She leaped toward the second sorcerer as the attack began and lost her grip. The thud was eclipsed by the pain catapulting into her side. The sorcery edged through her shield. She tried not to scream, the path lay up ahead and she ran using her energy to hold the path. As she turned into the corridor she hesitated, her path was blocked. The panic rose, she hurled her energy against the wall. It hit too hard and sparks screeched into the air cascading past. Then the roar bellowed from beneath and she froze.

The sound terrified her as she realised what she had done and screamed. The stallic energy rose and the Keep shuddered. There was nothing holding it back. The sorcerers behind her fled as the clanging filled the air. The raw stallic energy swelled upward. Saranon's mind raced, she wanted to run, but if she ran it would catch up. The horrid gurgling sound deepened, there was no escape. The floor creaked and she could feel the stallic energy flooding the lower levels. The crashing grew louder as the energy of the Keep grew close. It was almost upon her and she closed her eyes.

The wave hit as the energy pelted through scrambling her mind and the world grew dark. The sound of the Keep blocked her ears and she clung on as the wave swept past. Then the rush was gone and it slowed. She wanted to open her eyes, but the fear held her back. She stayed hidden in the sea of stallic energy until she could hang on no more. Saranon reached out. Climbing above the surface and made her way to the upper level. The walls still held as the Keep creaked. She reached out grabbing hold of a balustrade. She pulled herself out of the lower level as the mass of energy stagnated. It turned to a darker shade.

Gallagher caught sight of her as he held his blade free. He motioned for her to follow, and she glanced up. Her whole body screamed and her head throbbed as she ran. The chaos filtered through her ears as Gallagher headed straight toward the fight. She gasped as his blade hit into the attack of the Razen sorcerers and she hesitated. The Keep made no sense, the lower level was flooded and she had no way to communicate with it. Before she had time to think a bolt of sorcery swung to close. She held up her hand as it hit, watching it dissolve. Gallagher glanced in amazement before returning to the fight.

The Razen sorcerers regrouped as shouting rang out. Lord Shakar's voice boomed overhead. Gallagher fought hard but gained little ground. They heard Lord Shakar in the distance. He shouted back at Saranon, 'Cut a path.'

'What?' She shouted above the noise as her shield held

against the attack.

His voice was blunt, 'Use your bond-breaker.'

Saranon fumed and used her energy to blast a gap toward Lord Shakar. Gallagher ran through and she followed. He ran into the shield blocking the room and fell backward gasping in pain. The Razen sorcerers behind them were gathering. With no way out they would be trapped. He gazed at her with the same thought and she moved toward the shield. Saranon held out her hand. The stallic energy held inside her, ran along the shield's web, it flittered and she ran through. The shield faded to a dull glow. Holding on with utter defiance yet it was enough to let the Vandragamond through.

The small group of Razen were closing in on Lord Shakar as the shield lost its strength. Isen Quinn glanced at her with eyes that pierced straight to her soul. He was an even match for the Lord as they fought. Lord Shakar's bond-breaker, Evermoor, flared as he kept Isen grounded in the fight. The Razen closest to her broke away and she held out Corsavere to its full length. The bond-breaker sang as she charged. The sea green blade made from the heart of Odana Temple. It slashed through the nearest bond-breaker. With a piercing sound that made her skin crawl. The Razen sorcerer who held onto the remnants of his blade ran as the group broke away.

The only Razen sorcerer left, stood fighting Lord Shakar. Isen shouted as he fled into the depths of the Keep. Lord Shakar waited, lowering his blade. Saranon thought he was calling off the attack. Instead he signalled to

Gallagher and they parted in separate directions. Leaving her to wonder what was going on. She stared down at her blade as the dark night held on.

CHAPTER TWELVE

A fight for the worthy

Sounds creased through the Keep from the deep as Saranon ran to catch up. It was all she could do as she moved toward the direction of the bond-breakers. Evermoor made a hiss as it swung through the air. A stale burning smell greeted her as she ducked. The blast of sorcery whooshed overhead, heating up the air as it went. She slid across the ground as it hit the floor. The sound from the impact reached her ears. The floor lifted with a jarring crack and silence followed. She could feel the floor rise, as she jumped it, came to a halt above where she stood.

Her heart thudded in her ears and she ducked as the sorcery scorched the wall where she had been. The heat flickered past as she winced. Saranon tried to breathe, but the air had been wrenched away. Panic rose inside and she tried to scream, yet no sound came out. She concentrated as the clang of the two bond-breakers ahead reached her ears. She saw Isen Quinn's face. The Razen sorcerer thrust his blade against Lord Shaker's, his eyes locked with hers. She opened her mind to the energy within. The draft echoed into a gust as she blasted through the shields that blocked her out. Before the shield broke apart she braced herself moving forward. The energy hit, the pain reached her lungs and she gasped. The air flooded with sparks in as the shield fell.

The sorcery sparked in wild arc as it shattered and the Razen sorcerers ran. All except Isen Quinn. Lord Shakar's blade fell by his side. Isen stood for a few moments before he dropped to the floor. She ran forward and Isen held up his hand as the colour drained. He let out a cold laugh that sent shivers down her spine. Lord Shaker picked up his bond-breaker. The Keep creaked again from the deep but he did not run. He stared straight at Saranon, 'We are buried.'

'What?' She asked.

Gallagher met them, 'The Keep fell, we are buried and so are the Razen.'

Saranon's face went pale, 'We can't be.'

She was not about to believe the unthinkable. Yet, she could not determine where she was in the Keep. Lord Shakar smiled, 'Shall we finish the Razen?'

Gallagher gave the first hint of a smile that enjoyed pain and nodded as they began to leave. Saranon stood aghast, 'Wait, are you giving up?'

Lord Shakar smiled and held his hand on her shoulder,

'You were never meant to live.'

Saranon stood in shock as the Lord revelled in the cold words as he spoke them. 'How dare you?' She shouted, and he backed away.

The Lord continued, 'You should have died at Antavagon. Now you will die at Garduend.'

Saranon fumed, she wanted to hit the Lord, but at that moment the Keep rumbled and slid. Only this time she could sense it drop. She drew her bond-breaker Corsavere, 'One day I will take you on, but not this day.'

She swung her blade close and drove it down into the Keep. The floor began to meld with the blade as it seeped further into the walls. She watched Lord Shakar and Gallagher leave. As she spoke, 'Not this day, this day is for Garduend.'

The slow rumble of the stallic energy crept higher with an eerie drone as the Keep rumbled. She waited as she remembered Antavagon. The Keep had reached out to her, clinging onto life. Antavagon had survived, yet the sounds that crept upward were from a dying Keep. She steadied herself waiting as the sounds grew louder through the gaping hole beneath. The sparks rose as the Angeon surfaced from within and for a moment all became calm. In the darkness she heard a voice and Garduend spoke in the void.

The Angeon reached out to the dying Keep as it held on to the last spark of life. The central core was boiling underneath. It melted deep into the ground as it broke apart. The stallic energy flowed without a guiding source, and she clung to the wall. The Keep spoke over and over, let go, yet she held on. The shell of the core cracked deep beneath as the Keep held on in its last moment. She concentrated and the stallic energy narrowed just a fraction. She focused as it relented to her and the Keep creaked as it shuddered upward. The Angeon held on under the strain as the building moved toward the surface.

A boom rattled from below as the shell of the core fell in. She held out her arms as the blast catapulted toward her with the last rays of energy from the Keep. The hollow sound rang out in the void as the vacuum filled the gaping hole. The building began to groan under the stress. The eerie echo from the pressure droned around her humming the sound of death. Her concentration waned under the weight as she held her grip with every ache. Then the crashing came as the building crumbled above her. Her heart skipped a beat as the explosion followed and it was all she could do to hold on. Saranon strained under the pressure as the building began falling in on itself. Then a sound came from below, the last sound the Keep ever made.

In the numbness that followed the Angeon reached out. She compressed the last of the energy that was left. The Keep had given it to her, the last and most concentrated energy left behind. She held onto it so tight. That before she realised it the last remnants of Garduend collapsed in on itself. She could feel the energy writhe in an uneven swirl as it compressed. She held back the collapsing building in a deafening stalemate. In the dim haze that followed the clouds and misty vapour unveiled the Orb. She gasped though the sound was completely absorbed in the chaos around her. Her astonishment melted away into panic as she scanned around. She spotted a small opening in the distance.

As the energy subsided she grabbed the massive Orb. She floated back to the ground stumbling before she could run. The building crashed in behind her with nothing left to hold back the pressure. Saranon went to shield herself from the blow and the new Orb in her hands glowed. She ran, and thanked the Keep as she went. She held the last precious remains of Garduend in her arms close to her chest. She rushed to find a way out. The sky was filled with a charcoal ash. A mix of clouds not fit for daylight as the shadows met her in the croaky outside air.

It was all she could do not to choke as she held onto the energy of the Orb, clearing her way and the air ahead. Saranon could sense the Razen sorcerers in the distance and stared down at the Orb. She could not let them take it. She ran along the hillside heading toward the end of the smoke and dust that clung in the air. As the rocky forest became clear up ahead. She found the last remnants marking the edge of Garduend. She leaned down, her hands were so numb that she struggled to move the Orb. She stared at it in amazement, it was the largest she had ever seen. 'Goodbye Garduend,' she whispered.

Then she used the last strength of the Angeon to send the Orb into the ground surrounded by a seal. She hoped it would be enough to keep the Orb hidden. The dust began to settle she took a deep breath and ran toward the Razen sorcerers. The explosion left a blackened crater confronting her as she drew near. Deandra Lythen stood near the edge peering over the ruins as she glanced up. There was no sign of the Vandragamond. She wondered if Lord Shakar had ever intended to deal with the Razen. Deandra laughed aloud as she catapulted a blast toward the sorceress. Saranon blocked as she stepped back with the impact. Deandra waited with an amused smile then she attacked again. The blast hit Saranon in the back and she fell into the crater. Hollie Zimmerman stood where she had been peering over the edge.

She tried to aim but the two Razen attacked, sending her down into the crater. Deandra laughed and Saranon dived back into the remnants of the Keep. The hollowed out cavity creasing across the ground arched back into the rocky hillside. It left more than one trail to follow as she hid. The pain arched through the numbness as sensation returned. The dark caverns in the crater held an eerie tone as a draft flowed through. She could sense the Razen moving closer as the cold set in. The Keep was gone, it offered her no protection, as she glanced around. She would have to face the Razen head on. Saranon took her bond-breaker Corsavere. She held it up to the dim light it glowed as it sang through the air.

She held the bond-breaker firm in her hand as the Razen advanced. She could only just sense them as she waited in the silence. They were closing in and still she waited not daring to make a sound as she hid her location.

Yet it would not work for long as the sorcery of the Razen cut through. She sensed them searching and clenched her fist. Her shield had almost faded and she lunged toward the nearest Razen. Hollie ducked as the blade hit straight into the rock wall. It just missed her shoulder. Saranon tilted the bond-breaker toward her neck. Holding the blade before it touched Hollie's skin.

Deandra came up behind her, 'You won't win.'

The Razen sorceress blasted her in the back. The pain seared through and she winced. She relented taking her bond-breaker. Swinging the blade toward Deandra as Hollie made her escape. Deandra stepped back and Saranon advanced as she struck a shield. She swung Corsavere as the blade carved through, yet the shield held a moment too long. She could sense a blast building in magnitude as it rushed through the tunnels. She was too close. The air drew back in a vacuum as the sorcery rushed forward, then nothing. A giant flood of sorcery roared from behind. She found herself standing in the middle. The sorcery melded in a frozen embrace as each blast neutralised the other.

Deandra and Hollie had long disappeared by the time the energy settled. There remained an unsteady stillness. Saranon glanced outside. Edred, the administrator, loomed over her and held her arm, 'Come with me.'

It was not a tone to argue with as his dragon emerged from the hillside. Tarketh snorted with a sense of purpose. The mighty marmoz dragon leaped above the looming clouds. Edred held on behind with a tight grip. As he steered away from the last pounding plumes marking the end of the Keep. The air dissipated into an open sky with a warm dry stillness. Silence followed the rest of their journey. The dragon swooped with an elegant grace before touching the ground.

The Keep was the tidy home of the administrator. A lone figure came out to greet them. Tom was a taller version of his brother Jack, if that was at all possible. Edred, the administrator motioned for them to go inside. The sky filled with lurking dragons and their riders. She went out to greet Katholomu, now covered in a grey mucky coat of ash. He rubbed himself against her until she was completely covered. The dragon had an innate ability to let her know he was not impressed at being left behind. A rumble broke from the sky above. The dragons circling above broke into two clear packs.

As Saranon approached the open grounds a dragon broke from the clouds sweeping fast. She turned in time to see the claws reach out toward her. Tom struck first, the bolt of sorcery knocked the rider off-balance. She ran past him to the Keep as the group of riders were upon them. Hollie rode the dragon in the lead. Yet she did not strike as she landed between Saranon and the Keep. The Razen sorceress stood facing Saranon with a hard face. 'You were inside the Keep when it died,' Hollie said.

'No. Do I look like I was?' Saranon said as she tried brushing of the muck that Kat caked her in.

The tender soft stance that Kat had shown a moment ago vanished. His great body flexed. He jumped the last distance as his mighty claws dug into the other dragon's side. Katholomu eye-balled Hollie as he held the other dragon, pinning it down with ease. Hollie became uneasy as her dragon screeched out in pain, 'We'll see.'

She made the statement as Kat let go, then flew back into the open sky.

The dragon lowered his head and gave a low deep chuckle as he stared at Saranon who was as dirty as he. She frowned at the great beast, 'You do realise that we are both in need of a bath.'

The dragon snorted in open defiance at the suggestion. He stretched out his muscles in a show of strength and size, before curling his tail by his side.

The administrator's house was deceptively small. As part of it lay hidden underground in a maze of corridors. She made her way along to the dragon pens. Saranon rinsed her hands under the warm water. Katholomu lowered his shoulders to fit under the archway. A clump of dirt scraped off, it fell onto the ground spattering her from a distance. Then the dragon threw himself into the waiting pool. He soaked her from top to bottom. She snapped at him. He replied by rubbing her with his drenched shoulder before returning to the pool.

'You can have a bath in there if you like?' Tom suggested.

'Don't encourage him!' She shouted in haste.

Tom grinned at the sight trying not to laugh, 'The bathroom is that way.'

Katholomu lifted himself in one fluid motion out of the pool. He shook every drop of water out. Tom laughed as he held back the spray with his energy. He said, 'You had better go before you get soaked again.'

The dragon smiled looking pleased with himself, before squeezing out under the archway. He flopped on the ground with a hearty rumbling purr. That reverberated down his body. The bathroom was too small for a marmoz dragon and she washed in peace. There was no one about so she took the chance to peek around and crept upstairs. It was the first time she could remember being in a Vandragamond Keep. She felt a pang of sadness for Garduend it was not what she had wanted.

Saranon crept along to an open door and looked inside. It was full of books along one wall. She leaned over to pick one up and saw Jack Heath's name on a piece of writing near the desk. A sound caught her attention and she turned, knocking the ink all over his work. She froze unable to think, then used her energy to remove the ink spill from the writing. She gave a relieved sigh as she held it up to the light, with no mark to be seen. A creak of the door made her jump, and greeted Tom as she went red with embarrassment, 'Ah…'

There was an awkward silence. She made her way to the bright open room leading out to the courtyard. The meal on the table steamed as Saranon remembered how hungry she was. She dived into the thick stew. It was the first time Edred the administrator appeared at ease. She wondered if it was a facade. A tingling sensation stopped her from relaxing. She peered out the high glass windows to the sweeping view of the low mountains. She tapped her spoon against the bowl waiting for the tension to ease. Tom glanced at Edred then at her, keeping an uneven peace. She glanced up and the sky filled with a dark terror. She dropped her spoon and pushed Tom to the ground.

A crash came shattering through the window as she turned to the site of the blast. A group of dragons swarmed overhead with the sound screeching through the sky. She ran out into the courtyard looking for Katholomu, but he was nowhere to be seen. She scrambled back toward the Keep as the dragon riders circled in. The shield held as the Razen sorcerers blasted against it. She scrambled to the edge of the Keep trying not be seen. Then a great whir came overhead as her friend Galven rode his dragon toward the group. He hurled his sorcery toward the Razen. It was enough to send the dragons in every direction.

She could sense the Keep underneath as it rumbled away deep underground. She let her energy reach out and the Keep answered. She clung on to the energy of the Keep. The razon sorcerers who had attacked her friend were now in retreat. A sickening feeling reached her stomach as the dragons regrouped. They swooped down through the sky and the sound gave an eerie tone in the grey clouds. She stood her ground as best she could and kept the energy within her. The dragons came close and she could see Deandra. She raised her arms to the sky the energy flooded through as she aimed high.

This time it hit singeing the dragon's side. Deandra answered with a blast of sorcery. She managed to block it with the aid of the Keep. Deandra fell to the ground as the dragon rolled in pain. It screeched as it tried to get up. Then the beast ran toward the nearest pond not thinking of anything else. Its screams chilled her before it finally calmed. She hesitated as Deandra fled and she was too shocked to go after them. Even though the Keep held, it did not feel safe as she returned.

The grey sky darkened overhead as the night set in. Edred the administrator stood in the alcove waiting as he allowed her to pass. A great crash rumbled through the sky. She lost her balance and glanced back to find the sorcerers gathered once more. She could see Katholomu in the distance as one of the dragons struck out, her anger flared. She ran toward him. She gathered her energy preparing to strike. She ran as a new fleet of dragons gathered on the horizon. They loomed from the darkness toward them. Lord Shakar flew in close. She could sense him, but could not see his face. Deandra's attention swerved toward the newcomers. Saranon took a chance and blasted her energy toward Deandra.

The Razen sorceress retaliated before Saranon could shield herself. The Lord blocked the Razen's sorcery. Then without warning he turned his full attention on her. His dragon Dregora swooped close. This time there was no Keep to stand in her way. She held her bond-breaker Corsavere. In the form of a sword, high above her head to challenge him after what he had done. The Lord stepped down from his dragon holding his bond-breaker by his side. For a moment he watched waiting for her to move. She was frustrated by his calm stance and her anger swelled as she raised the blade. Her swing fell short as she raised her hand and used her sorcery to follow through. The Lord staggered back as his face showed a hint of surprise. Yet it soon turned into a cold harsh glare.

He raised his hands and his sorcery strengthened. She could see the Razen sorcerers flee and only then did she begin to panic. She stood back and let out a gasp. When she realised she had stepped back toward the administrator. Her sorcery swelled from deep within and the Lord laughed, 'That will not work.'

Saranon glared at him as she fumed, yet he did not relent. Lord Shakar aimed for her. She absorbed the energy before he had time to think. He began to raise his arms again, the second blast hit and she absorbed it. She waited for him to close in. Yet at the last moment he pulled back as though sensing what she was prepared to do. 'Perhaps another day,' He said.

Lord Shakar smiled in a manner that took away any trust she may have had. 'You let the Razen escape,' she glared at him.

The Lord laughed, 'They will not get far.'

She struck out catching him off guard and held his arm, there was nothing. Gallagher whispered underneath his breath as he put back his bond-breaker, and stepped away. There was no sign of the energy she had absorbed. It was not the first time Lord Shakar had been lost for words. He waved his hand toward Edred, the administrator. Edred leaned over. 'It appears you will need to leave,' he spoke. He gave her a map for the Asdenard Keep, Endorell, 'It would be best if you stayed there.'

Saranon felt like she was being passed off, but said nothing as she left. She wanted to put as much distance as she could between her, Lord Shakar and the Orb. The Razen sorcerers would already be searching. It would be best not to draw attention. With the map in hand she darted out of the courtyard. Tom ran after her, 'Wait, aren't you going to say goodbye?'

She smiled and waved as he grinned. He gave her a small present, it was a book, 'In case you become lost,' he explained.

She was not sure what he meant, but accepted it with gratitude.

Katholomu met her with a calm gaze as he let her climb on. He was watching the sky with an anticipation that made him tense. The shadows of darkness crossed the evening with the smell of ash. The dust was still thick in the air from what remained of the old Keep. She closed her eyes as the image flashed through her mind, yet she would have to forget. Saranon motioned for the dragon to go and he flung himself hard into the still night air. The tiredness rolled in as she managed to keep awake. The great dragon darted down near a small cave well worn by dragons. He took her into the heart of a dragon colony.

It was the first time she had seen so many marmoz dragons, yet she was too tired to be scared or excited. She took the dragon's suggestion and setup camp for the night. After she had lain down the dragon wrapped himself around her. She was thankful that the dragon was clean.

Katholomu closed his wing over her in a small cacoon. She wondered how long the sweet smell would last.

Saranon drifted off to sleep, a familiar face haunted her dreams. No matter where she was Tasha found her, waiting just beyond the darkness. Tasha's spirit came to visit across the void holding out her hands. Saranon could not make out if it was a warning or an invitation. Her dream held the image, yet it did not answer her question, as she fell into a deeper sleep. The image of her friend faded into a deep resounding darkness.

CHAPTER THIRTEEN

Friendship of old

Saranon found herself staring out at several sets of small eyes. The three infant dragons began losing their shyness. One small dragon, the same size as her, stuck her head into the sleeping bag. This provided a cue for the other two who felt as though they had just been left out. She heard a sharp rip, as her sleeping bag was torn into shreds. All three young dragons froze at the sound. Then realised there was no danger. The last remnants of the sleeping bag became even smaller.

She sighed as any hope of saving her sleeping bag evaporated. It was too difficult to be angry with three of the cutest creatures she had ever seen. They revelled in the attention. The landscape was beautiful, untouched by people. It had an array of paths well-worn by the dragon inhabitants. Saranon stood out in the open contemplating the map to Endorell. A giant snort of warm air rushed down her back. She turned her head to see the largest female marmoz dragon she had ever met. She walked away trying to avoid doing anything to draw the dragon's attention.

As she sidestepped backwards she felt something large behind her. She glanced up in a silent horror, as a male marmoz dragon bent his head down and glared. Saranon wanted to scream as she remained silent. She stepped away and glanced around, hoping not to bump into any more dragons. Her heart sank as she walked along she would have to dart through the crowd of dragons up ahead.

Saranon began treading over the uneven ground. Every small move or grunt from the dragons made her quiver. She took her time, with more than one set of eyes keeping close attention. She made her way to the end of the group letting out a sigh of relief. As a low rumble of a dragon voice bellowed behind her, 'You're welcome.'

She stared in astonishment. As the dragon near her curled up into a tight ball with one eye left open. She had just wasted more than an hour when the dragons were content to let her pass through.

She wanted to say something, but the sheer scale of the group gave her an uneasy feeling. She unfolded the small map before choosing a pleasant spot to sit down. The map was well drawn, yet she was having a difficult time locating any bearings to go by. She felt awkward heading deeper into Darkonia. It was not a place where she could ask for directions, given there would be people searching for her. There were several lay-lines nearby. Yet without knowing where she was going it could be dangerous to become lost. She trudged on. The open paths were silent and a welcome relief. A faint light beamed from her talik as she opened the small circular device. It had picked up a faint signal from Endorell, as she changed direction.

Saranon strode along feeling confident with her decision to avoid the lay-lines. She followed an old path that had seen better days. It was overgrown with scrub amid the sparse trees. As she looked up to the beautiful clear sky a spark of wizardry whizzed up into the air. Endorell Keep was a wizard stronghold and she was not bothered by it. As she trudged along the path a few buildings became visible in the distance. She bent down to check her map.

She stood up and turned just in time to see a large ball of wizardry heading straight for her. She reacted using her sorcery to snuff it out. The wizardry burst into a cloudy haze raining tiny sparks over the ground. The sound of muffled voices reached her ears before she saw anyone. As the sparks settled two groups of annoyed wizards appeared on either side. Captain Verkin shouted, 'This place belongs to the Asdenard.'

She was not sure how to respond to the wizard. Yet before she could Roger spoke up, 'Saranon was sent here by the administrator.'

Captain Verkin was a large man who looked much taller as he stood beside her. 'You don't look like you could cause that much trouble,' he said.

Roger smiled, 'Believe me she can.'

The Captain was not impressed. He did not give her

any welcome as he walked in the direction of the Keep. Roger waved her over as they marched together in unison. 'I thought you weren't supposed to return?' He said with a wry smile.

'That was not my fault,' she grumbled as she ran to keep up.

Endorell Keep was mighty indeed. Its great buildings and walls loomed high into the air with a statuesque grandeur. The wizards slowed as they entered the vast courtyard. They were be met by a few quizzical stares at the sight of Saranon. 'Wait here,' the Captain spoke to her and Roger.

She rested on the stairs leading to the main entrance. She took in the view from the raised platform. The Keep was well spread out with its own town huddled close. The buildings were followed by sprawling low hills. The open fields were broken by the rocky ground and small forest. A firm hand leaned on her shoulder as the Captain reached down, 'You are expected.'

He walked away, assuming that she would follow. The wizard moved so fast that Saranon ran forward when he stopped. She almost ran into the Host Matthew. After her last experience with a wizard bonded to the Keep she backed away. The Host's dark eyes watched her. Captain Verkin made a small bow to the Host then turned to leave. She called out, 'Wait, where are you going?'

'I said, you are expected,' then the Captain left.

She was not sure how to respond to Matthew. She stood there in stunned silence as the Host spoke first. The melded part of the Keep just showing above the neck line made her shiver. She knew it was not painful but it looked out of place. Matthew was calm, in complete contrast to the way the Host Nathan had been at Greddin Fort. She was not prepared to let go of the uneasy sensation whirling away in her stomach. She waited for the moment he would change as she listened. The Host wished to show her around the Keep and she accepted.

Endorell was a massive stronghold by any comparison. The wizards around her knew it holding an air of confidence. The few sorcerers she saw welcomed her, yet the whole scene made her uncomfortable. She had been exiled from Darkonia and the sentiment could not have vanished. The old detention camps had not been forgotten. Pennie had not spoken of any forgiveness for what she had done after breaking free. Yet here she was in a small piece of tranquil paradise. The Royal Darkonian Army had made Endorell its headquarters.

She wandered off, thankful to be away from the Host's company. She peered over the balcony taking in the vast landscape. 'Beautiful isn't it?' Galven asked.

She almost jumped and gave him a scornful look. While he continued, 'The Asdenard will give safe passage until the Razen are finished.'

'I thought that was finished?' Saranon asked.

He replied, 'It hasn't begun.'

She found her room and flopped down across the bed letting the breeze fill the air. Her tired eyes woke with a clunk near the open window. She sat up to see Roger making himself comfortable sitting on the sill. 'The Captain wants to see you,' he spoke without giving anything away.

She gave him a puzzled look before stepping over the sill. Following him along the balcony in the afternoon as the shadows began to creep.

A rowdy sound echoed from below as they made their way down through to a great hall. There was an abundance of food to choose from, yet she still felt uneasy. Captain Verkin sat through the whole meal without uttering a word. She wondered if he wanted to speak to her. As the table began to clear she rose and the Captain motioned for her to sit. It was the last thing she wanted to do. The Captain gave no hint away as he spoke, 'I don't know what you've done to Matthew, but it has to stop.'

She asked. 'Pardon?'

'You heard me,' the Captain spoke with a firm tone.

Saranon wore a puzzled expression, with no idea what he was talking about. The Captain showed his annoyance. She glanced around hoping for a sign of help and found none.

Captain Verkin leaned forward clasping Saranon's hand. He said, 'You have no idea what I'm talking about?'

She felt uncomfortable underneath his gaze. The Captain led her away from the table, 'You are a novice.'

She grimaced at the response, after everything she had been through. He continued, 'Your visit here will not be long.'

The wizard left, yet he did not answer the question. Leaving her to wonder why Matthew was being nice to her.

She peered around and she spotted Galven. She wanted to throttle him for not helping.

He quizzed her about the Host without giving anything away. Saranon was not impressed and found an excuse to leave. She left the window to her room open to the night sky. A small welcome breeze offered relief. She knelt and placed a small ward on the windowsill. She glanced up to see the Host standing on the balcony. Matthew stood silent for a moment then he spoke, 'I knew you… from before.'

She gazed up at him, unsure what to say as the Host struggled to find the right words. He sat on the windowsill peering at the tiny ward. 'I wanted you to stay, but it was before…' Matthew trailed off.

As he turned away staring out at the night sky. 'You mean before you were a Host,' Saranon filled the gap.

He nodded without looking at her. It was not what she had expected, but it would explain his odd behaviour. 'I called out, but the Asdenard didn't listen,' Matthew spoke in the breeze.

From the thoughts of the Keep that melded with his mind, she felt the weight of the Host's words. She hung her head without uttering a sound in the silence that followed. The Host stood composing himself. He tried to shift away from the Keep's emotions and left. The hour was growing late and too much had happened in one day as she climbed into bed. Yet her mind would not calm itself. The remnants of Garduend washed over her dreams. A lone figure stood haunting her. The sorceress turned in the radiant light with her long dress flowing.

Tasha her old companion through the dark days. A memory from the detention camps returned in her dreams. She stood more elegant than she had appeared in life. Saranon walked up the slope to greet her friend. Tasha held out her hand pointing to the land below. In the distance she saw a large holding with an aged castle rising up from the landscape. Yet as she focused on the building it was gone, disappearing into the embers of her dreams.

The sound of the door crept into her precious sleep as she tried not to notice. A voice followed. 'Are you awake?' Galven whispered in the faint morning light.

His shadow moved overhead and she open her eyes, 'Can it wait?'

'Acwellen has disappeared,' Galven spoke in haste.

Saranon did not understand the significance of his tone as she mumbled her way out of bed.

The morning light filled her head with a stubborn ache, as she rubbed the sleep out of her eyes. Galven shook his head upon seeing her emerge from the room. Her head still ached as he explained along the way. A familiar thread tugged at her thoughts, the Host had been too calm. A small group had gathered by the edge of the habitable area. They were dwarfed by the size of the great entrance into the indolin chambers of the Keep.

Captain Daina Ressinden was busy as she held out a tracer device, larger than a talik. The doors below were open with two officers not far from the entrance. 'Ah, just who I've been waiting for,' Daina said as she spotted the sorceress.

Before Saranon had a chance to say otherwise the Captain held her arm. They walked down the stairs. 'If you don't find Verkin's son, he will turn you into ash,' Captain Daina said.

'What?' Saranon gasped.

The Captain smiled, 'You heard me, now give me your talik.'

She handed over her talik not sure what to expect. As the Captain calibrated it to the tracer, and tossed it back. 'If you pick up anything don't wait. Just go in and get him out,' the Captain instructed.

Before Saranon could reply the Captain had moved on. She wondered if it was Captain Ressinden who would turn her into ash.

The chambers were warm, and she wondered if the talik would pick up anything. She trudged through the underground corridors trying not to become lost. She leaned down and used her sorcery against the jammed door. It refused to budge as she sensed the Keep willing it to stay shut. There were other ways to get in to the lower chambers. Yet that would mean going further out from the wizards.

The Keep and the Host did not want to talk. She felt like there was something she was missing. The confusion hindered her thoughts. She stepped back as Captain Verkin rushed down shouting as he went. The Captain was in no mood to listen as he ranted with an incessant desperation. He hurled a blast against the door, the wizardry shattered and she stepped away. The Keep had shut them out, and she needed to reach Acwellen. Captain Ressinden rushed down with her officers to calm the scene. Captain Verkin's shouts ran through the air.

If the Keep would not let her in she would have to find another way. Saranon took a few steps back then she held out her arms, leaned backward and fell. She let her mind clear and the energy wrapped around her. She melted straight through the floor, in a freefall as the energy softened her landing. She felt something soft and furry underneath and opened her eyes. The soft sweat purr of the zennigh trickled through. The giant cat was so large its fur covered her. She sat upright trying not to wake the creature.

She slid down the zennigh's back landing on the sandy floor. The creature shifted closing the gap between her and the wall as she ran out of the way. The walls of the imbenik chambers were older than she expected. She leaned close to the Keep that did not want to be heard. There was something there as she sensed the walls, something else.

A tiny ripple that caught in her mind as the Keep came to life behind its vale of silence. Endorell gave a tremor from above as it reverberated through the walls. She ran trying to hide from the flow of stallic energy from the Keep. She stopped running as all the walls appeared the same. She ran back, but there was no trace of the zennigh. She was lost. Panic began to swell up in her throat as she tried to quell her rising thoughts. Saranon ran, and glanced around at the blank walls.

The heat filtered through the dry air and she searched for her talik. As she fumbled a small glow appeared it was the small book Tom had given her. She opened it and the pages changed to a show a moving map. A wall moved on the map and she heard a faint noise and smiled. She was in a moving maze but she still had to find a way out and Acwellen. The walls moved again. Soon she would have to choose, she held the book in one hand as she moved with haste.

The Keep had annoyed her long enough, she raced to move ahead of the maze as it closed in around her. A way out revealed itself on the page. Yet as soon as she made her way there the walls moved back around her, to form a large room with no way out. She hit her fist against the wall and felt the Keep's reaction. She wondered what that meant as she looked at the page again, yet there was still no way out. She put the book away it was no use against a stubborn Keep.

The wall opposite moved as she ran toward it, and she stopped. In the alcove Acwellen laid on the ground almost still. She slumped down beside him and wondered if he knew. It did not take long for the wizard to wake up as he panicked looking for a way out. Saranon watched in an awkward silence as desperation set in. The wizard used his energy to blast against the wall. It was not enough. She was not about to argue with an angry wizard as she watched on.

She waited until the wizard stood exhausted. She asked while he caught his breath, 'Has your father met me before?'

Acwellen turned acknowledging her for the first time. 'If you help we can both get out,' he said.

'I don't think so,' Saranon exclaimed to his amazement. 'Has your father met me before?'

The wizard who was not much older stared at her, 'I have.'

Saranon could not hide her astonishment. Acwellen read her thoughts, 'Fine, I'll tell you, but then we are getting out of here.'

She nodded in agreement, not wanting to change the subject. 'Oriana requested sanctuary for you, but the Asdenard would not give it,' Acwellen explained. Saranon sank to her knees. 'Your mother came here before we knew what was happening.'

A large crack began to form down the ceiling and it spiralled out. Saranon and Acwellen gazed in silence. A jarring sound rang out as wizardry pelted from above them, and they ran. The labyrinth moved as the blast fell through. Saranon slammed her fist against the wall as it blocked them away from the blast. 'We're safe,' Acwellen said.

She was not so sure, 'Really?'

A rumble made its way from underneath as the Keep stirred. She could sense the wizards breaking through and pushed against the wall in frustration. Acwellen did not look impressed.

She felt the Keep whirring underneath, it wanted her to follow. She hesitated as the floor began to melt away. Acwellen panicked, the wizard could not enter the central core. She ran and dived through as the hole vanished behind her. Endorell Keep reached out pulling her down into the central core. The vast shell defied gravity. She floated above the unnatural storm spiralling up from Tordoren. Endorell reached out and her mind blocked the Keep. It rumbled from beneath then it gave her what it had held onto. A memory of what was, what will be, and what should be. She saw the Angeon, but it was not her. The image was Zeralden Hadenvar, the last Angeon.

She recognised the walls of the great hall in Endorell, a cold silence hung in the still air. The walls were charred and in her hand Zeralden held the Eye of Escora. The Orb glowed, yet the Angeon did not need it as the night wrapped around. All she could see on the ground were remnants of the Dreshans. The army had occupied Zyanthia. Zeralden placed gave the Eye of Escora to the Keep. She stood back, the energy flowed through. The energy of the Angeon glowed, it glowed beyond all reason and then the image was gone. Saranon gasped. 'You had the Orb,' she spoke to the central core and it spoke back. You and I are the same, its voice lingered in her mind.

She stared in disbelief. As the stallic energy lighted up the swirling storm trapped in the core. It sparked rushing up the great rod embedded in the unseen depths. She could feel the panic rise as the Keep continued. The rumble blasted upward igniting the rod. Instead of sending it through the outer shell the Keep sent it toward Saranon. The shock rang through her ears as the Keep rumbled hurtling her to the surface. The light of the Keep shone as she reached out to touch the surface of the end node. At the farthest part of Endorell. Her hand brushed against the sorcerer's stone to make sure it was real. She was alive, yet the Keep had known.

She stood up, bathing in the sunlight as it streamed down. Perhaps, just once, she could be who she was. Saranon reached inward as the Angeon rose, this time she let it go. The energy grew beyond what she dared to hold. The creases of energy glowed as it concentrated. She held out her hands and let it flow back into the Keep. The moment of peace lasted for only a short glimpse as the voices of wizards rang out. The group approached her and Captain Verkin spoke, 'Where is Acwellen?'

Saranon stood on the end node unswayed by the Captain's tone. She stood in the centre as the stone surface retracted into the Keep. She floated above the gaping hole as Captain Verkin stood near edge. The stallic energy rose in a soft wave that filled the morning air. It brought with it the wizard. Acwellen was overwhelmed with awe as the Keep closed the end node underneath. He touched solid ground. Saranon stepped from the stone's surface, moving away from the elated wizards. She flinched as she watched Captain Verkin greet his son, Acwellen. Her greeting had been far different.

She hung her head and walked away, perhaps one day she would feel the same. Her senses reached across the grounds of Endorell as a figure approached. Mitch had made it to Darkonia. The wizard still managed to astound her, though he did not look impressed. Saranon was in no mood to talk as she attempted to ignore him. 'When were you going to tell me about Lord Shakar?' He asked.

'You didn't come all this way for that?' She replied.

He placed his hand on her shoulder, 'Lord Shakar is dangerous.'

Saranon glared at him. 'I'm serious,' he said.

'You are too late,' she did not want to elaborate.

Mitch fell silent. He could read her immediate thoughts but gave no hint of what he thought. The grounds belonging to the grand fortress of Endorell softened its edge. With the grass fields and low shrubs. The long walk gave ample time for a crowd to gather as Captain Verkin followed them. For the first time she saw the Captain smile as he passed them. She stopped at the top of the stairs leading to the main courtyard. 'That wizard knew my mother, Oriana,' she spoke to Mitch.

He nodded in silent agreement before adding, 'Do not hassle the Captain.'

The thought was tempting and Mitch gave her a stern look.

CHAPTER FOURTEEN

Acquaintances past

Saranon dodged the wizards who were excited to see Acwellen again. She had managed to clear the commotion when Galven picked her up in a tight hug. He lifted her clean off the ground. She wanted to shout at him. He had put her down with a large grin, 'I just thought I'd share in the excitement.'

Saranon could feel her cheeks grow hot with embarrassment.

As she waited a moment it became obvious that none of the wizards were going to thank her. She let out a sigh. She managed to sneak her way in to the kitchen before the lunchtime rush. She munched on a piece of warm toast. If there was one thing she could say about Endorell, the food was delicious. It reminded her of Mrs Harper's Tavern in Redadere. As she reminisced, a sound crept along the floor breaking her concentration. Captain Verkin stood near the doorway while he spoke, 'I forgot to thank you.'

Saranon was not impressed by the attempt to appease the Keep. She wanted to shout at him in the silence, but instead nodded a curt reply. She stared up at the wizard who appeared reluctant to move. As he added, 'Stay away from Matthew.'

She almost choked on her toast while the Captain walked away.

The Keep itself was welcoming in stark contrast to its occupants. She placed her hand up against the wall sensing Endorell. It lulled in the background. A small whimper escaped from the darkness at the end of the stairs. She made her way down while no one was looking. The distinct sound of the zennigh drew her as she peered around the corner. Saranon smiled at the sight of the young creature. The kitten was as tall as her, as the zennigh glanced back with deep amber eyes. Before she had a chance to reach out her hand it purred and she stood mesmerized. A voice drew her attention as Galven called out and when she turned back the zennigh was gone.

'Back to the wizards I suppose,' she spoke aloud.

'You'll be gone soon enough,' Roger said, startling her.

She tried to work out where he had come from, and he smiled without giving an answer. She was too astonished at being caught unaware to argue. As she ran up the stairs hesitating and stared back into an empty space. Galven waited, a solitary figure. He gazed out the window toward the rugged terrain below. They headed off to gather some equipment before heading out.

He appeared edgy though Saranon was unsure why as she followed him. They left the main building along an uncommon path. It took her a moment longer to catch on to what Galven was up to. A misquew waited in the shade as he motioned for her to go. He patted the riding cat with a heavy hand on its back and it leaped into a steady run. She leaned down and held tight to the misquew. It padded along with its soft paws not making a sound.

It was dangerous to stay in Darkonia. The ground cover hid the full strength of the sun as the misquew avoided open ground. Saranon kept her head close to its fur as she glanced around hoping that they were alone. She sensed an end node just as the creature stooped to let her down. She patted the misquew feeling the sweat along its back. She wiped her hand as the creature left. The end node looked as though it had hardly been used. Yet the Keep reacted when she reached out her senses, opening a door to let her in.

Kaythar felt solid and sturdy, filling her mind with a flood of conversation. She brushed her fingers along the walls. The Keep knew she was being sent here. She enquired as to why. The Keep let out a chuckle that ran along her senses as it responded to her question. Answers given by a Keep did not always make sense, but she thanked him all the same. The Keep appeared quite pleased to be visited by the Angeon. She was not sure the occupants would be as enthusiastic. So she kept to the less travelled path leading below the habitable area.

Kaythar talked away even in the silence. It encouraged her to go below the indolin chambers. She smiled as he continued to talk and the image of a bond-breaker filled her head. The Keep was talking so much because it wanted something. Still, after Garduend it made a pleasant change. She listened as Kaythar chattered away in the background. The Keep felt alive and well looked after as she opened the door, trying not to make a sound.

The room was laid out with the equipment needed to refine a bond-breaker. A few skada rested under the bench, the only hint that the room had been prepared in a rush. She leaned down and held one of the mechanical spiders in both her hands. It gave a sign of recognition. She patted it as though it were alive and tucked it under one arm. She rummaged around the room. The Keep was silent, then it began chatting even more. Saranon held the spider level with her eyes. 'Well do you think I should create a bond-breaker?' She asked.

The skada moved in response nodding its head and she let it run across the ground.

She placed a couple of tools on the table with a clunk. She froze in surprise forgetting the need to be quiet. She waited to see if anything had been heard. The Keep reassured her, she set to work while faint noises echoed from above. The lower chambers were warm and welcoming with a hint of age and dust along the stone walls. The strength of the Keep showed in the well-kept skada who tried to pre-empt her. In truth it had not taken much for the Keep to convince her. Saranon had been itching to make more bond-breakers. Hiding away in Kaythar seemed like the perfect opportunity.

The Keep came across with a thrill of sheer excitement. Reverberating into a faint hum along the walls and she smiled as she worked at a steady pace. Kaythar was not eager for her to meet the occupants of the habitable area. She was not willing to meet them. Before long the sorceress had five blades ready. With great care she carried each one from the pool of sheal where she had made them. The potent liquid energy running through the Keep lay silent. Absorbing any noise she made when lifting the bond-breakers out. The fine blades shone in the light, with the heart stone well formed from the elements. The Keep and her energy condensed into a solid mass.

She wrapped them up after one last gaze. She took them back to the quarters that had become her temporary home. As she made the finishing touches leaving two behind for the Keep. Saranon patted the skada that had kept her company. It was a small gesture, yet it was a relief after the end of Garduend. She slipped the three new bond-breakers into a sova bag. It shrank back into a tiny pouch. Then she made her way out into the warm night air.

She followed the lay-lines. Hoping that the advice the Keep had given her would be enough to make it north over the border. The warm breeze played at her cloak as she tried not to draw attention. There was no one there, but still she had to be careful. Travelling along the lay-lines was common this far north. The night air broke with the occasional sound. Each time she glanced around trying to assure herself it was nothing. The night grew late and she managed to find a small alcove for some much needed sleep. Her weary muscles told her how far she had gone.

Even though the lay-lines quickened her pace it did not ease the toll of the journey. She used her energy and a tiny sacra seal to conceal her location. She curled up in a comfy sleeping bag. The morning light broke long before she woke. She pretended not to notice the brightness of day. Her muscles were still weary from the night before. The warm air rustled through the branches of the trees. There was a short gap in the lay-lines up ahead as she scanned the area.

She hesitated wondering if she should risk being seen. The safety of the sacra seal remained as she stayed close by. Preferring to wait as the movement passed. The small snap of a dry twig caught her attention as she looked up to see a misquew. The creature lay there. Unaffected by her attempts to remain hidden from the outside world. She was reluctant to shoo it away, hoping that no one travelling by would notice.

Another sound emanated through her senses. As she waited ever so still, hoping the travellers would pass. Saranon could sense a group of wizards scouting the area to the south-east. The group was in the direction of Kaythar. She could hear the voices as they closed in, they showed no sign of noticing her. Though it was clear they were looking for someone. A larger group appeared behind the first. She sat while the misquew rolled over bathing in the sun's warm light. It stretched out its paw ever closer, as she held back a surge of panic.

A few voices became raised and she recognized Captain Ressinden's voice through the clearing. She shouted at the Captain from Kaythar. Her tone carried with it a menacing threat as her opponent refused to back down. Saranon found herself in an awkward position. She watched the Asdenard ready to fight amongst themselves. Her chances of leaving soon were dwindling with every moment.

Before she could wonder what would happen, Captain Verkin rushed in, igniting a massive shield, it forced the wizards from Kaythar to step back. The open threat had an instantaneous effect. Saranon gaped in disbelief as Captain Ressinden tried to gain control. The wizards nearest her were intent on each other. She stayed in the protection of the sacra seal. The misquew stood up from its rest to sit right beside her. She felt sorry for the creature as she patted its shoulder. The misquew rubbed its head against her in gratitude. She froze realising how stupid she had been.

She glanced around to see if anyone had noticed and there was no sign. The arguing dissipated as the voices faded. She was beginning to think she would have to wait until nightfall. The first of the evening shadows stretched across the fading light. As she leaned down to pat the misquew goodbye. She picked up her sacra seal. She tucked the three bond-breakers, in the form of daggers, under her arm. She surveyed the landscape one last time before heading out into the open.

The north of Darkonia felt like a country she had never known. Yet she had to remind herself she had been here before. Acwellen's words stuck fresh in her mind as she mulled them over. The Keep Endorell had met her mother. Kaythar had given her some old directions albeit in its own language. She headed out towards the lay-line. The warm breeze swept along providing a cool relief. Saranon held onto her belongings as she covered the last patch of ground. Then the air changed as it took her a moment to realise it was not the lay-line.

The ground rushed away beneath her feet as she was thrown backwards. Before she could land she reached out her energy. It shielded the blow of her descent. Shouting rang out around her, the confusion set in and she panicked. She let the blast of her sorcery scorch across the ground. Breaking the distortion, as soon as she did it she knew it was a mistake. The energy would act like a beacon for any sorcerers close by, as she mumbled under her breath. The words of a wizard cut through as he screamed, 'Stop, I yield just stop!'

Saranon stared on as Captain Edevon crouched close to where she stood. She gaped in amazement unsure what to do next. Captain Ressinden smiled with a calm sense of satisfaction. 'Don't mind him, you are coming with us,' he said.

She spoke the truth, 'I can't.'

Captain Verkin spoke, 'The Arroada know she's here. Leave before I change my mind.'

The Captain spoke the last sentence as he stared straight at her. Saranon could feel the sorcery stir in the distance, she had to go.

She handed the bundle of bond-breakers over to Captain Daina Ressinden. As she spoke, 'I made them at Kaythar.'

The Captain whispered the words, 'Thank you.'

It was not the grandest way to give the Asdenard the bond-breakers. Yet it would have to do as she ran straight into the lay-line. She hoped that she had enough time to cross the border. The night air took away the heat, replacing it with a breeze. That did nothing to sweep away the agitation from being caught unaware. As it was she could not help thinking she had left the journey too late. She hoped, in the silence, that nothing else would come as the darkness settled in. Every sound made her nervous as she quickened her pace.

She hoped she could make it. The lay-line ended as the large head of the dragon rose into view. Katholomu saw her expression. He grunted with a loud snort then picked her up with a twist of her neck taking off for the sky. The great beast wasted no time with a strong flight. Straight for the shadow that was Ardaguar. The Keep shone in the moonlight with a grey silhouette. Marking the end of her journey as the dragon swooped down. Mitch climbed part way up Kat's shoulder, and held her in a firm embrace. He helped her to the ground.

Saranon went to walk and stumbled as the wizards around her burst out laughing. Mitch whispered, 'They know you took on Captain Edevon.'

She picked herself up, trying to block the laughter out. As she headed toward to her room and slammed the door too loud. A headache sank in as her head hit the pillow, yet she was too tired to sleep. She stayed awake in the dark when a noise disturbed her. She looked up to Pennie's silhouette in the light. As her friend crouched down, 'Captain Edevon is here.'

Saranon sat bolt upright. Pennie giggled, 'That's the least of your worries.'

'What do you mean?' She asked.

'You gave him a bond-breaker,' Pennie explained.

'I did not,' Saranon shouted and her friend glared at her. 'I did not,' she whispered, and Pennie giggled.

Saranon could not sleep before, she was not going to be able to after that. Pennie's laughter taunted her. As she closed her eyes and tried to count dragons to fall asleep.

The face of a dragon stuck in her mind and she stood up in annoyance. She tip-toed to the water jug, as a torrent of glass exploded behind her. The shards from the window shattered through the air. Saranon caught the motion with her sorcery and slowed it down almost to a stop. She stared at the bloody object as it rolled along the floor. The dragon's claw had been broken clean off with the toe still attached. Before she could think Pennie grabbed her arm and they ran.

An explosion thundered from the courtyard, vibrating through the Keep with a deep rumble. It left her with no doubt they were under attack as she stumbled and tried to catch up. A flash broke across the night sky. The thunderous sound roared again, with an unwavering tone. She stopped at the sight. Pennie ran down into the heart of the Keep and Saranon hesitated. The Glyrondagar swarmed in a mass near the breach of the outer shield. Lord Dackren's blade burned in the raging dark as shouts rang out. The wizard clan was losing ground, as the smell of charred dragon choked the air.

The Razen surged forward. She could almost sense the stolen sorcery wrapped in their souls. A blast rang out through the depths they were heading for the core. The wizards gathered holding on with all their strength resonating from their sheer numbers. Saranon ran toward them, and Lord Dackren hit the ground. The blast of dark sorcery ran through as it spiralled out of control. Saranon leaped into the blazing night sky, and met the blast head on. The impact evaporated as she glided through holding Corsavere high. The bond-breaker shimmered. She used her energy to take down the first Razen sorcerer mid-air. She landed on firm ground and the Keep reached out from the depths below.

The impact sent a shock-wave splitting along the ground as the sound caught up. The night went dark as all the light from the Razen sorcerers went out. Saranon could sense the wizard clan charge in the dark. They ran past with only the sound of their feet connecting with the ground. Screams rang out up ahead and she circled in. Lord Dackren had regained his senses and raised his blade toward the Razen sorcerer. 'Ardaguar belongs to us,' the Lord shouted as his blade swept through in a long arc.

The wizards lit the sky as Lord Dackren turned to face her. 'Saranon, the Keep belongs to us,' he repeated.

She stood silent for a moment, 'It is not the Keep you sense,' then she let go of the Angeon.

The Lord's bond-breaker fell to the ground in disbelief, 'For the love of Odana.'

He regained his composure. He held her close, 'I know why the Emperor of Normisia wants you.'

'What?' She asked, but he left without an answer.

Mitch ran up beside her and gave her a hug that shook the air out of her lungs. She tried to speak and he let go. Even though it felt like such a short time had passed, she was exhausted. She managed to make her way back inside the walls of the Keep. Pennie had cleaned their room yet neither wanted to be there. They made their way to the quarters of the Vandragamond. Jack welcomed them, this time she did not have any effort drifting off to sleep.

In her dreams Tasha waited grabbing hold of her arm, and beckoning her to follow. There was haste in Tasha's movements, as though she could not move fast enough. Saranon ran after her friend and stumbled, as the ground moved underneath. She glanced up, and the horizon that shook as she lost sight of Tasha. Then something stirred, something deep beneath the ground. The reverberation hit the surface of Tordoren like a flood. She placed her hands over her ears. The sound rang out, only this time she knew what it was, as Tordoren called from the deep.

No amount of blocking it out would make it fade. She closed her eyes wishing the dream to stop. Yet it went on long after mocking her without remorse. The darkness that followed filled her dreams with a hollow resonance. Every time she searched she found the same answer. The one she had been hoping to avoid. No matter how much she ran, the flood was there. It waited just below the surface beckoning with a slow march. It called, without whispering a word from the silence that crept with it. Washing away the hurt and leaving a solitary numbness. Lady Alvere had warned her, the Angeon has the ability to make or break the world.

CHAPTER FIFTEEN

The quest begins

The light streamed through with the brightness of the mid-morning sun. Saranon was still wrestling with dreams that had haunted the night before. Pennie popped her head around the door. Her friend smiled, 'Nice to see you're finally awake.'

It was not the response she was hoping for. The sorcerer's quarters were like a small labyrinth. As she made her way through, Pennie tried not to laugh. The sun was far too strong and only added to her headache.

A bustling hub of jovial voices greeted her ears as she entered the corridor. She rushed down to the great hall. She arrived in time to see Lord Dackren waving the new bond-breaker about with a steady sway. He kept his ale steady in the other hand. She gaped in amazement as he just missed slicing the table in half. Lord Dackren staggered and smiled as he caught sight of her. She glanced at the door, but he was closer. He placed his mug down then scooped her up in the same arm and planted a moist kiss fair on her cheek. Without thinking she pushed him away and he held her even closer.

He grinned before letting her down and she breathed a sigh of relief. She darted away and a voice spoke from over her shoulder. 'I see Lord Dackren thanked you,' Ben Waterworth remarked.

She was about to say something then changed her mind, 'Yes.'

'It was not as bad as it looked, we only lost two souls,' Ben spoke as they walked. 'I was wondering if you would come for a ride.'

His request caught her off guard and she nodded in response.

Captain Edevon was waiting near the dragon pens, 'It's time to return to Darkonia.'

'What do you mean?' Saranon asked.

'The Razen have not been defeated,' Ben explained.

'We must leave,' Captain Edevon answered.

Ben Waterworth nudged her toward Katholomu, 'See you in Darkonia.'

With that he climbed up on the grandest marmoz dragon Saranon had ever seen. Thrack was the same size as Katholomu. They followed the Captain and his dragon into the blue open sky. She had so many questions to ask as her mind raced, yet all her thoughts closed in on one, the Razen.

Captain Edevon took her back the way she came. They flew the rolling hillside straight to the Keep Kaythar. Katholomu glided with ease keeping less than a wing span between them. The dragons sped towards the Keep, and skimmed along the open courtyard. Then with the last momentum, ran into the stronghold of the Keep. As the great doors lowered behind them she stayed firm atop the dragon.

Ben Waterworth extended his hand, 'You can come down now.'

It was not how she wanted to arrive back in her homeland. After all the trouble Galven had gone to help her leave. She made her way down from Katholomu's shoulders. He was calm. For an absent-minded dragon he understood an awful lot, which made her wonder.

The hum from Kaythar was more distant as though focused on something. She turned her attention to the wizards who greeted Ben as they would an old friend. The walls of the Keep held strong, yet the marks from the damage were clear. The far tower to the north had been obliterated. Only the broken remains scattered along the grounds hinted to its location. Saranon strode closer to see the outer sheen on the rim. The light reflected off the stone seal covering the once hidden floor. It was testament to the enduring Keep that the seal held stronger than ever. Yet it made her shiver to think of what had been.

The marks scorching the ground lay fresh as the pungent smell filled the air. The shallow forest surrounding the Keep gave an overbearing silence. She gazed down at the seal. Captain Edevon approached. The sun beamed down on his bare arms showing the bruises of the night before. He stood in the silence transfixed by the seal, 'If I were to make a bet I would say you know where the Orb is.'

Saranon glanced toward him and her eyes gave away her secret. 'I thought as much,' he said, 'Do you know how many people we lost?'

The Captain left the question without pressing further.

'Not enough' she replied.

The Captain was aghast. 'The Razen do not have your Keep,' Saranon explained.

She glanced across the open courtyard to the distant fields. 'You stand the same distance away from Validain as does Ardaguar,' she spoke.

'That we do,' the Captain replied. 'We defeated them once, long ago, they care not to remember.'

She wondered why the Vandragamond would take an interest in the wizard clans. Then let the thought be.

'You haven't seen wizards take on sorcerers. Have you?' The Captain strode by her side, 'That is a sight to behold.'

Saranon was not sure she wanted to stay to find out. Yet as she passed through the corridors one thing was clear. The Asdenard were preparing for battle. She found Ben in the control room overlooking the fields beyond the Keep. He stooped over a map that made no sense. 'You certainly make an impression,' he said.

'What?' Saranon asked.

'An Orb that everyone wants and you have no need

for,' Ben mused.

'Is that why I am in Darkonia?' She asked.

'The Orb belongs to the Asdenard. The Keep was theirs before the Razen destroyed it,' Ben replied.

'The Orb stays where it is,' she spoke in a firm voice.

Ben laughed and the tone caught her off-guard, she had not expected his reaction. The shadows grew as the sun set across the still landscape. Kaythar was not where she wanted to be and the wizards made her feel on edge. Everywhere she went their eyes were on her, the one who had the Orb.

For once Saranon found herself in the unusual state. Where the Angeon was no longer the issue and she wondered how important the Orb could be. She had not spoken of its size and she had been the only one to set eyes upon it. The night air swept across the open grounds mixed with a warm breeze. Katholomu was resting, content in the dragon pens. She wanted to shout at him, all someone had to do was offer him a warm bed and food. This did not bother Kat in the slightest, as he taunted her with one eye creased open. He rolled over on his back and gave a rumbling purr of affection. Then he flopped over whisking his tail around to encircle her.

She was not impressed as she crossed her arms and he laughed in a mocking gesture. 'What's so funny?' She snapped, and he laughed even more.

Captain Edevon spoke and sound of his voice made her jump, 'Even your dragon can tame you.'

Saranon's face went bright red. The Captain stepped

closer as Kat relinquished his captive. 'Bring me the Orb and I will demonstrate. You are no match for the Asdenard,' the Captain spoke as though she were an unruly child.

'I am not here to fight you,' she said.

The Captain smiled then walked away. She glared at the dragon that pretended to be asleep. The smug smile showed underneath. Night covered the Keep as the lights warmed the outside walls with a soft glow. She was not ready for sleep. The wizards had not slowed their pace and the Captain had left her in an agitated state. She had seen the underneath of Kaythar Keep. Yet in the habitable area the wizards held it strong. They had been blocking her access to the inner workings of the Keep.

She went down to where the wizards trained, the open room sat just below the main entrance. The Captain greeted her by throwing a staff her way. She caught it with great reluctance, training with wizards did not appeal to her. Captain Edevon nodded and she saw no polite way out of accepting. The wizard was quick he left several bruises before she managed to make a mark. He stopped and gave a short bow in acknowledgement. The Captain ceased much to her relief. 'Most sorcerers use their energy to win,' he explained.

'I told you I am not here to fight,' she repeated.

A thunderous roar shuddered down the columns making the building shake. 'Well, not you...' She added.

The Keep came to life as the wizards rose to the challenge, only this time they were prepared. Saranon ran out onto the courtyard to watch the Razen attacking from above. The wizards streamed into the sky as they rode on their dragons. A gaping hole opened as the courtyard moved. It made way for the wizards riding the misquew. The large riding cats ran without fear. She found herself standing in the middle with the Keep on one side and the wizards on the other. The Razen sorcerers swooped in from the sky. Their dark sorcery pelted against the shield protecting the Keep.

The Razen wanted Kaythar with the Keep then they would have an unbeatable stronghold. The wizards fought, picking at the edges as the shield began to flicker. The Keep had not been able to recover. Saranon ran away from the protection of the wizard Keep, she had to protect it. The Razen dragon riders continued their attack against the Keep. Kaythar gave everything it could to hold the last remnants of the shield. Soon the wizards would be on their own. She ran as the energy surged from within. Floating high above the sky as the Angeon revealed itself to the world.

The Razen sorcerers changed their aim and blasted their sorcery toward her. It was all she needed as the energy was absorbed and cascaded downward. Kaythar latched onto the Angeon. The stallic energy rose from below the Keep surging upward from the central core. The Angeon held the energy as it flowed into the shield. It pummelled through the air with a solid tone. Her frustration showed as she remained caught. Holding up the shield for the Keep, rather than taking on the Razen. Yet as her anguish showed, the wizards rushed forward eager to hold their fort. Captain Edevon charged into the fray. She lost sight of him as the wizards surged ahead in an almighty wave.

The flanks held strong against the Razen sorcerers yet neither was giving ground. The Angeon began to feel the wane of the stallic energy crashing from below. She held on hoping that it would be enough. The wizards crashed forward as a Razen sorcerer fell under the stampede. The dragon it had been riding shrieked in pain. The wizards downed another Razen. The screams cut through the air piercing at her ears. Yet still she held on as the stallic energy creased through and the hold began to slip.

The wizards divided the last of the Razen sorcerers. She could only just sense their movement as her hold reached the end of its grasp. The stallic energy ebbed back through the ground with an impenetrable sound. It filled her mind as it fled. Saranon glanced up at the rolling sky and freefell, until her energy cushioned the final gap. She lay back expecting to feel the ground and gasped as she fell into Ben's waiting arms. He stayed by her side as the last cries rang out, marking the end of the attack. Darkness covered the night sky as a chill set in. Time flowed again as the events caught up with her weary muscles.

Mitch ran to her side from the battle's edge, his face showed the pressure of the fight. She had not seen him go and she had just been able to sense him as she held onto the shield. 'They were after you,' he said with a grim tone that made her shudder.

Saranon strode toward the battle where the Razen sorcerers had fallen. The wizards stepped aside to let her pass through as she went. Athera stood in the middle. The wizardess showed the signs of a weary fight and her eyes shone with a fiery temper.

The ground beneath revealed the ashen scars from the defeat of the Razen sorcerers. It filled the air with an acrid trail of smoke hovering with a heavy weight. She gazed over the maze criss-crossing the boundaries of the Keep. 'We need the Orb,' Athera said what the wizard clan was thinking.

'No,' she answered with a steady determination and left with all eyes on her.

Mitch ran after her, his expression said it all, he was not impressed. This time as she entered the Keep Kaythar welcomed her. It opened the great doors that led below the habitable area. Mitch followed behind her. The sparse foyer opened to many corridors and all were silent. Saranon fumed as she leaned down near the pool of sheal. The liquid stallic energy resembled water at a glance. She removed her shoes and waded in. As the last of the stallic energy left, she made her way up to the solid floor. She rested near the liquid's edge. 'The Orb is not for the Asdenard and is not for the Vandragamond. It was made for the Angeon,' she spoke.

Mitch listened, but the wizard did not change his stance. 'The Asdenard will guard it,' he said.

'An Orb so large even I struggle holding it,' she said.

Her voice echoed through the corridors. A small pebble came loose and drew her attention. She sensed Pennie along the corridor near Mitch. She changed her open astonishment, before he had a chance to investigate. 'It's only Pennie,' she explained.

Wondering how the sorceress had managed to make her way into the wizard's Keep. 'I'm stuck,' Pennie's voice called out.

'Of course you are,' she rolled her eyes as she stood up.

Mitch observed Pennie trying to pull something through the wall. It was clear she was not stuck, but the object she was trying to bring through would not budge. He melded into the wall, and handed the empty staff to Saranon.

'What is it?' She asked.

'It's for the Orb of Garduend,' Pennie snatched it back.

Saranon produced the small Orb from Hedavin and placed it in the staff. 'Very funny,' Pennie said with a flat tone.

'The real Orb won't fit,' she explained.

Mitch took the staff, 'You put it in a Darkonian staff.'

'Does it matter?' She asked.

'Yes,' he replied.

Saranon tried to remove the Orb and he waved it out of her reach. 'It belongs to me,' he said.

Pennie was about to argue, but Saranon shook her head. The Orb was Normisian and she was not about to take it from him. Pennie folded her arms, 'You have to get the Orb.'

Saranon grimaced. 'It was formed from a wizard Keep, and belongs to the Asdenard,' Pennie explained.

'Wizards,' she grumbled and Mitch stared at her.

The last thing she wanted to do was expose the Orb of Garduend, yet it appeared she did not have a choice. As they headed to the habitable area Mitch's staff gave way to confusion. Before Captain Edevon confirmed the Orb was not from Garduend. The presence of the second Orb only made the tension worse. Everywhere she went all eyes were upon her. The evening was late. The exhaustion of supporting the Keep set in as she made her way to a heavy sleep.

A jarring scratching sound filtered through her mind. As the morning light shone in, Katholomu's claws scraped across the floor. He had managed to open the window and his forearm stuck through. The dragon twisted his paw sideways clasping her in the blanket. He dragged her out the window. She scrambled up his arm and yanked at his ears, while shouting at him. Kat curled his tail around he batted her away from his ears. Pennie came running to the courtyard and burst out laughing. Saranon swung down off the dragon while shouting at him.

'I asked Kat to take you to Garduend,' Pennie explained.

'I don't need help,' she snapped.

'All right then, but you need to have the Orb here in three days. The Asdenard will not be forgiving,' Pennie replied.

Before she could respond Mitch tapped her on the shoulder. 'I will come with you,' he spoke as he steered her away.

She felt unprepared as she spied the staff strapped to his pack. 'Where are we going?' She asked.

He stared down at her the wizard towered over her when up close. He was not about to be dragged into conversation. The cloud of silence hung over them as they crept toward a lay-line at the edge of the Keep. She was reluctant to travel through it, but Mitch did not hesitate. The Orb lay hidden near the remnants of Garduend protected by the seal from her energy. She shuddered to think what the Razen would do with it.

A warm breeze met them at the end of the lay-line. They were still some distance from the ruined Keep. They stood in the sheltered hillside marking the entrance. Mitch raised the staff as he glanced around. A warning blast rang out and he used the staff to shield the blow. Saranon ran up behind him as the Vandragamond circle in. She could see no sign of Lord Shakar and waited. Andwyrdan made his path through the legion of sorcerers that gathered around them. The eldest son of Lord Shakar stood tall with the same menacing glare. 'Hand over the Orb of Garduend,' he said.

'It belongs to the Asdenard,' Mitch spoke.

Saranon gasped, then regained her composure, 'Hand it over.'

She eyed the staff and Mitch gave her a disapproving glare. For a moment she thought the wizard was going to take on Andwyrdan. He relented and threw the staff toward the sorcerer.

'You are coming with me,' Andwyrdan spoke. The

Vandragamond circled around them in a tight group.

Mitch remained silent as they entered the camp hidden in the hill. The fresh dry air whispered through with light from above. The band of sorcerers were not well organised. She wondered how long they had been there. Equipment lay scattered all over the floor. Faeryn was caught between telling her what to do and apologising for the mess. Saranon began making a mental map of the place as she went. Faeryn showed them to a small room with scant furniture. She sat on the bench and watched Faeryn leave.

Mitch stood inspecting the wall for any sign of an opening. She wondered if he was still cross about handing over the Orb from Hedavin. 'Look I… Get down,' she screamed the last two words.

The blast of sorcery thundered through the wall. It sent rock and dirt in every direction. Saranon shielded Mitch from the damage. As the rubble settled she glanced out to the sky, 'I found a way out.'

Mitch ran grabbing her arm as he went. She heard the Razen behind her, but there was no time. If they stayed to help she would lose the opportunity to uncover the Orb. She ran ahead and he followed. She struck down at the dirt revealing the seal and placed her hand on it. The solid seal twisted open and the Orb glistened in the sun as she held it in both hands. Mitch gaped in amazement and stood back, 'We have to return it.'

Saranon opened a sova bag and placed the Orb inside. Mitch was about to protest then he changed his mind.

There were more elegant ways to transport an Orb. Yet it had already attracted too much attention. The path to lay-line was clear and they ran toward it. Shouting rang out from behind, but she did not turn back. The lay-line offered a pleasant relief from the fighting. They reached the end too soon. Captain Edevon greeted them flanked by the wizards of Kaythar Keep. 'Hand over the Orb,' he said.

Saranon took out the tiny sova bag and let it expand before she reached in to reveal the large Orb. A hush fell upon the crowd and Pennie ran through, 'I can see why you didn't want to use it.'

The Orb for all its magnificence could be too dangerous to use. She had had enough of dealing with it and placed it in the Captains waiting arms.

The Captain treated it with care. She hoped that it would be as safe with the Asdenard as it was guarded by the seal. The wizards gathered around as they led her into the great hall of Kaythar Keep. An air of sadness clung in the room. Saranon remembered what little time she had spent with Garduend. For all the damage it had been graceful in defeat. Worthy of the final remnant she had created. The moment slipped past as music brought the hall to life. Mitch brought her a steaming bowl of soup and she sat near the open fire. The flames danced with the music. She wondered how long it would take for Andwyrdan to discover that he had the wrong Orb.

The evening filled the sky as she followed the trail of lights toward the dragon pens. A dull thudding spread from underneath the door. As Katholomu heaved it up out of the way and squeezed underneath. He took care to make sure the last wisp of his tail was clear. He let the door fall to the ground with a sudden thud. The dragon opened his wings to the warm breeze.

Katholomu waited holding his head high in the air, listening in a poised stance. Then it came, the eerie call in the distance a hollow sound that grasped her soul. The sound clung in the air long after it began fading with the sun. The sensation left her cold as a chill ran down her body. Kat nudged his head forward and she clambered up his shoulder. The dragon waited in anticipation and a voice called out. She turned around while holding on tight. 'Are you ready?' Ben asked from below as he patted the dragon's side.

She wanted to express her annoyance. Katholomu leaped into the air with jolt as she held on. The dragon paid her no attention gliding through the sky with ease. Saranon fumed at being led into something she did not understand. The warm night air did little to soothe her. The sorcery in the air became apparent. It trickled through like a dry wind brushing against her skin. The sensation prickled along her arms. Her mind registered where it came from. The Razen sorcerers were heading for Kaythar. She could sense the dark sorcery as they drew near.

The dark haze spread along the ground and then she saw it or she thought she did. It moved with the wind and Kat moved with it. He swooped side on and gave a small flinch of discomfort, yet he went on. The darkness grew in haphazard patches criss-crossing the ground. She let go, falling from the sky as her energy softened her descent. She saw the underbelly of the great dragon as he flew past. The great wings pounded the air into the ground. For a moment all time stood still. The dark sorcery leeched across the ground covering Tordoren.

The whooshing of wings rushed against the air behind her. She glanced up to see Mitch land beside her. 'What are you doing here?'

'Getting back my staff,' he explained.

She was not about to argue as the dark sorcery began to spark. It glowed in lines scattering the ground. It appeared as though a section of Tordoren had shattered underneath.

CHAPTER SIXTEEN

In the great hall

Saranon wondered how Mitch could remain calm. The faint lines deepened in the ground. The surface split from beneath, she dropped down losing sight of her companion. The sky lit up above as the corner markers flared forming a shield over the dark sorcery. She was being trapped in. She tried to rise upward and the dark sorcery sparked into life. It expanded like an open wound tearing deep into Tordoren.

A hollow screech stretched across the withered sky burning her ears, a piercing sound. So shrill she clenched her teeth as it reverberated through her body. The patterns of shadows came to life. They moved underneath the full light of the golden yellow moon. A haze of smoke wrapped around it in a smothering embrace. The smell of charred dirt filled the dry air. The shadows moved above in an unnatural path, vexing her from a distance. A chill ran down her spine mirroring her thoughts.

The chill ran deep as the smell of the deadening of Tordoren lay thick in the air. It filled her lungs with the remnants of the seared earth. An angry flame sparked in the distance rising above the ground. It shot out without warning as the air absorbed its glow. The rip of the blast hurled closer. Narrowing the distance as her energy surged into the gap. Its strength hit with a staggering speed. It hit with a heavy jolt pounding through the air. The explosion lit up the sky with a thunderous boom whipping along the hillside. The air beat hot with an acrid sound reverberating across the night sky.

Saranon reached down, as the energy of Angeon rose, seeking Tordoren below. She called out through the open wound willing for an answer in the silence. Dark sorcery flared from above. Mitch responded in kind keeping the Razen at bay. A well began beneath as the first sensation rose, she could almost feel it yet it was there. Tordoren rose from the depths searing the dark sorcery as it went. She allowed the energy to rise within. The Angeon broke through the dark prison. Sparks lit up as the links shattered, pounding along the open ground.

The Angeon rose into the night sky as the dark sorcery dimmed, creating a void where she had been. Mitch managed to hold on as the movement settled. She could make out the Vandragamond up ahead. They rushed toward the Razen under the cover of darkness. Andwyrdan led holding the staff high as he closed in. The Razen struck and the Vandragamond blocked. The staff began to glow and she held her breath. Andwyrdan's sorcery spiralled outward from the Orb with a crashing force. It sent the Razen back. The Angeon glimpsed Hollie and Deandra in the distance, then they were gone.

The lines of dark sorcery came alive as they lit up the sky. The lines connected in a pattern around the Vandragamond. If she did not act soon the Vandragamond would be trapped. The Angeon let her energy run into the ground. It ran along Tordoren searing through the dark sorcery as it went. The explosion shattered the ground as the two forms of sorcery collided. The Angeon held out her hands as the energy strengthened into a burning sphere. Then it sheared through the air. Screeching as it expanded toward the front row of the Razen. The night went dark for all except the Angeon whose energy glowed from within.

Andwyrdan turned and raised the staff toward the Angeon. Mitch yelled out and used his wizardry to drag her down. The blast of sorcery flared past just missing her in mid-air. She managed to soften her descent and the Angeon left. Mitch grabbed her hand and they fled. Shouts rang out behind them as the Vandragamond turned their attention to her. 'Next time let them die,' Mitch said.

Saranon stopped and ran toward the Vandragamond. 'What are you doing?' Mitch asked, shouting above the noise.

She was already in front of the group, they surrounded her as Andwyrdan stared her down. 'That does not belong to you,' she said.

Andwyrdan held up the staff and broke it in two, disconnecting the Orb, 'This is a fake.'

He held the Orb in his hand and it began to glow. Saranon shouted, 'Hand it over.'

Andwyrdan laughed, 'You are not Vandragamond, it won't be long and you will die.'

Saranon fumed as the Orb grew stronger Andwyrdan aimed it at her. She caught the blast and absorbed it, then drew the Orb toward her. Andwyrdan refused to let go as it became too hot to grasp. He screamed and let go, the Orb flew toward her. She used Andwyrdan's energy from the blast to form a new staff stronger than the old. She held the staff high and the Orb grew so bright, the sorcerers had to look away. She brought down the end of the staff, it hit the ground with a thunderous crack. As the last of the dark sorcery scourging the ground, lifted up to the sky, the energy crackled across the sky as it fled. It sent millions of tiny sparks raining downward.

'At least I know how to hold an Orb,' Saranon shouted.

The Vandragamond ran from the commotion. Mitch stood beside her. 'We have to leave,' she said.

She gave the staff to him and he smiled, 'You had to annoy Andwyrdan.'

He said no more as they rushed toward Kathomolu who was busy rolling in the dirt. The dragon shook himself and grinned as they clambered up. He headed north at hurtling speed and she had to stay low to hold on.

Ardaguar Keep came into view with the morning light, as the sun's first rays hit the Keep. She could see the troops gathered in the grounds. A great cheer rose as Mitch held up the staff and the Orb glowed. If she had wanted to make a discreet entrance any chance of that was gone. The dragon gave an almighty roar, before skidding across the courtyard. Whipping his tail around as he came to a stop in the opposite direction. Ben Waterworth came out to greet them, 'The Vandragamond have attacked Kaythar.'

Saranon's weary eyes revealed her exhaustion. 'This is not your fight,' Ben added.

She was in no frame to argue with him, but the frustration showed. Ardaguar welcomed her with caution, it was a wizard Keep and remained guarded. The faint whirring hum from the central core filled her mind. As her head slumped on the pillow she fell into much needed sleep. The black sea in her dream filtered into a clear stream as she followed it from the shore. She gazed into Tasha's eyes, the image of her friend stood over her. 'I have let you down,' she whispered.

Tasha leaned in close and answered, no. A space nearing eternity lapsed in the silence that followed. The image of her old friend stood over her in the dream. She tried to block out the last remnants of the attack, until the sound faded. In the warmth of the afternoon she managed to stumble out of bed. She landed with a thud on the floor yanking the bed sheets with her. Ben ran to see what all the noise was and burst out laughing before he kneeled down. He lifted Saranon to her feet. 'Not so nimble after the fight,' the wizard grinned as he helped her up.

The Keep was silent with few people as she glanced

around. Katholomu made his presence felt by flicking his long tail in the air just outside. He moved his head to stare eye to eye with her. She did not need the dragon and yet he followed her. He gave an amused smile and a deep rumble from his belly that sounded like a chuckle. As the sun's rays crept lower in the sky she faced the dragon. Katholomu pulled himself up in anticipation. Ben waited near the doorway as she clambered on Kat's shoulders. He spoke with a firm resolution, 'I cannot go with you.'

Saranon turned to face him, 'I know.'

The dragon itched to reach the sky as he steadied his legs and jolted forward. She clung on tight to the fold around his neck and nestled herself close to his skin. She glanced down at the broken earth along the surface of Tordoren. The scorched remnants stared back at her. It was a stark reminder of the strength of sorcery used in the attack. The night was settling in fast as Katholomu spread his great wings across the sky. Through it all Saranon could pinpoint where she had been holding her own ground. A chill trickled down her spine. If Andwyrdan could not control the small Orb, she did not want him to get the Orb of Garduend.

As the dragon moved on, she could see another large track where Andwyrdan had been. She peered over and the dragon tilted gliding to the ground. She made her way down, careful not to disturb the marks as she went. Saranon examined the pattern, tracing the markings back to their original location. First she went to where Hollie had stood, the struggle still showed on the ground. She tried not to step on the scuff marks as they lay all around. Then she went further ahead, following the tell-tale signs that lead to where Deandra had been. She turned, looking over the whole landscape, there was an odd sensation. Yet she could not describe it.

She glanced around, a spark glinted in the ground and she reached down. The small remains of a seal shone, only it was unlike any she had seen. The air was calm and still. It cleared her head from the rough night before as the last aches left her body. She found herself standing where Andwyrdan had been. A familiar sound thudded behind her. Katholomu rolled on his side in the charred dirt. His tail swished flicking clumps everywhere. Before she had time to yell at him he had rolled over the area where she had been.

Saranon ran forward. The dragon darted over the top, landing where Andwyrdan had been. 'Katholomu get here now,' she yelled, but it was too late.

He had already rolled and rubbed his back straight over the top of the site. She wanted to throttle him and used a small amount of energy to shift him sideways. The dragon pounced in one massive leap. He rolled in another patch of charred earth. She ran after him, the dragon flicked his tail and moved again. It had turned into a game, as she realised that chasing him would remove all sign of the attack.

She shouted and the dragon gave her a quizzical look. Then he ignored her while scratching an itch. She stood closer staring him in the face. Kat pretended to ignore her, without a care in the world at what he had just done. She could only hope that no one would notice the dragon's work. It would be impossible to miss the trail and Katholomu wore the evidence. As she stared at the ground Kat nudged her with his grimy chin, showering a spray of ash over her. She was too angry to be upset as she shook her head in disbelief.

Saranon brushed her shoulder then stared down at the remnants in her hand. Then she smiled as the attack made sense. She hugged the dragon and Kat looked astounded not expecting her response. The Razen sorcerers were making it difficult. They would not be able to fight them without the Orb of Garduend.

A voice called out from over the edge of the hillside. It bellowed so loud she jumped with fright as Gallagher yelled out again. She stood frozen behind the dragon hoping not to be noticed. It was a lame attempt. He yelled out again, 'I leave you alone and look what you do.'

Saranon's face went pale as she met Gallagher. He continued, 'Not you,' then he stared at Katholomu, 'You.'

The dragon sat upright looking rather skittish from the accusation. The great beast glanced sideways in a bid to avoid his gaze.

Gallagher leaned over to pat the great beast and Kat snorted in a cool response. 'Wreaking havoc on the land, I see,' Gallagher said.

He spoke in a softer tone near the dragon's ear. He turned to Saranon adding a firm comment, 'You need a tighter grip.'

He climbed on Katholomu's shoulders, 'I'm taking the dragon. How are you getting to Validain?'

'Are you forgetting something?' She asked.

Gallagher leaned down, 'You are as good as the Lord at keeping secrets. You are not the only one.'

She could feel her face grow warm. 'We thought the Armythral were hiding something,' he offered to help her up.

She clambered aboard. Gallagher spoke, 'You've got a lot to learn if you want to fly with me.'

With that he moved his leg and the great dragon flew into the sky. All she could do was cling on and she did not trust her odd companion. They circled around the grandest sorcerer Keep she had ever laid eyes on. The pearl Keep glowed through the night. In stark contrast to the rough sorcerers who wore light armour. The same colour of darkness. The image took her breath away and she gasped in astonishment. They descended into the main courtyard as the lights flared an audience greeted them.

The balconies were full as all eyes followed the dragon. The Keep was the largest she had seen. It appeared out of place in the hands of the Vandragamond. They were renowned for holding out against the Dreshan Occupation. As she glanced around she could sense why the Dreshans feared them. Her legs trembled as she held her gaze. The great sorcerer warriors parted as Lord Shakar marched through the crowd. She saw the horns on his helmet and rough dark fur around the shoulders of his cape. She stared into his eyes. The high Lord had a menacing glare even at peace and this was the closest it would be.

Saranon followed as the Lord swept through. The crowds parted in a wave of strength and respect. This was not a place for the weak as the glances held steady. Gallagher closed the great doors behind them with a bang. The sound reverberated through the enormous chamber. The light from the Keep bounced off the pale walls. The thick columns reached to the high ceiling looming in a tall arch overhead. Lord Shakar turned to face her. As he reached the centre of the grand chamber, 'This is where the last Angeon stood. She forced my predecessor to his knees. If you ever do the same I will make you wish you had died at Antavagon.'

Gallagher began clapping behind her, the sound echoed through the chamber. 'Welcome to the clan,' he said. 'Now what will we do about the other Angeon.'

'Kill him,' Lord Shakar said.

'Merrick is in Serenphel,' Saranon spoke.

'He will come and I will deal with him,' Lord Shakar answered without a hint of doubt. 'Daughter of mine, the call of Angeon will grow. You will be given a choice, one chance and if you miss it, all will be lost. Then, I will kill you.'

Saranon gasped and Gallagher spoke as he circled around her. 'The high Lord Vandragamond will kill the Angeon who chooses the wrong path.'

'How will I know?' She asked.

Lord Shakar bellowed with a hollow laugh that rang out, echoing in her ears. 'If it was that easy I would tell you.

I could rule Zyanthia with an Angeon,' he said.

The conversation left her feeling cold. Gallagher led her away from the grand chamber. Validain was vast by any standard for a Keep. The building stretched on over the rocky hill taller than any other. The ambient lights glowed filling the night sky. Gallagher grinned before opening the door to the largest bedroom she had ever seen. The floor half-filled the space creating a mezzanine. She glanced over the edge and there in the dark below was her dragon. Katholomu had his belly showing as he relaxed in the dragon pen. 'You can keep an eye on your dragon,' Gallagher said before leaving.

The room filled a high tower on the same level as the grand chamber. It stood several floors above the fields below. The wind swept around the building reminding her of how tall the Keep was. The hour was late and she could not relax. She did not expect the Lord to be the one who would know about the Angeon. Yet the Vandragamond never fell to the Dreshans. They had a complete history and the Lord did not fear her. Saranon's mind held onto the thoughts, long after she went to sleep.

A crash in the dragon pen below woke her in the morning light. Katholomu gave a low growl as he bashed into the gate again. 'Hold on,' she sang out and slid down the small staircase. 'Wait for me.'

Kat glared at her as though it were her fault he had been shut in. The gate sprang open with a rush to the surprise of onlookers. The courtyard and walkways were filled with people. Gallagher shouted from the balcony,

'You are late.'

Before she could answer Katholomu hurled himself into the air and flew off. She asked, 'What's going on?'

'This,' he opened his arms, 'is Validain, welcome to the chaos. Your wizard has arrived.'

'Pardon?' She asked.

'The one you attached yourself to,' Gallagher smirked.

Saranon went red with embarrassment.

The great hall filled with voices, shattering the peace, as she opened the door. Lord Shakar eyed her from the head table located in the centre of the hall, 'There you are. You can tell my administrator that he has nothing to fear.'

Edred Heath the administrator explained, 'Andwyrdan is in possession of the Orb of Garduend.'

Saranon went pale, 'Ah…'

'He will be fine,' Lord Shakar reassured the administrator.

'Ah…,' she continued.

'He will be fine,' Lord Shakar stated to her.

'It's twice the size of an ordinary Orb,' she spoke.

The Lord threw his metal chalice at the administrator's head. Edred held his book up blocking it without flinching, as though he had done it before. The chalice bounced off and Gallagher caught it. 'This is your fault,' Lord Shakar pointed at Edred.

The administrator responded, 'Yes sire.'

'Why can't I have an Orb like that?' Lord Shakar asked. 'Oh well, he will find out soon enough. Now, your wife…'

'My ex-wife sire,' Edred the administrator responded.

'Your wife…' Lord Shakar repeated. 'Is a…'

'A difficult person to deal with,' Gallagher spoke.

'…A wretch,' Lord Shakar said. 'Can I burn her at the stake?'

The administrator went pale. Gallagher interrupted, 'That was taken off the list a while ago.'

'Who removed it?' The Lord asked.

'You did sire,' Gallagher responded, 'As part of reconciliation with the wiccan.'

'Oh, well you can think of something,' the Lord spoke. 'Garridan, take Saranon to her wizard.' Lord Shakar then turned to her. 'Next time you visit I would prefer that your wizard was not attached,' he said.

Gallagher shook his head when he saw that she was about to respond. Saranon took the hint and followed Garridan out of the great hall. He was as tall as the high Lord, yet his youth showed behind his small beard. He wore the uniform of his station with a plain dark fur covering his broad shoulders. The bond-breaker on his belt shone in the light and he grinned when he caught her staring at it. 'You are not the only one who can make a bond-breaker. He held it out with pride and Saranon took it. The dark blade of heart stone shone the colour of burnt blood and she gave it back. 'Were you weak when you bonded the wizard?' Garridan asked.

He waited for a reply then laughed. 'You won't last long with a wizard.'

'I will be fine,' she retorted.

Garridan opened the door then left. Saranon glanced through to a large room with tall glass windows. They opened up to the balcony overlooking the inner courtyard. The balcony stretched onward. It joined up to the many walkways that wrapped around the towers. Mitch sat as he spoke to Commander Iona. She appeared formidable even for a sorceress. Her uniform wore the heavy toll of a life in the harsh terrain. Iona spoke first, 'I hear my daughter Faeryn and Andwyrdan have the Orb.'

The Commander did not look old enough to be Faeryn's mother. Yet she did not doubt the resemblance. Iona was a dark haired beauty with a trace of grit on her cheek from the night's travel to the Keep. Mitch gave an expression as though he had been picked up from Kaythar. The Commander answered the unspoken question, 'We found your wizard not far from Validain.'

'I was looking for you,' Mitch clarified.

'The wizard can stay with you, try not to lose him,' the Commander left them in peace.

Mitch relaxed, 'I was outside Kaythar. Andwyrdan took the Orb before it had been sealed within the Keep.' He continued. 'What are you doing here?'

'I'm not sure,' Saranon said as shouts reached them.

The door burst open. Gallagher entered, 'You have been invited to the central core.'

She asked, 'Pardon?'

'It is an instruction from Lord Shakar. All Vandragamond meet Validain as a curtesy,' He explained.

'The custom dates back more than a thousand years,'

Mitch said.

'Do I have too?' She asked.

'Yes,' replied Mitch and Gallagher at the same time.

'You are not supposed to agree,' she remarked.

The last thing Saranon wanted to do was visit the central core yet it intrigued her. A Keep of such grandeur would have a spectacular core by any standard.

While they spoke the walkways around the tall windows filled with spectators. A slow chant rose through the crowd. 'Really,' she whispered, and glanced at Mitch.

Lord Shakar's voice boomed from outside the open door, 'Saranon.'

She asked, 'Now?'

'You will meet the central core…now,' the Lord's voice boomed above the noise.

She did not see what the urgency was, 'You want me to meet the core now?'

'Yes,' the Lord replied.

Saranon raised her arms catapulting her energy downward into the depths of the Keep. Validain answered with a rising surge of stallic energy. It melted through the floor creating a vortex. The vapours spun around in a tight whirlwind gaining speed. 'Not now,' Lord Shakar shouted.

Mitch stepped back as the vortex grew, the central core was no place for a wizard.

'Stop, wait,' the Lord's voice carried above the whirlwind.

The energy from the central core crashed into her. It flooded up through the whirlwind that held her. The vortex began to close and the core took her deep beneath the ground. Validain whirred with an electrifying storm in the deep as she peering above her. Gravity had no place in the central core, the magnitude of the core made its own. Validain whirred in the darkness, it sped raising the energy from the deep. Faster and faster it sped as the energy coiled up from the giant rod and into the core. She reached out to the core and it accepted.

In that moment Saranon was Vandragamond, she was Validain and she was the Angeon. The energy ran through her, concentrating as the central core whirred in the deep. The storm in the heart of the central core began to move with a rapid pace. It wrapped around her with a droning sound. The deep rumbling of the core began to fade, in the centre of the storm began a calm that filled her soul. She focused outward toward the sky. With a deafening roar the central core answered. The outer shell of the core opened creating a funnel to the sorcerer's stone above. The vacuum pressed against her and Saranon brought the might of the Keep with her.

The sorcerer's stone stood above the grand chamber. It formed a platform above the heart of the Keep. Saranon, the Angeon, rose into the sky and Validain with her. The brilliant light from the energy shone, radiating throughout the Keep. She locked onto her target, the old Keep that once was Garduend. A thunderous pounding erupted from the deep and she waited in anticipation. The central core drove the raw energy with such force it flew up into the air. All sound was lost as she focused the energy on the old

Keep.

The stallic energy catapulted across the sky in a giant arc. Sparks sprayed through the air. Then it landed deep in the ground of Tordoren. The energy formed the seed of hope that would give rise to a new Keep. Validain rumbled from beneath and Tordoren awakened. They both sensed the new central core forming a Keep from deep below. She floated down until her feet touched the sorcerer's stone. Garridan stood beside her, 'Most sorcerers flare the shield. They don't create a new Keep.'

Mitch ran onto the sorcerer's stone toward her, 'The Lord wants to see you.'

'I bet he does,' Garridan replied.

Saranon made her way down the elegant tower that wrapped around the grand chamber. It was not what she had expected, yet Garduend did not deserve to die. The Asdenard wizards needed their Keep. Lord Shakar greeted her. They strode towards the great hall as the cheering around her began. The Lord reached the great hall, 'This is why we are Vandragamond. We are the greatest sorcerers to walk Tordoren and nothing will break us.'

A great cheer rose up and the Lord welcomed her to the main table at the centre of the room.

He leaned over, 'If you ever make a wizard Keep again do not use Validain.'

'Now where were we,' the Lord spoke aloud.

'Sire,' Gallagher interrupted.

'Yes,' replied the Lord.

'Andwyrdan has attacked Ardaguar Keep,' Gallagher

said.

'What? Well he had better succeed,' the Lord spoke. 'Send the troops, if he flags, fall to plan B.'

Saranon tried to interject. The Lord remarked, 'This is Andwyrdan's fight do not intervene.'

'But…' She began.

'We do not interrupt a Vandragamond in battle. The last time involved removing the Dreshan Occupation from Zyanthia. That will not happen again,' Lord Shakar glared at her.

The Lord repeated, 'That will not happen again.'

'I am the Angeon,' she stated.

Lord Shakar raised his hand. Saranon blocked his sorcery before it hit and he was caught off-guard. The Lord stumbled and fell, slamming into the floor on his knees. 'Leave,' he shouted. 'Leave Validain and do not come back.'

Saranon ran from the great hall. Mitch grabbed her arm and they fled toward the courtyard. 'Jump,' he said.

'What?' She asked.

Katholomu swooped from the sky. They both jumped landing on the dragon as he sped into the sky.

CHAPTER SEVENTEEN

A wizard out of place

The dark mood clung in the air long after the midday sun shone bright over the Darkonian sky. Katholomu flew north to the border then turned left toward the fledgling Keep. 'What are doing?' Saranon asked the dragon.

'We cannot fly to Ardaguar in the light,' Mitch explained.

It was not what she wanted to hear, Andwyrdan was at Ardaguar and so was the Orb. She wanted to scream, as the dragon landed in the shelter of the building. Mitch helped her down and she glanced around, 'Wow.'

The new Keep had the immediate structure emanating from the ground. The building reached above the lower chambers in places stretched far apart. It showed the true size of the central core below. She gasped in astonishment, 'Did I make that?'

'Yes,' Mitch opened the main door to the great hall.

The place felt empty. With little more than the great hall spreading back into the hillside. The columns continued up to the high ceiling above. Facing the great doors at the opposite end a platform loomed. The size and scale dwarfed them as they glanced around.

The hum of the central core warmed the Keep with a radiant glow as the sun sank in the afternoon sky. Mitch went to the platform and opened a panel, glancing at the inner workings of the Keep. 'It's a wizard Keep,' he shouted with delight.

He took her by the hand and swung her round in the excitement. 'Yes,' she stared at him wondering what the fuss was about.

'You made a wizard Keep,' Mitch repeated.

'I still don't get it,' she said.

'That's impressive,' Mitch explained.

Saranon sat on the platform gazing out the high windows. The frustration showed plain on her face. She wanted to be at Ardaguar, yet as she waited, the exhaustion set in. Validain and making the Keep had been draining. 'Have you thought of a name?' Mitch asked.

She gave him a puzzled look, 'Pardon?'

'You need to name the Keep,' he replied.

'Oh no,' she shook her head, 'You can name it.'

'Angore,' Mitch responded.

'Really,' she stood on the platform and raised her arms, 'I name you Angore.'

The Keep hummed in response. 'I think he likes it,'

she said to Mitch.

They rested through the afternoon in the darkness of the great hall. They waited for the cover of the night sky. Saranon took out her small sova bag. It changed size and she opened it laying her bedding on the platform. The exhaustion of the day sank in and she slept.

As her dreams settled in, a figure stood over her and she recognised her old friend. Tasha was insistent trying to say something, yet no sound came out. In her dream she reached out, the more she reached the further away Tasha appeared. Her friend's eyes were filled with a solid determination. Saranon moved and every part of her body felt heavy, weighing her down. She fell over and could not get up.

The dream had crippled her. It frustrated her as every time she tried to lift herself she failed. It should have been easy, yet something was weighing her down. She shouted out to let Tasha know. The figure of her old friend stood there without emotion, her eyes looking past. Saranon gazed over her shoulder and there was nothing. She turned back and a different face appeared it was Hollie. She tried to wake up but she could not move, she tried to shout out and the sound was muffled. She screamed over and over again, yet the dream did not stop.

She screamed louder and louder. Until the sound filled her head to the point where she thought she would burst. Then it broke out into the silence, into the void, into the nothing. It reached beyond the dream that held her tight in its grip. Angore reassured her in the dark as she woke. Mitch was ready and Katholomu had his head through the door. The dragon snorted warm air into the room as he watched with impatience. 'We have to go,' Saranon scrambled to her feet.

'Andwyrdan has not breached the shield, we have time,' Mitch said.

'How do you know?' She asked.

Pennie answered, 'Because I told him. You made a Keep and didn't tell me.'

She was about to apologise, 'It's okay, the Glyrondagar need you.'

Galven appeared beside her in the great hall glancing around in amazement, 'She's beautiful.'

'Angore is a he and a wizard's Keep,' she explained.

'Next time I want a sorcerer's Keep,' Pennie stated with a hint of amusement. 'The Asdenard will be pleased. You make a solid Keep.'

'I saw Tasha, I have to leave,' she said.

Pennie eyed her with suspicion, 'You still see her?'

'Yes,' she remarked.

Pennie was not impressed, 'We will talk later.'

Saranon climbed up on Kat's shoulders with Mitch behind her. The dragon was itching to fly, and took off in the cover of the night sky. She clung on hoping they were not too late. They had to save Ardaguar from Andwyrdan and the Orb of Garduend. The fiery haze wafted through the air as they flew close, yet it was not the sight she expected. The Glyrondagar held out strong attacking in the night sky. The great weapons built into Ardaguar made the

Vandragamond look easy prey. The sorcerers hung back. 'He doesn't know how to use the Orb,' she remarked.

'It's just as well,' Mitch spoke.

Katholomu veered behind the Keep avoiding the main thrust of battle. Mitch sent up a wizard light for the Glyrondagar to know who they were. At first there was no response then a welcome flare sparked through the dark. Kat glided in with no more than hand's width for grace between the walls of the building. She closed her eyes as he passed through. 'Show off,' she exclaimed and the dragon roared with amusement. Zara came into the dragon pens to greet them, 'You took your time.'

'What do you mean?' She asked.

'We were expecting you a few days ago,' she explained while leading her to the great hall.

The air simmered with the dark mood that had fallen over the Glyrondagar. Lord Dackren gave a grim smile as she strode toward his table, 'We have a problem.'

'Yes,' she responded thinking he meant Andwyrdan.

'Andwyrdan does not have the Orb,' the Lord said.

'What?' She exclaimed.

'…and we have to pound him into the ground before we can find who has it. Do you care to join me?' Lord Dackren asked.

All eyes in the great hall fell on her and waited. 'I will fight with you,' she answered. Applause erupted through the crowd and Mitch spoke, 'Are you sure?'

'We have to end this and get the Orb,' she replied.

He nodded in acknowledgement. The air was thick

with smoke from the Keep. It was mixed with wizardry from the battlements. She made her way up to the sorcerer's stone. Where Lord Dackren's finest soldiers stood. Ben Waterworth glanced her way, 'I thought you were going to stand me up.'

'Never,' she humoured him.

'How do you want to do this?' Ben asked.

Saranon went toward the centre where Ben stood. The sweat ran down his face, yet he managed a smile. A wave of sorcery aimed toward them in the night sky. Screeching as the sparks ripped through the air. She sensed the central core below, Ardaguar wanted vengeance. 'Wait,' she answered.

The stallic energy from the core surged below. She summoned it forward calling to the Keep. The sparks grew ever closer and she repeated her words, 'Wait.'

The sparks flung down toward them. 'Now,' she shouted.

Ben and the wizards gathered around the stone. She attacked with the full might of the Keep. The stallic energy raged into the air like a cloud enveloping the night sky. The sparks evaporated and the shield shone a brilliant fiery golden haze. It flared out toward the sorcerer clan. The Vandragamond hesitated at the sight, then a small group at the rear ran. The rest followed, breaking off in sections as they went. Shouting rang out below as the dragon riders disappeared into the darkness.

'We must do that again some time, when the Keep is not under attack,' Ben peered over the low wall. Watching as the Vandragamond clan scattered in disarray. His great marmoz dragon Thrack flew down from the sky and Saranon climbed on. 'Hey, he doesn't fly without me,' Ben spoke as he climbed on. 'I could get used to this.'

She said nothing as she focused on the Vandragamond below. 'Andwyrdan is in the sky,' Ben responded as though reading her thoughts. Thrack plunged in the darkness he flew hard then turned looping around. 'What is he doing?' She asked.

'Hang on,' Ben clung on low to the dragon as Thrack sped faster making tight turns, as he went. Her heart thudded, they were gaining ground as she spotted Andwyrdan's dragon up ahead. Thrack dived in close, as the dragon swooped and sped toward the border.

Thrack beat his wings hard and dived again on his prey. This time he knocked into the other dragon. His claws ripped through flesh and the dragon screamed on its descent. Saranon watched on in horror. The dragon plunged to the ground with a screech that pierced through her. They flew down hitting the earth hard. She rolled off summersaulting along the grass. Above her stood Edred the administrator. He turned his attention to Andwyrdan, 'Where is the Orb?'

'You cannot have it,' he fumed.

Commander Iona hit him to the ground, 'The administrator asked you a question.'

'You won't get it,' Andwyrdan spat the words out.

Edred hurled his sorcery at Andwyrdan who let out a horrible scream. 'Stop, he doesn't have it,' Saranon shouted.

From the darkness Faeryn spoke, 'We lost the Orb to the north of Validain.'

Commander Iona stared at the administrator. 'I bet your former wife knows where it is,' she said.

Edred glared down at Andwyrdan, 'You had to take the Orb from Kaythar.'

'You attacked Ardaguar with no Orb,' Commander Iona yelled. 'Wait until Lord Shakar hears of this.'

Ben watched in a silence stance as the band of wizards grew around him. After the sorcerers had left he spoke, 'That is how the Vandragamond apologise. Andwyrdan will be punished for his actions.'

'Now can we find the Orb?' She asked.

Captain Edevon strode through the crowd, 'You have permission to search for the Orb.'

Ben glanced at her, 'That was meant for me.'

She grew impatient as the Captain waited for a response, 'Are we going to Kaythar?'

'Ah, that would be splendid,' the Captain replied. Ben shrugged then climbed on Thrack.

'Oh no, this time I'm directing the dragon,' she said.

She did not want to fall off the dragon again. They followed Captain Edevon through a silent sky and made their way toward Kaythar. The Keep appeared as she had last seen it, standing solid in the night.

Thrack touched the ground with a smooth glide much to her relief. A great thud landed next to them. Katholomu pounded against the ground with Mitch riding high. The dragon riders took it as their que to follow them into the dragon pens. The day's events had caught up with them. Saranon almost tripped as she fell backward into Ben. 'I think you need to rest,' he said in a serious tone.

She was not about to argue as time slipped away, the Orb was still out there somewhere. Again it would have to wait.

Captain Daina Ressinden showed her to a small cosy room. The wizardess wanted to talk then refrained from doing so. Saranon could not relax so she invited the Captain to sit by the fireplace. 'Did you bring Lord Shakar to his knees?' The Captain asked.

'It was an accident,' she replied.

'The Vandragamond are comparing you to the Angeon of old. They say you made a wizard Keep.' Captain Daina said.

'I did. Angore stands where Garduend fell. Mitch named him,' she replied.

The Captain smiled, then she added, 'Sleep well.'

Tasha came haunting her dreams, the Orb held in her hands near the black ocean. The grass moved in the wind and Saranon ran toward her. The Orb of Garduend gave a blinding flash and she could not see. The ground changed and she found herself in a cave with no way out. She yelled and no one heard. The dream racked at her thoughts as she slept through the night. Mitch appeared in the morning light and startled her. Even with the bond the wizard could still sneak up. 'Captain Edevon has a lead on the Orb,' he said.

'Of course he does,' she did not think much of the

Captain.

She raced down to the dragon pens, and Mitch ran after her, 'Not that sort of lead.'

'What do you mean?' She asked and he pointed outside.

In the courtyard stood Jack Heath, she had not seen him since her first trip to Ardaguar. The Vandragamond sorcerer gazed at her. His eyes confirmed her thoughts, he knew who had the Orb of Garduend. Gallagher patted her on the back and she almost jumped. 'Now you just need to humiliate Garridan,' he said.

Her face went red and he laughed.

After Andwyrdan she had not wanted to be among the sorcerer clan. Yet there in the courtyard a garrison from the clan made themselves ready. To her amazement the Asdenard prepared with them. It was the first time she had seen the wizard and sorcerer clan talk with ease, united by a common foe. Gallagher asked, 'What of your dragon?'

Saranon turned her head. To her embarrassment Katholomu was scratching his back. He pelted the outer wall of the dragon pens. He paid her no attention as she called his name. Gallagher whistled and Kat scurried over rubbing his head against the sorcerer.

Kat glanced at the two clans getting ready to leave. He stared at her with a silent expectation. She was dreading the word before he spoke, 'Coward.'

Jack gaped in astonishment, 'I didn't know he could talk.'

'Yes,' she answered.

'Your dragon has a point,' Gallagher spoke, 'You have done nothing to prepare.'

She dreaded the thought of having to meet the Razen again, yet they had the Orb. 'I am ready,' she replied.

The dragon scoffed at her. 'I am,' she repeated.

Captain Daina Ressinden came up to meet them, 'We are set to go.'

Kat glared at her in a grump, as her dragon riders began to take to the sky. 'No, you can wait,' she said.

Katholomu beckoned, yet he nudged Jack instead. 'I know who you're riding with,' Ben said to the dragon then he climbed up on Thrack.

Before she could decide Kat flew into the air with a giant leap. She climbed up next to Ben who spoke, 'You need to earn your dragon's respect. He'll keep flying off otherwise.'

'Thanks,' she gave a flat response.

They followed Katholomu through the air at a steady pace. The clouds grew thick in the hazy sky. She reached out her hand then the dragon swooped down. The thin sprawl of trees changed into a rocky hillside rising above. They landed as Jack waited, 'We are close.'

Saranon could sense the dampening of sorcery emanating from the ground. It gave an eerie sensation, one that filled her with dread. Jack's stony face showed his determination. Yet there was no sign of the other dragon riders.

She held her bond-breaker Corsavere in the form of a sword. He glanced at it and their eyes locked. Ben drew his bond-breaker, an elegant blood red the colour of the Glyrondagar. Ben quickened his pace, taking the lead, as Jack stepped aside. She followed the wizard and he ran. The dark sorcery made it difficult to sense anything below the surface. A glowing ball grew in the distance the light filled their vision making it hard to see. Ben yelled out in pain, the dark sorcery caught her off-guard. The strength of the blast pelted down, knocking the air out of her lungs and she began to choke.

She charged forward attacking with her energy. It was just enough to block the blow. She reached Ben sheltering him as he regained his composure. He ran forward and she shouted, but he did not stop. More than one blast headed toward them and Saranon had to choose. She took out the blast to the right and held up a shield as the second came shattering down. Ben dived back under the shield as the blast hit. Sparks pounded with a fiery eruption above them. He pointed to the left and she nodded. They ran and she blasted her energy forward. Ben ran past the flames that lapped along the ground. His blade hit the shield of a figure in the haze up ahead, she could almost make them out.

A blast hit her from behind, it pummelled her to the ground. Pain seared as the air sparked and she dived for cover. She lost sight of the wizard Ben. In the distance the figure stepped forward, Hollie glared at her. The dragon riders broke through the sky from the clan Vandragamond. In the confusion Ben Waterworth rushed toward Hollie. He knocked the Orb of Garduend out of the Razen's hands. It rolled as it hit the ground. A scream pierced the air as Ben held Hollie tight. The hold was broken when he was flung backward. The dark sorcery seared and Saranon blocked the blast as she stood in front of Ben.

Deandra picked up the Orb as the Vandragamond sorcerers closed in. The shadows of the swooping dragons dimmed the sun's light. Then the blasts hit the ground toward the Orb. Deandra ran from the fight leaving Hollie alone. As the dragons landed Saranon turned to help Ben. A surge of pain ran across her back and she fell to the ground, as the air caught in her lungs. She looked around, but only darkness greeted her. She realised her vision had blurred. Yet she could still sense Hollie as she gathered her energy to block the Razen. Hollie took aim again and the fractured remnants broke through knocking her back.

She heard the Vandragamond rallying around her, as she stood regaining her strength. Before she could take aim Hollie hurled another blast straight toward her. Saranon managed to absorb the impact and regain her stance. She sent a massive flare of energy hurling across the open ground. The blast hit its mark, yet Hollie did not falter to her amazement. The Razen kept on going as the energy drew back toward Hollie. She gasped as she felt the vacuum pull around her in the void. She was missing something, but it was too late.

She braced herself as the blast flared. It raged through the air with a mighty strength. Every breath she took stung, as she just managed to hold on through the attack. A movement caught her eye, and she squinted in the haze.

A figure stood where it should not have and she gasped trying to reach out. Yet the blast was too great and she held on trying to battle her way forward. Another blast rang out thick and strong, yet it was not her as she sensed Jack up ahead. She tried to reach him through the thick haze.

Hollie struck again and she managed to hold it back. As the sparks flew with a deep roar and the blast hit her energy. Jack ran toward Hollie as Saranon struggled to hold on. Then a deep loud thunderbolt cracked along the ground. It roared with a pounding against her ears, blocking out every other sound. She hurled her energy forward and had lost sight of Jack. She ran forward as another blast struck her. She fell as the remainder of the blast cascaded over head with a fiery rage.

She reached out her hand and caught his. The sparks dimmed in the grey sky and she stood over him. He looked up with the last gasps fighting for every breath and it was too late. Tears welled in her eyes flooding down her cheeks and she wanted to scream. A sound rang out, but it was not her not this time. As the last breath of air left his lips, Jack Heath's head sank to the ground. She clung on not knowing what to do. As the haze cleared Hollie's hysterical screams filled the air and Gallagher moved in. He swung his bond-breaker deep. Saranon hung her head as Hollie's final scream cut through the air. Gallagher stood silent as the Vandragamond sorcerer's ran through the hillside. They ran past with one goal, to find the Orb. Gallagher gazed down and did not speak.

She stared down in disbelief, her arms were numb, yet

they would not relax. She stared down into Jack's dull eyes and the tears blurred her vision. She wanted to scream, but no sound would come out. Her voice had gone hoarse from the pain. Yet she felt numb inside as she knelt down and she let him go. She trembled as she stood trying to make her legs work as the exhaustion set in. The tears continued to creep down her cheeks. A constant reminder of what had been lost.

Saranon stared down at the lifeless body. She touched Jack's face closing his eyes from the unseen world. She was in too much shock to be angry. Before she could say anything Gallagher patted her shoulder. With a reassuring tone asked her to leave. She felt numb, every muscle in her body ached as she walked away. She turned back one last time it was all over. She felt completely drained as exhaustion set in. The darkness of night covered them and all she could do was cry.

Katholomu waited, his face was hard, the dragon showed no sympathy as she wept. He backed away before letting her climb on. 'Okay Kat you have your wish, find Deandra.'

The dragon's ears tilted back realising what he was being asked. It was the only hesitation he gave as he pelted into the dark sky blending into the cover of night. The image of Jack Heath stayed with her as she clung on to Katholomu.

CHAPTER EIGHTEEN

Vengeance with a cost

The night covered them as Kat flew through the sky. Saranon felt like the only one who was trapped in a cloud of unease that clung in her mind. She was caught in the middle of something she did not understand. The loss of her Orb only made it worse. The dragon swooped low along the hill side, he almost stopped. Mitch ran out of the darkness joining her on Kat's shoulders. 'Validain,' he ordered the dragon.

Saranon was not impressed as Katholomu did as he was told. They took off into the sky. 'I asked Kat to find Deandra,' she said.

'She's heading to Validain,' he replied.

She asked, 'How do you know?'

'Deandra carved through a legion of Asdenard on her way,' he replied.

He was almost out of breath. Saranon gasped, 'We are in trouble.'

'You have to stop her,' he said.

'Don't tell me what to do,' she retorted.

'If she gets Validain she could do more damage than you,' he responded.

'Thanks,' she said in a flat tone.

She not sure she wanted to be compared to a Razen sorceress with an Orb. Kat flew straight for the Keep. The dragon blended in as he swooped low and she saw the first signs of the attack on the outer rim. The Vandragamond were clustered around the perimeter near the damage. It took her a moment to realise Kat was taking her to an end node. A barrier beamed faint around the low tower at the perimeter. The dragon tilted away in frustration. His claws carved into the ground catapulting both riders into the scrub nearby. She wanted to shout at him, but there was no time.

Validain called out creating a void. That sucked her in as she moved backward toward the end node. As she touched the sorcerer's stone it flared. She realised it was not the Keep that dragged her in. She wanted to scream as the air left her lungs. Mitch read her thoughts and he went to lunge forward onto the node. She shouted in her mind, 'Don't.'

Katholomu tilted his ears back and leaped straight over the top of Mitch. He plunged his claws into the top of the sorcerer's stone. It broke releasing the pressure. The dragon screeched in pain. He hurled himself away from the stallic energy as it shot into the sky.

The raw energy of the Keep coursed through piercing her skin. The energy of the Validain was more than she had ever known. The Razen appeared on the outskirts surrounding Mitch and Kat. All she could do was look on as the stallic energy held her above the ground. In the distance the Issola came, she sensed Pennie and Galven riding on the misquew. The riding cats rustled through the trees. That clung around the grounds of the Keep. Silent and deadly. Katholomu roared as he joined the fight, and Mitch followed. Validain was beginning to seal the sorcerer's stone beneath. The tide turned and the stallic energy fell into the closing void.

Saranon rushed down with it and the sorcerer's stone closed above her. It blocked out the night sky and the noise above. She landed with a thud, hitting the floor as the stallic energy drained away. The ledge broke off at a sharp angle. She peered over into the depths as sparks flew up from the stallic energy. The void closed and a rumble resounded through the Keep. The sound echoed through her mind jarring at her senses and her eyes grew wide. She ran down toward the central core as the doors began to close in the imbenik chamber. 'No,' she spoke her thought aloud.

The Keep was being sealed off she ran using her energy to speed up. The doors were closing and she ran down toward the middle of the Keep. She had to make it to the centre, but the path was blocked. She thumped her hands against the sealed path, 'No.'

The sound began to fade as the doors below sealed off

the central core. One last strand remained in the middle, but she was standing on the wrong side. The Keep would not let her in. She sensed movement along the tunnels, the Razen were coming and she was trapped.

The Keep was trapped, and she had to get through she pounded her fists on the wall. The Razen approached, a blast rang out and she blocked it. The dark sorcery disintegrated shattering back through the tunnel buying her time. There was only one way to get to Validain in time and she did not want to use her energy. The Razen were closing in and she had a moment of grace before they would descend. The way to the central core was blocked and her options were fast running out. 'You left me no choice,' she whispered toward the oncoming Razen.

She let Validain in and the Keep dragged her into the centre. The stallic energy wrapped around her and she was in, but at what cost? The energy from the Orb trickled down as the Keep repulsed against it, not wanting to let it in. It clung to her, using her to block the Orb from creating a connection. Saranon winced she would have to block the Orb of Garduend from below. The Orb pounded from the other side of the sorcerer's stone. The stone sealed the floor of the grand chamber above. The energy seared through as giant fractures creased along the stone. The fractures let the energy of the Orb seep in and with it the dark sorcery.

Deandra held control of the Orb and her sorcery flared in the darkness, it was not her own. The sorcery stolen from her victims leaked through into the stallic energy. Saranon reached out weaving the stallic energy around the walls. A whirlwind picked up from the depths as Validain took the hint. It created a void to prevent the dark sorcery from connecting with the energy of the Keep. Then a jarring sound split the air as the sorcerer's stone shattered. Sending shards down in the vacuum created by the whirlwind. The shards flared, hitting her shield as she protected herself from the damage.

The blasts of sorcery filled the ceiling of the void. The Razen and the Vandragamond fought above. The whirlwind kept the dark sorcery from reaching the stallic energy in the void. She hoped it would be enough, yet Deandra still had the Orb. She tried to reach up but the sorcery surging downward was too great blocking her path. Validain called to her and she hesitated. The Orb of Garduend shone bright through the damaged floor. She tried again and could not make it, Validain called out even stronger. She had to get access to the grand chamber. Lord Shakar's shouts filled the air. He was flung into the void held over the damaged floor.

Validain called out and she relented before the Lord's screams filled the void. She may not be able to enter the grand chamber, but someone else could. In that moment she gave the Keep something more than it could ever have on its own. She gave it life. The Angeon joined with the stallic energy melding into the flow. The embodiment of the Keep appeared above, an exact imitation of her. 'There is just one thing I need to tell you,' she said to the Keep. 'Just one thing, Deandra cheats.'

The Keep knew what she meant in the void, then the

screams rang out from above. She wanted to block them out, but they ran through her mind. Such was the cost of being part of the Keep.

***

She stood near the wall. Lord Shakar's screams filled the air as Deandra used the Orb against him. The Razen sorceress held it in her hands as she laughed. The Razen followers stood surrounding the fallen Lord. Saranon froze and Lord Shakar shouted at Deandra. The sorcerer's stone on the floor had been blown to pieces. The damage lay in the centre where Lord Shakar floated. Deandra turned to face Saranon giving her captive a small reprieve. The Razen directed the Orb at her. The energy emanating from the Orb crackled through the air so close that it hissed.

She waited holding out her arms as the energy from the Orb hit. The pain split her skin before she was ready and the Angeon began to show. Deandra hit with the Orb's energy again. The skin ripped away showing more of the Angeon underneath. The Razen sorceress screamed, 'Die.'

Deandra aimed again and again, yet more of the Angeon showed through. The Razen made the Orb shine bright. Then she sent the sorcery toward her in one giant blast taking the last of her old self away. The Angeon stood before the Razen. If she held out her hand she could touch Deandra but instead she touched the Orb.

Her hands racked with pain as the Angeon held on, and Razen sorceress would not let go. Then Angeon pushed Deandra toward Lord Shakar. Deandra screamed, 'Why won't you die?'

The Razen sorcerers tried to attacked, but the Angeon had locked on to the Orb. Just as Deandra tapered on the edge of the gaping hole in the floor Andwyrdan attacked. The blast broke Saranon's lock on the Orb and the Razen sorceress attacked him. The blast from the Orb sent Andwyrdan flying and he hit the wall of the grand chamber hard.

Lord Shakar shouted at him for interfering. The Razen sorceress laughed, as she began her attack on the Lord. He was struggling to hold on as Deandra floated toward the void. Then the Angeon melted the sorcerer's stone closing the gap. Lord Shakar laughed dragging Deandra down with him. She screamed through the darkness as the gap began to close over. The last remnant sealed them in. Deandra's screams could still be heard echoing from below the chamber.

The Razen sorcerers closed in. The Angeon raised the Orb of Garduend through the sorcerer's stone. It hung in the air above the centre connected to Validain. The Keep used it to attack the sorcerers. The Angeon watched as they disintegrated. Andwyrdan gazed at the Orb she did not want him running off with it again. He placed his hand so close then pulled it away as though taunting her. Deandra's screams echoed up through the walls. She shivered as the Lord held the Razen sorceress in a tight grip. It was all she could do to remain calm, as he bled the sorcery from Deandra down in the void.

Saranon could sense the pain of the Razen sorceress. She leaned over clutching her stomach as it showed on her face. She clenched her jaw tight as the screaming continued. Andwyrdan studied her face, 'You can feel it.'

She wanted the pain to cease but the screaming continued as the Lord attacked. The Orb glowed as Deandra reached out. Saranon gripped the Orb and held it steady. The Lord attacked from below and amidst the pain came sweeping relief. It was so sudden, she fell back.

Lord Shakar melded through the floor. She waited for him to emerge before stepping through the Orb. When she passed through her old self returned. A fine web of deception covering what lay beneath the surface. Andwyrdan tried to remove the Orb and it would not budge. Saranon wanted to berate him but it had taken all her strength not to succumb to an old trick, that Deandra had used to gain the advantage. She was not sure if she would ever thank Lord Dackren for his effort by cheating with the disc. The knowledge had been invaluable.

Lord Shakar gazed at the Orb with open awe, 'Can I have it?'

She reached over, then hesitated, I think there is someone else you need to ask. Saranon placed her hand on top of the Orb. The lady that was the embodiment of the Keep stood where she was. Lord Shakar gaped, 'Validain.'

'Yes my Lord,' Validain spoke.

'Can I...' He stammered, 'Can I have the Orb of Garduend.'

Validain smiled and gave the Orb to the Lord, 'You can have the Orb, but you will always be mine.'

Lord Shakar nodded in agreement as the embodiment

of the Keep vanished. 'Where is Saranon?' Andwyrdan asked.

The question brought Lord Shakar back to reality. 'Saranon,' he yelled.

His voice boomed in the grand chamber but no answer came.

***

She heard their voices from above and did not answer. It had taken all her strength to stay out of the fight with the Razen sorceress. Deandra was gone. The Keep had asked her not to intervene. All she wanted to do was block the memory of the screams from her ears. She waited for Validain to settle. Then she disentangled herself from the flow of stallic energy. Letting go was much harder than she realised. The exhaustion hit as she floated in the void. She had given all she could to take back the Orb of Garduend. Her muscles pounded with the lasting pain. She made it to the ledge forming the opening to a tunnel.

She gasped as the air filled her lungs and cradled her head against the wall. Down far below, the Keep had destroyed the last remnants of Deandra. Part of her wanted to be normal, yet then the Keep would not have stood a chance and that frightened her even more. Validain hummed away in the silence content with the outcome. Saranon glanced toward the sealed tunnel. She murmured under her breath, 'The least you could do is open it.'

The Keep seemed amused by the request.

It was all the warning she had before Validain opened the sealed tunnel. The blasts from the Razen sorcerers rushed in. She blocked and answered them with a thunderous catapult of energy, that whirled around as it swept the length of the tunnel. The Angeon rose to the surface as the pain faded. She ran after the few Razen, who were brave enough to remain in the Keep. The blasts flew along the walls. Cascading through the air with thousands of sparks as the sorcery clashed up ahead. She did not hesitate as she ran through to the open sky raising her arms in an open embrace. The night air met her in a cool stance as the Angeon slipped away.

Pennie greeted her, 'You always did make an exit.'

Saranon turned with great reluctance to face Validain, 'I have to go back.'

They stood in silence before Pennie asked, 'Will you stay.'

'No,' she exclaimed and her friend laughed.

'Where is the Orb?' Pennie asked.

'Lord Shakar has it,' she was doubtful, but the Keep was certain the Lord would look after it.

Pennie left her comment unsaid, as they walked toward the Keep.

The sky lit up with the fires still raging around the rim, yet the walls held strong. Commander Iona came out to greet them, her garrison close by. 'Lord Shakar is looking for you,' the Commander said.

The lights from the energy of the Keep glowed fierce. They revealed the signs of the attack along the walls and the internal courtyard. The Vandragamond appeared at ease with the last remnants of their opponents almost gone.

Pennie stayed close as the sorcerer clan stared at them.

The grey sky waned before the sun rose over the hillside giving the first hint of dawn. The doors of the great hall were wide open as shouts rang out through the air. Lord Shakar chose not to notice her. She approached the main table in the centre of the hall. A sense of disarray and exhaustion hung over the atmosphere in the great hall. The sorcerer clan re-grouped after a long night. Edred the administrator stood. The only one who gave a sense of calm as his heavy brow revealed the toll of losing a son. The Orb of Garduend rolled on the thick wooden table and she stopped it with her hand.

'We need to talk,' Saranon stared at the Lord who had drowned his sorrows in a bottle of wine.

'You are too late,' the Lord replied with a broad smile, 'the war is won.'

An exhausted round of cheers went up through the crowd gathered in the great hall. All eyes were on her. 'You were too late,' Saranon spoke the words with a sense of finality. 'You let Garduend fall and I helped you destroy Deandra.'

Lord Shakar stood and the crowd went silent, he moved toward the Orb and she held it out of reach. 'The new Keep Angore goes to the Asdenard,' she spoke.

Before the Lord could answer Edred did, 'You have an agreement.'

The Lord glared at Edred, 'You…'

'You can have the Orb,' Saranon interrupted.

'Validain gave it to me,' Lord Shakar stated.

'Yes we did,' she replied. 'We both did. I took control of Validain, perhaps next time you won't be so careless.'

'That is not possible,' Lord Shakar spoke in an even tone.

'I am the Angeon,' she said taking a deep breath. 'I have the power to make or break the world, and I took control of your Keep.'

The Lord's face changed with an expression of anguish. 'You were there when I killed Deandra,' he said.

Saranon wanted to scream out, but she had made an agreement with Validain. The cost of retrieving the Orb had been to watch Deandra die. She avoided his unspoken question, 'The Orb stays with you. Angore goes to the Asdenard.'

Lord Shakar looked into the Orb perplexed by the choice before him. Losing a new Keep was difficult to fathom. 'You drive a hard bargain the Asdenard may have the Keep,' he said.

'But…' Andwyrdan began.

'Silence,' the Lord shouted in disgust. 'A wizard Keep is for the weak.'

Lord Shakar became pensive and was almost about to say something. He changed his mind at the last moment. 'I will place it near the other one,' he said.

Saranon asked, 'Pardon?'

'You are not the first to make a large Orb,' he replied.

He strode through the enormous doors of the great hall and into the waiting crowd. A cheer rose up as the flames burned near the outer rim of the Keep. Lord Shakar turned to her, 'That is how I will kill you.'

The words sent a chill through her. She froze watching the Lord walk into the gathering crowd. The thankless sun rose over the new day. Showing the marks spread across the fine pearl building. It stood strong with minimal damage below the surface, as though mocking the Razen. The Vandragamond paid no attention to the burning flames, that shot up around the perimeter. The sun shone bright as it rose in the morning sky warming the air.

Saranon glanced up and the wings of Katholomu spread across the light. The beast cast a shadow deep along the walls of the Keep. The great marmoz dragon let out a stomach curdling roar that bounced off the walls. She walked toward him and he lowered his head. She wanted to cry, she wanted to let all the pain out, but it stayed inside. She patted the dragon's head and he rubbed his chin against her. Deandra's screams still filled her ears, she wanted to cry and could not. The memory lay like an open wound on her mind. Mitch climbed up on the great beast. He held out his hand, 'I think it's time you told the Asdenard they have a new Keep.'

'How often do you read my mind?' She asked.

He laughed, 'You confronted Lord Shakar I didn't need to.'

Katholomu took to the sky in the full light of day casting a shadow deep on the ground. The breeze caught her hair and she smiled, the dragon knew how to ease her mind. Kaythar Keep shone with a brilliant glow in the sun. The large fortress had a soft edge that blended into the background. The dragon swooped low before gliding into the courtyard. The Keep was calm with no sign of the previous events. Ben Waterworth ran to greet them the wizard appeared out of place so far into Darkonia.

'I should warn you, the Asdenard are not impressed about losing the Orb,' Ben said. 'They had the opportunity to take care of it,' her voice held a bitter edge.

She was not about to argue with the Darkonian wizards over the Orb of Garduend. Captain Edevon strode toward them, his face an image of stone. She prepared herself but before he could speak Captain Daina did. 'Welcome back to Kaythar. You cannot stay long. The Arthrose know you are here,' the Captain continued. 'I'm not sure how that happened.'

Captain Daina glared at Captain Edevon as she spoke.

'The Orb of Garduend is with Lord Shakar. In return he has agreed for the new Keep Angore to go to the Asdenard,' Saranon said.

'The Lord does not enter into agreements,' Captain Daina spoke.

'This time he did,' she replied.

Bells rang out around the Keep breaking the silence. She found herself at the centre of a growing crowd. The official word had been given from the Vandragamond. The new Keep Angore belonged to the Asdenard.

In among the cheers she collapsed with exhaustion, Mitch held onto her as she fell. 'Mitch,' she whispered and he took her through the crowd into the Keep. 'I thought the Angeon was not supposed to sleep,' he spoke.

The joke was lost on her as she tried to stay awake. It did not take long to make her way to a warm cosy bed. She could just keep her eyes open long enough to settle as sleep stole her away. As she rested the Angeon crept into her dreams towering over her thoughts. The inner turmoil had taken its toll as she struggled with the Angeon within. It gripped her even still as the energy moved restless. It waited just beneath the surface. The energy dragged her into its depths as she fought against who she was. Validain appeared and in her dream she sank down below the surface. She fell into the heart of the Keep. She was not the first person to arrive. The figure turned and she came face to face with her old friend Tasha.

Tasha's fawn coloured curls flowed down her shoulders. Each time her old friend grew older as though still in the world of the living. She reached out her hand and Tasha stepped back shaking her head, not yet. The Keep disappeared and she was left alone standing on an open plain. A worn path trailing along the ground led to one place. She stepped on the path and Tordoren shuddered. It called, weighing her down as she tried to clear her thoughts. Yet the disturbance remained long after the thought was gone.

A sharp light broke through the slit between the curtains. She ignored it and went back to sleep. She opened her eyes again and sat up. Realising she had slept a full day to the following morning. Faint shouts from the courtyard below and the building shook. Katholomu blocked out the sun as he peered through the window. She shouted at him but he would not leave. Shouting rang out below and she rushed downstairs to the impatient dragon.

CHAPTER NINETEEN

A faded memory

Katholomu bowed his head scooping her up onto his shoulders. He moved before she had time to argue. He leaped into the sky as she wrestled to stay on. She shouted in his ear to no effect as he flew on with a purpose. The great beast refused to take any notice. Kat began a slow decent as he circled before touching the ground. She slid down as he dropped his shoulder to let her off. Saranon took a step back before facing the large marmoz dragon. He lowered his head nudging her with a rugged kindness and the anger she held, ebbed away.

She found it difficult to stay angry with the beast. She patted the dragon with a mingled frustration. The dragon nudged her again and she hugged his thick neck. He nudged her again and she patted his cheek. He nudged her sideways and she took a step back. The small rocks slipped underfoot. Before she could blink she toppled over the unseen edge. Her arms flew up in the air, with only a moment to use her energy to soften her landing. Still the hard ground felt real as she picked herself up glaring up at the stunned dragon. Katholomu did his best imitation of being meek as she shouted at him. His gleaming fangs gave his silent chuckle away.

The ground had given way years before leaving a small hole. It led down into a labyrinth of tunnels on the outskirts of Validain. The grass had covered the sloping earth that led down to where she stood. She strode toward the path when something moved and she froze. The dry air whooshed with a hollow beckoning drone. It called in an uneven tone from the labyrinth. The dragon had a habit of getting her into trouble and this felt no different. She made her way along the old tunnels and a musty smell filtered through. She crept forward to a sealed door. Without thinking, she placed her hand up, and melded through the solid frame.

The acrid stench from inside the room lay thick in the air. She pried around a dismal mess left behind. All the signs told her it had been abandoned by the Razen, yet something was still there. She could feel it on the edges of her senses, when she focused, it slipped away staying out of reach. A small tapping caught her attention and she turned to find nothing. In her haste she knocked a glass tube off the bench and it hit the floor with a shattering jolt. A thin haze shrieked out of the shards as she stumbled back in fright. She caught her breath while the last wisps evaporated in the dank air. Saranon let out a gasp and covered her mouth. She stepped around the remnants lying on the floor, as a chill crept down her spine.

She hesitated, not wanting to admit what she had seen. Her heart thudded in her ears filling the uneven silence. A draft rippled past from beyond the room. She froze in place as the hair on the back of her neck stood on end. She willed herself to move, yet the message only just made it to her limbs. A rising panic gripped her, almost holding her back with a frightening numbness. Saranon counted the seconds in a silent whisper as she opened her eyes. She moved in a fluid motion as she kept the panic at bay.

She steadied herself against the rising sensation, warning her to stay away. Still her heart thudded louder. She held out her hand trying not to tremble and pushed against the door. It was stuck, she should have known. She belted against the door in a rush and it would not budge. The door slid away as she melded through with an uneasiness that would not settle. The floor was slippery underneath, as she made her way forward, staying away from the edge.

The narrow walkway wrapped around the centre leading down into the great void below. She could not sense anyone. Yet the uneasiness still remained as she peered into the murky darkness. She stepped closer and almost slipped grasping the railing in front. A whirling motion caught her eye. Instead of running away the panic vanished in the shock of what lay in the deep. She made her way down standing on the edge of the murky glow.

She was mesmerized by the slow moving whirlpool. Its stream edged off into the darkness leading straight toward Validain.

Saranon took out Tellembre, awakening the bond-breaker into the form of a sword. The heart stone blade shone like steel in the dim light. She held it above her head and the blade shimmered with an internal glow. She pitched it down hard into the dark liquid. It hit the ground below before she had time to cease the plunge. It gave a short acknowledgement before sinking in. She waded in making her way along the tunnel as it lead ever closer to the Keep. It was high enough if she did not stand tall. The draft grew stronger with a stagnant smell, creeping into her lungs.

The tunnel began to widen and she peered straight into a large cavern on the edge of the Keep. At the far end lay the outer wall thick and strong. The barrier stood impenetrable. Yet lapping at its door in great volume, the dark, unstable liquid lurked. She was standing in it. She had to move. She held Tellembre up and its light gave a soft glow. It was enough to make her way across to a narrow set of stairs hidden near the edge of the wall. A sense of relief swept over her as she lifted herself out of the liquid.

She clambered up the slippery steps to a small alcove. She began to meld through the thick outer door and stopped. She glanced back at the liquid below. The volume was too great, enough to break apart the wall of the Keep. She trembled as she put Tellembre away. If she left the unstable liquid, it could be used to break into the Keep.

She could not leave Validain helpless, not after all it had done. The ledge of the small alcove extended back into the open cave. She peered down staring into the silent gloom. She had to make a choice, yet the choice had been made for her. The resentment sank in as the Angeon rose to the surface.

The energy of the Angeon bounced off the walls. The vast space of the cavern revealed itself in the light. Saranon waited for the sorcery to strengthen like a rising tide and held it in. The walls glowed radiating from the sorcery held within. The web of sorcery criss-crossed the room in an uneven maze, that glistened in the light. One spark, just one spark and she held her breath. 'Forgive me Validain,' she spoke into the blinding flame.

The Angeon ignited the web. A thunderous blast rang out and the result was instant. She melded through the sealed door guarding the Keep. 'Forgive me for what I have done,' she whispered into the darkness.

Validain shook and she ran as the liquid trapped in the cavern evaporated. The immense volume managed to shake the building. She kept running not wanting to turn back. The impact resounded through the lower levels of the Keep. Echoing above, as the commotion flooded in. Saranon rushed through not wanting to turn back. She ran until she reached the surface. The midday sun pelted down as a shadow of dust rose up through the air and she this time she turned back. A giant dust cloud rose out of a deep hole in the ground. Arcing its way around the wall where she had stood. The crevasse gaped like an open wound staring up at the sky.

She stood in astonishment as panic rose and she glanced around for Katholomu. She had forgotten about the great dragon. She gazed along the hillside for sign of his presence. Her head sank as she realised what she had done. The dragon did not deserve such a fate even if she was angry with him. The tears welled in her eyes and a booming voice shouted, 'Saranon.'

Andwyrdan charged toward her in a fit of rage. He pushed his way through the crowd, yet she did not move. He ran driven by a steady anger as he came toward her, 'You endangered Validain.'

He hurled his energy toward her with precision. Saranon put her hand up to block at the last moment. Andwyrdan continued as she edged out of his way. The blows were unrelenting, yet she could only block the sorcery. When all she could think of was Katholomu.

She had grown fond of the dragon and now it was too late. All she wanted to do was leave. It showed on her face as Andwyrdan forced her farther away. She moved toward the edge of the courtyard. She had no desire to stay, yet Andwyrdan would not let her go. She moved away from the Keep, and he kept at her with a steady ferocity. Forcing her back and still she would not strike out. They were alone as the crowd stayed well out of the way. Andwyrdan struck out again and again.

She kept her eyes locked on him as she moved backward. Then she trod on something soft, and fell. The world went hazy and for a moment she lost her bearings as she scrambled to refocus. A loud snort rumbled from above. The stench from the dragon's breath wafted past. She shouted with excitement, 'Katholomu.'

The haze lifted and her smile disappeared. Andwyrdan was still standing there waiting for her.

This time she struck, he flew back and stumbled. Saranon did not waste time as she rushed toward him. Andwyrdan shouted at her, but she did not listen. She blasted him as she held her ground. A roar of laughter shot up from the balcony above. Lord Shakar watched on with a small audience and she gaped in astonishment.

Andwyrdan turned his back on her. He rushed into the haven of Validain away from the crowd that had gathered. Saranon was so mixed with emotions it was hard to know what to feel. She smiled up at the great dragon that still wore the dust from his ordeal. Before she had a chance to speak the beast shook his coat. He poured the grimy dust straight over her. Then he rubbed the side of his chin on her shoulder. He gave a loud grunt of satisfaction and jumped over her head. He flew straight up into the clear blue sky spreading his wings to the sun's warm rays.

She had managed to stifle most of the blast, but the crevasse still showed. She made her way back to the Keep. Her limbs ached as she stood, trying not to let her annoyance show. The Vandragamond set to work restoring the Keep. She coughed from the dust and used her sorcery to remove the rest of the grime. Her head continued to rush with the thought of almost loosing Kat. The great beast had shrugged it off far quicker than she. Saranon had no idea how the dragon had survived.

The crevasse ran deep in the earth leaving part of Validain exposed. The Keep could not stay vulnerable for long. Voices travelled along from the open courtyard. She hastened her step trying to avoid Andwyrdan who spotted her. He announced to Lord Shakar that he would mend the damage. Saranon refrained from speaking, while Andwyrdan made a glorious exit. He rode high on the back of Dregora. The great dragon paid no attention as he flew in one fluid motion. The beast headed straight to the edge of Validain and the deep crevasse.

'You shouldn't let him get to you,' Tom Heath spoke beside her.

Saranon jumped. She had been so busy glaring at Andwyrdan that she had not noticed Tom right next to her. His sad eyes still showed the pain from the loss of his brother. He invited her up to the main platform to watch the display. She hoped Andwyrdan would fail in his attempt. The sorcerer's stone shone with a brilliant darkness in the full light of day. She took care making her way around the edge of the raised floor.

The view was spectacular and awful at the same time. She stared down at the full extent of the damage. The crevasse carved deep into Tordoren, Andwyrdan flew toward it on Dregora. She fumed as she recognised the Orb of Garduend. He held the Orb high floating it above the dragon. Saranon gripped the low wall so tight her fingers began turning white. The Orb shone a brilliant pale blue in the clear sky. Andwyrdan's sorcery spun around the outside strengthening the glow. The sight was impressive though she was reluctant to admit it. Calm fell across the land. He directed the sorcery toward the crevasse in a widening arc. The blast flared across the sky hitting hard near the edge of the gaping hole.

Andwyrdan blasted the crevasse again and again. Yet the wall of the Keep remained exposed. The blasts of sorcery became desperate and with a great reluctance he ceased. He flew Dregora straight for the platform. The dragon swooped in at speed causing her to duck out of the way. The talons in the hind legs almost hooked her as the great beast landed. He threw the Orb at her and she caught it, passing it to Tom. Andwyrdan shouted, 'This is your problem, deal with it.'

Tom turned to her, 'Are you going to leave that unanswered?'

Saranon took a moment to realise what he meant. A smile crept across her face as she ran to the centre of the sorcerer's stone. The Angeon flowed in with the void. Taking her high above the platform as the energy surged from deep inside. The circle beneath her shone with a fiery embrace. The energy resonated through the Keep. The central core stirred from deep within. The raw stallic energy flowed up to the surface. The sparks caught the last glimpses of light. It raged across the golden sky with a brilliant white shimmer. It flowed through the sorcerer's stone.

The Angeon absorbed the energy and compounded it. Until it grew into a giant fiery ball above, glowing red hot.

As the last ray of light ebbed across the ground, she severed the connection. The flaming ball stood there in a void of reality. The Angeon hurled the raging sphere toward the open wound. A great roar of thunder shook the Keep as the sphere sank into the damaged ground. Pulling the wound shut as it melted into Tordoren. The shockwave pummelled its way back. Saranon stood strong, shielding the Keep from the blast. The waves rushed overhead in a storm of energy as the sparks flew in every direction.

The Angeon held on with a renewed purpose as the land below healed. She covered the exposed Keep to the world. The last crackles of energy simmered along the shield in a final wave. Then it ebbed away. She floated above the circle for one last moment before the stallic energy disappeared. The Angeon slipped away leaving her drained and she descended onto the sorcerer's stone. The circle once again returned to its brilliant darkness. It lay dormant once more in the shadows of the early night. Tom smiled, 'That was not what I meant, but it will do.'

Saranon took one last glance over the low wall to admire her handy work. It was hard to see, even though she could sense it in the dim light. Music filled the walls inside as she headed down to the great hall where a feast was underway. Ben Waterworth waved her over, he had already made a start. The wizard looked better than he had for days, with no sign of his earlier struggle. As he spoke, 'I guess you'll want to head back to Ardaguar after all this. You're welcome to stay if can you deal with this lot.'

Commander Iona sat at the other side of the table,

'Are you saying you don't like my company?'

'No,' the wizard sighed.

Saranon smiled and took no noticed as she dug in to a hearty feast. She could sense the humming of the Keep in the background, it was content at last. She took a moment to answer Ben, 'I have somewhere else I need to go.'

Ben responded between mouthfuls, 'You will always be welcome.'

As the night grew dark the exhaustion from the day set in. She took one last glance back at the hall filled with song and laughter. The shadows danced across the wall from the glow of the Keep's energy. She made her way to a soft warm bed. The night filled her head with a myriad of dreams, yet one returned over and over again. It called out from a distance with a shimmering white glow. All her dreams turned to a white soft silence. Someone was trying to reach out calling across the void.

Saranon woke with a pounding head as the light crept in. She peered over the sweeping staircase to check on Katholomu. The dragon was stretched out in a relaxed sleep with his belly showing. The warm sun beat down with the last days of summer as she made her way downstairs. The morning was still early and the sounds of life began to trickle through the Keep. She took a deep breath and steadied herself. There was something she had been meaning to do. She had been running away from the inevitable.

The sunlight sparkled glowing across the dry grass. She descended down the steps with a heavy heart. She wanted to run away. It would be easier than facing the truth as she walked along the stone path. There was just one thing that remained, as she felt her breath catch in the morning air. She found him, his name engraved in the stone above. Saranon knelt on the grass peering down at the sewn earth.

She hung her head with the weight of all that had happened. She wondered if it could have been different. It was all she could do to stand and whispered the words. 'Goodbye Jack,' and touched the grave stone one last time.

She walked away as though leaving would somehow make Jack Heath's passing final. She took one last glimpse back as she closed the gate and a figure caught her eye. Standing at the edge of the open field, as she gazed up, stood the silhouette of an elegant sorceress.

The lady removed a scarf from around her shoulders. She uncovered long golden locks that shone in the light. Oriana wore a beautiful pale dress in stark contrast to her dark grimy garments.

'Saranon,' Oriana's soft voice froze her to spot.

'Do I know you?' Saranon asked.

'You are my daughter,' Oriana's eyes welled with tears.

She stood in disbelief, as though moving would make the image disappear. Oriana placed an arm around Saranon for the first time in years. She gazed into the eyes of the mother she hardly knew and stood spellbound by the moment. Not sure if she should look away in case it was a dream. Yet the dream was real enough, as the tears escaped down her face.

ACKNOWLEDGEMENTS

Life has been a journey filled with many challenges, and the people I would like to thank would not fit on this page. To everyone out there who has been part of this incredible journey thank you, your support has been appreciated.

– Please Leave a Review –

For all the wonderful people who have read the book it would be fantastic if you can leave a review, this helps other readers find it. Thank you.

BOOKS

The Legacy of Zyanthia series:
Made in the Image of the Goddess
Running through the Rising Tide
Deep in the Shadow of the Fallen

AUTHOR

If you love fantasy with adventure and a hint of the unexpected the quest is about to begin. Escape into fantasy, and the mystical world of magic mixed with adventure. You are in good company although chose your company wisely. There are anti-heroes, wizards, and a range of chaotic characters ahead. Not to mention dragons. A fantasy world set in an ancient mythical world has to have dragons. Tales of sword and sorcery captivated Chantelle from a young age. Reading until all hours of the night to find out what would happen to the characters. There was just one problem the story would finish far too soon.

Hidden away in the distant past the life of a fantasy writer began. The real life struggles have been a saga all of their own for author Chantelle Griffin. Originally known as Chantelle Lowe and born in Tasmania, Australia. Her dreams haunted her from an early age. Vivid tumultuous dreams carrying adventure and danger. It took the author into a fantasy world filled with sorcery and treachery. The story continues to captivate her writing. If you love fantasy with adventure follow the Legacy of Zyanthia series.

www.chantellegriffin.com

GLOSSARY

ANGEON: 'The Angeon is Darkonia's answer to the Oracle, a sorcerer born with the ability to break down all defences and render a civilisation powerless.' There had been no Angeon since shortly after the Dreshan Occupation ended over 200 years ago with Zeralden Hadenvar the last Angeon who ruled Darkonia (as Queen) by marriage to the King's second son.

BOND-BREAKER: A weapon made by sorcery when dormant resembles a dagger, when activated resembles a sword it acts as a catalyst to magnify and aim the user's energy and can be used equally well by wizards as well as sorcerers. 'The most feared swords a sorcerer could use made of heart stone a melding of the elements to form a solid material that resembled crystal and sharp enough to cut through stone.'

CENTRAL CORE: The working core mechanism which powers the Keep, usually hidden away deep within the earth. It is a large engine created by sorcery which then continues to thrive on a combination of energy drawn from deep within the earth and sorcery. The combination creates a very raw and powerful energy which is difficult to manipulate.

DEAD ZONE: This is created when part of the Keep is not receiving energy from the central core or when energy has been diverted.

END NODE: Last outpost of a Keep's main energy source located at semi-regular intervals around the perimeter.

FERMADICIDE: Dark skeletal creatures.

FIRE MARK: A mark on the right shoulder to, the symbol of the fires of chaos given to the Issola in the camps.

HILAZEN: Bonded wizard.

HOST: Wizard joined with a Keep, it takes 60 hours to complete a union.

HYRIK: Restraint on sorcery, like a collar.

IMBENIK CHAMBER: Near the central core within the Keep, in between the indolin chamber and the central core it contains alters where a sorcerer can meld with the Keep.

INDOLIN CHAMBER: Inside the Keep, in between the habitable area and the central core.

KEDRIL(S): Tools to fix a Keep.

KEEP: A building protected by a central core powered by sorcery and energy from the earth. 'The tunnels led down to the primary systems and the central core that transferred energy from far below the ground into the core and turned into a usable energy source. Most central cores were located deep in the ground where the temperature was constantly warm…'

KULTIER: Long giant cockroaches.

LAY-LINE: Fast method of travel.

MAZETTE: Small (bird size) dragons.

MISQUEW: Riding cat.

NEFRELLE: Small creature (cat size), part human with very sharp teeth and claws.

OCKREN: Big cat, the soul of the Keep.

PALAFON: Tiny dragon.

QUADMAR: Aquatic creature from the murky depths, larger than a mermaid.

SACRA SEAL: Small, can hold it on your hand.

SHEAL: Liquid inside the Keep, very potent compressed raw energy.

SKADA: Small mechanical creatures that help maintain the Keep, they resemble a large spider.

SOVA BAG: A deceptive small light pouch that can become an enormous bag and hold a lot of objects, it will not hold living things.

STALLIC ENERGY: Energy from the Keep.

TALIK: Communication device. 'The sorceress held up her talik a small round disc that could open small enough to fit in the palm of her hand and placed her thumb on the centre of the outside…'

TRIDEN: Giant crab/spider, dark brown.

UVALEN CODE: '…A complex masterpiece describing the natural laws that governed sorcery.'

ZENNIGH: A large cat that normally lives within a Keep, they are too big to fit in a house but that has not stopped the occasional one from trying and getting their head jammed in the doorway.
ZYANTHIAN REGION: Armedicia, Taria, Normisia, Darkonia and Alveron were formed from one country called Zyanthia.